To Jennie

Hope you have a wonderful birthday

best wishes

Chris Scott

x

A Quiet Island

by

Christine Brooks

AuthorHouse™ UK Ltd.
500 Avebury Boulevard
Central Milton Keynes, MK9 2BE
www.authorhouse.co.uk
Phone: 08001974150

First published by AuthorHouse 2/27/2008

ISBN: 978-1-4343-5321-4 (sc)

Printed in the United States of America
Bloomington, Indiana

This book is printed on acid-free paper.

For Paul and my wonderful family and friends with all my love.

Prologue

Barbados - West Indies - August: Samuel Johnston walked home along the quiet deserted beach. The dawn was just breaking. The early rays quickly strengthening to dispel any morning coolness. Although he had grown up with the beautiful scenery he could still marvel at its beauty in the early light. He admired still, the way the waving fronds of the palms were silhouetted against the awakening sky. He was a contented man. He loved his job as a night security officer at the prestigious Treasure Beach Hotel. He particularly liked the uniform, felt it gave him an air of authority. The navy serge trousers and the crisp sky blue shirt gave him a dignified paramilitary appearance. Although in reality he had very little to do, he felt his presence gave quiet assurance to the tourists.

The previous day had been the festival of the Kaddooment. An entire day of carnival and revelry. The annual event was the highlight of the social calendar. Sam smiled as he noticed a glittering fragment of discarded tinsel, which had blown across the sands. It had been a good festival this year. "Guess we'd better start planning next year's" he thought as he stooped and picked up the shining litter. He yawned. It had been a quiet night. By the time Sam had gone on duty for the late shift most people had worn themselves out. The exertions of the long procession, the street dancing, blending smoothly with the copious amounts of rum, which lubricated the entire proceedings, made for an early nightcap. There had been one or two party stragglers but they'd stumbled off to bed shortly after he'd arrived, clutching their bright streamers and singing half remembered lines from the current calypso songs. He had evicted a beach vendor from the bar and helped a wealthy but extremely drunk American back to his room, receiving a generous tip for his trouble. Walking along the beach, lost in reverie, contemplating how he would spend his bonus, he very nearly fell over the body of a man, lying face down on the soft white sand.

"Hey mister, you okay? Too much liquid sunshine eh my friend? Now you know why we call it rum punch. Come on then Mister rum head. Want a hand getting back to your hotel?" he grinned, someone had obviously enjoyed the Kaddooment. The man didn't move.

Sam frowned; hoping the man had not wandered away from his hotel. He was supposed to make sure the guests slept off any excesses in their rooms, not lying out on the beach. Leaning over he gently shook the man's shoulder. He was quite sure it was a visitor, he was wearing the typical garb of the tourist, shorts and T-shirt, the back bearing the logo of the local brewery. He carefully rolled him over on to his back and gasped in horror.

The man's shirt no longer urged people to drink the local beer - his shirt now told a different story. This man wasn't dead drunk. Just dead. A vast dark stain, spreading out from a small tear just under the heart, puckering the thin cotton, and leaving no doubt of its wearer's fate. The man's eyes were open and staring, flies buzzed around the congealed blood enjoying an unexpected yet welcome breakfast. There was so much blood for such a small wound. It saturated the white sand under the body. For a moment Samuel stood staring in total shock and disbelief at the gruesome sight. Glancing wildly around he spotted a beach vendor slowly approaching.

"Hey you!" He screamed.

"Oh man don't you go bugging me. What's your problem man?" Grumbled the salesman. "I ain't working yet - ain't a body round yet." He kept trudging through the soft sand, annoyed at being pestered by the hotel security so early.

"Get the police man!"

"What? What you talking bout?" He peered closer and suddenly caught a glimpse of the body. "What you done man? Sweet Jesus - what you done?" He gasped as he too saw the carnage.

"Just get help, Go, just go!" Sam wailed. The beach vendor turned and fled. The powdery sand flew up as he scrambled across the beach.

Sam fought to regain his composure - he was after all, a kind of policeman himself, he reasoned. He was a highly trained security officer, he told himself - he could handle any crisis. It was no use. His eyes were drawn back to the body. "All that blood" He gasped. A sickly stench filled the air as the virgin sand was turned an ugly liver brown. He clasped his hands over his mouth but he couldn't prevent the bile that rose in his throat spraying through his trembling fingers. He sat miserably in his ruined uniform and awaited the arrival of the police.

The new civic complex at Holetown on the West Coast of Barbados was a source of much community pride. It housed a post office, courtroom and police station. Candy-store paintwork of peppermint green with contrasting white shutters made it look more like a local attraction than an official government building.

Winston Alleyne, Chief of Police, Holetown division, groaned as he surveyed the building site that was supposed to be the new police station.

"I thought this was going to be finished last month?" he barked at the foreman as he picked his way across paint pots and ladders. It was his usual morning refrain as he arrived.

"Outside's finished, Boss." Proclaimed the builder proudly.

"What about the inside?"

"Jail cell's finished." Continued the builder cheerfully, "Ceptin the bars - they's coming soon though and we've painted a line to show where they be." He added helpfully.

"Oh terrific." He glared over towards the new prison area. A scruffy looking local man stood inside the recessed area. Their eyes locked and they both looked down at the painted white line at the prisoner's feet.

"Mango suspect Sir." The desk sergeant said brightly. The prisoner shrugged, reaching into his pocket he drew out a fruit and started to chew slowly.

"Sergeant." sighed Winston, "Don't let him eat all the evidence." He walked on into his office.

"Your office is finished." Called the builder after him, "More or less..."

He sat at his desk in his gleaming new office. It was at the front of the building, and from his window he could see the locals and tourists mingling in the small shopping mall at Sunset Crest opposite the civic complex. Above the shops an air-conditioned gym did a good trade for the island's fitness fanatics, many building up enough energy to enjoy a late breakfast in the cafe and bakery below. Brightly painted mini mokes lined up along the car park, patiently awaiting the arrival of the next tourist, ready to do battle with the bumpy roads. Their ranks giving evidence of the popularity of the small Caribbean island.

He stared with unseeing eyes out of his window - this was trouble - big trouble. He hadn't actually seen the body himself yet. It had been discovered very early that morning, hastily photographed and taken directly to the morgue at The Queen Elizabeth Hospital in Bridgetown. There was no question of keeping it at the incident site due to the intense heat. There was also the question of minimising publicity. Although there had been no form of identification on the victim it had been quickly surmised that the deceased had been a tourist. Winston sighed deeply as he contemplated the immediate future - a dead tourist - worse; a murdered tourist would not exactly enhance the Island's reputation as a safe holiday destination. Tourists were, unfortunately, occasionally robbed, but rarely harmed physically. The locals knew better than to kill the golden goose, they may steal a few eggs or pull a few feathers but everyone knew where to draw the line.

He gave a wry smile as he remembered he was supposed to be interviewing the prisoner. A local man accused of stealing mangoes. He wondered briefly if the suspect was still waiting. "Mangoes! If only that was the biggest problem!" he thought dejectedly, the murder overshadowed everything. It was bound to make the foreign press; people would surely be deterred from visiting. There are lots of Caribbean islands; it would be only too easy to find another destination. His eyes rested fleetingly on the name plaque on his desk. Under his name was printed the Island's motto. "Tourism is our life - play your part" Like most Bajans he was acutely aware of the competition, everyone worked hard to make their island the most attractive.

The shrill ringing of the telephone interrupted his gloomy thoughts.

"Chief" he answered abruptly, "Oh hi Malcolm, are you down at the QEH?"

"Yup, already on the case - we foreigners don't waste time you know!" Malcolm stated cheerfully in his strong English accent. He was a British pathologist who had transferred from England as part of an exchange scheme within the police force. He continued in a more serious tone. "Actually I haven't officially started the full P.M. on your stabbing victim as yet, but I thought I'd fill you in on what I found in the prelim. I think I've found something rather interesting. It might help to get you started in the investigation"

"What have you got?" Winston reached for a notepad, his hopes rising that perhaps this thing could be wrapped up quickly.

"Well I know this sounds crazy, but I don't think this guy was unlucky." Malcolm said slowly, remembering his immediate thoughts as he examined the body upon arrival.

"Maybe in England you have a different notion of luck - out here in the tropics we tend to think being found stabbed to death is pretty unlucky. We're funny like that!" Winston commented dryly.

Malcolm laughed, "I guess I should have phrased that better! What I meant was, this was not just bad luck. It doesn't look like a mugging that went wrong or even an accidental stabbing in a fight. Certainly there are no immediate signs of a struggle. It's early days yet, but from my experience, and the evidence so far, I would say this was a professional job."

"What the hell are you suggesting? What "evidence so far?""

"Look this is all off the record right? It's just that...well... judging by the entry wound, whoever killed this man, knew what he was doing. It was a neat job. It would have been an almost instantaneous death - no time to cry out and attract attention. Swift and deadly accurate."

Malcolm was standing with his back to the room, facing the wall phone his fingers traced the contours of the clinical white tiles as he spoke. He turned and looked over at the trolley behind him. The body was covered in a surgical green sheet that contrasted sharply with the ghostly white hand that had slipped out from under it.

"Someone who certainly knew how to handle a knife." He continued, "The blade entered under the rib cage. An old trick, removes any possibility of the blade being deflected by a rib. The weapon was intended to kill, not intimidate. Probably a stiletto or a boning knife, certainly a thin blade. Usually enters the heart via the spleen. That would account for the amount of blood lost. This wasn't your usual mugger, not with that degree of accuracy."

"You mean a professional, like a ... hitman? You're kidding! Are you sure?"

"No, I'm not sure - not yet. That's why I say it's off the record but I just thought I ought to warn you. I mean, if this man is someone important enough to be professionally killed - well the old solids are going to hit the ventilation system! Only a thought but you'd better be prepared and damn certain everything's being handled by the book right from the start. God knows who he is - was - but...I guess someone thought him a problem." Malcolm sighed, thoughtfully.

Outside Winston's office the prisoner finished his breakfast and strolled nonchalantly out the door. Winston caught a brief glimpse of him as he ambled past his window but his thoughts were preoccupied with the unknown murder victim.

"You don't recognise him at all do you? Does he look like a high ranking politician or someone?" He suggested.

"What does a high ranking politician look like? Anyway this guy just looks like Joe Public to me. I wouldn't say he was old enough to be a world leader - maybe someone important's son? I don't know - I leave that sort of thing to you lot!"

"Thanks Malcolm I appreciate you taking the time to warn me - when do you reckon you'll be finished?"

"I'll put it on priority, should be able to get back to you later on today - I'll keep you posted"

Winston hung up the phone and sat staring into space, his hand still resting on the phone as if to keep the line between him and the hospital open. His mind was whirling with the latest turn of events. A professional hitman? It couldn't be possible, no surely Malcolm was mistaken. After all, he wasn't Bajan. He didn't know the island and its people that well. Things like that just don't happen here - maybe in some rough inner city in England, London gangs or something but not here.

He wondered briefly what the chances were of keeping the whole thing quiet - pretty slim, he decided. Maybe if the guy turned out to be from some small Scandinavian country. The island's main tourist trade came from Britain and America - the likelihood was that he came from either of those. The officer who had seen the body seemed to think so but these days, you never could tell. All they knew for now was that he was a white guy and looked like a tourist. "Joe Public" Malcolm had called him - so who was he? Was he someone important? Important enough to be professionally killed? Winston couldn't afford the twinge of conscience that suggested he should feel more sympathy for the victim than the island. He was too aware of the possible consequences of this one act of violence.

"Tourism" he declared to the empty room, "is our life's blood." He sighed heavily and stared down at the phone under his hand. "You know Malcolm, something like this can bring on a very bad case of anaemia."

In the hospital morgue Malcolm unknowingly mimicked Winston's actions. He paused with his hand resting on the phone while he too pondered the identity of the mysterious victim. A faint noise behind him caused him to whirl around startled. To his surprise a stranger stood before him. The morgue was a restricted area and certainly not the sort of place anyone would casually walk into unannounced. For a moment the two men stood facing each other then the stranger smiled and reached into his pocket. Something in his manner made Malcolm step back.

Chapter 1

Miami - Three months earlier. Randall Westfield III was not a happy man. Slamming down the phone he glared at the young blonde manicurist perched provocatively on his desk. A young man, his arms full of papers and folders tried desperately to melt into the background.

"Get out!" The girl took one glance at his murderous expression and fled. The young man stammered nervously.

"Sir? We do need to have your approval today for these layouts..." Randall ignored him. He reached over to the office intercom. "I want everyone in the board room - now!" He bellowed. "Sir, your wife is on line one. She says it's urgent." the disembodied voice came back to him.

"I'm busy." He retorted, jumping to his feet he strode out, bursting through his secretary's office like a thunderclap. "But Sir...." she began leaning to speak into the intercom then straightening up as she realised he was already in the room. "She did say it was urg..." her voice trailed off as she too caught his expression. "Yes Sir, I'll assemble everyone." Her words fell on deaf ears as he swept on out of the room. The hapless young man trailing unwisely behind. Pausing at the door for a second Randall turned around and glared at him. "Perhaps if I just um...well... use my own discretion..." the man ventured timidly.

"Do that!" Randall snarled. He strode angrily across the thickly carpeted hallway and stormed into the penthouse boardroom where he stood staring out of the window. His fury mounting with every minute his staff kept him waiting.

To a casual observer it would appear that Randall Westfield III should be extremely content. Head of the hugely successful Westfield Inc. He had inherited the company from his father some ten years previously and more than trebled its assets in that time. The Company had been founded as a simple trading store by his great-great grandfather and each generation had added to the business. The original trading post had prided itself on its determination to keep the customer happy. The settlers wanted pelts to meet their needs and the Indians wanted supplies, great-great grandfather did a deal and everyone was happy - especially great-great grandfather who founded the family fortune. There had been a sepia picture of him standing behind a wooden counter beneath a sign reading "We try harder for our Customers" it had been on the wall of each successive owner for years.

Randall had, unfortunately, only inherited his father's business, not any of his more humble characteristics. His first act had been to remove the sepia print and have it replaced with a tasteful oil painting. He had his name changed to Randall Westfield III, although to the best of anyone's knowledge there had never been a I or II.

The Company still traded of course; it bought small companies now, broke them up and sold them off. It made vast profits. It did still fulfil its customer's need although the Company motto was now simplified, "You want it - we get it!" His declared business interests were, naturally, strictly legitimate, but there was an increasing amount of business which only a select few knew of. The Company had a customer who wanted specific weapons, no questions asked, they were obtained and sold. The customer was still kept happy. Randall Westfield III truly believed everything, and everyone, had a price, and if anyone wanted something badly enough - he was the one to get it for them.

Currently he was involved in supplying a small country in South America with enough plutonium to meet its needs - its need being to build a small nuclear weapon. Randall had discovered an Eastern European country which was rather anxious to lose a similar amount of plutonium and a very lucrative deal had been struck. The spirit of the family tradition lived on.

"It's a damn good deal." Muttered Randall, "Nothing's going to blow this one." He thought back to the Company's origins. "The profits on this would have kept the pelt business for years. Dad would be so proud...." his expression darkened once more, "well, maybe not!"

By now the plutonium should be safely out of Europe. It had left the country in two 40 gallon oil drums, lined with lead and properly sealed, on the back of a supposedly empty foreign aid truck. They had been transferred to a liner and were currently heading across the Atlantic en route for Venezuela. Randall, though by nature not a generous man, knew which palms to grease and in this case his judgement in picking corruptible officials had paid off. He'd received a tip off from the docks. Someone knew what to look for - someone had betrayed him. There was a scuffling of chairs and he heard his board hastily assembling. He glowered around the room, few people knew about this deal.

Ben Webb, the Company lawyer, shifted uncomfortably in his seat, Randall glared at him and the hapless man turned a delicate shade of puce. "Not him for sure!" Thought Randall with disgust, "He hasn't got the spine to sell anyone out." To Ben's relief Randall's gaze travelled on. Warren Schreiber, Head of Security, formerly a disgraced New York cop. He had narrowly avoided corruption charges when vital evidence went missing. He had left New York in a hurry and joined the Company six months previously. "Hasn't been here long" mused Randall, "Could be - I'll watch him." Schreiber had come highly recommended from New York though, and was very bitter about the authorities who had sacked him. "I could imagine him selling out to a higher bidder but not the authorities - that don't add up."

A nervous looking secretary brought in a tray of coffee. The cups rattled and she winced as she hastily deposited the tray and hurried out. Randall continued his silent appraisal.

"Al Garcia? Nah - never, he's been with me too long. He's like a brother." He beamed at Al briefly then moved on again, "Charlie?" His eyes narrowed as he looked across at Charlie Carson. Charlie's job description read "personal assistant", but in reality he was a bodyguard. A huge bear-like man not known for his quick wit or intelligence to be sure, but fiercely loyal. No, he couldn't really imagine Charlie had anything to do with this. He shrugged, maybe it was someone over in Europe, he didn't really trust foreigners. Time enough to find out where the leak had come from later, for now he had to find some way out of this mess. He was used to things running smoothly. He was not a man who took even minor setbacks in his stride and this was a major setback. The small group of nervous looking men glanced around at each other.

Ben Webb risked a brief glimpse at his boss then quickly lowered his gaze and carefully avoided eye contact. He wondered for the thousandth time why he ever stayed with Westfield Inc. He had been hired by Randall's father some fifteen years previously and was in fact an excellent lawyer. He knew every aspect of business law and was meticulous in his work. Now seeing his employer staring coldly at him he swallowed hard and tugged at his suddenly too tight collar.

"Why did I stay?" He thought desperately. "I should have got out as soon as...well as soon as ...well I should have left when the old man did."

At first after Randall took over the Company things remained much the same, but gradually Ben became aware of various dealings which, although perhaps not strictly illegal, were certainly of a rather dubious nature. Randall, recognising the Ben's talents as a lawyer and also acutely aware of the man's Company knowledge, doubled his salary, by now, Ben Webb was in too deep. A mixture of greed and fear bought his loyalty to the Company. Now he sat in a cold sweat wondering what had caused his boss's current wrath, and hoping desperately that it wouldn't involve him.

Seeing Randall walk over to the huge window and stand staring out at the Miami coastline Ben seized the opportunity to try and find out more. He leaned over towards Warren Schreiber who was sitting beside him at the oval conference table.

"What's up?" he whispered hoarsely, keeping an anxious eye towards the window.

Warren shrugged unable to offer any information, nor indeed reassurance to his colleague. He too, although less visibly nervous, sat wondering what was the cause of the hastily convened meeting. Few people knew much about Warren Schreiber, rumours abounded in the Company about his being thrown out of the police force for alleged corruption, but no one seemed to know any details. He was officially head of security at Westfield Inc. but most people suspected he was Randall Westfield's eyes and ears around the Company.

Warren reached over and casually poured himself a coffee. Adding sugar, his spoon scraped the cup as he stirred the contents. Al Garcia glanced over disapprovingly and Warren met his look. He paused for a second then slowly and deliberately recommenced stirring. Al glowered at him and Warren shot him a brief defiant smile as he gently tapped the spoon against the cup and rested it on the table. He reported directly to Randall, and was unafraid of his rival, Al Garcia. Most of the others were afraid of them both and conversations tended to flounder when either of them entered a room. The tension mounted in the room as the silence seemed to envelop them all in an air of grim foreboding. Suddenly Randall turned away from the window and walked over to the head of the table. Ben resisted the urge to jump up and hold the man's chair for him.

"Gentlemen" Randall spoke quietly as he took his usual seat. "We appear to have a problem." Despite his quiet manner his voice sounded menacing. He paused and looked around the table, he had their full attention as he continued, "It would appear that certain...officials, have become interested in our little shipping venture." He didn't need to elaborate as to which shipping venture he was referring to - they all knew instantly.

Ben gasped, "That's it! I knew it would happen, I should never have got involved - I'm going to jail!" He thought frantically. "Of course Hillary will probably divorce me. Her mother will have a field day...."

Randall's voice cut across his thoughts. "Of course, I'm sure you all know there is no need to panic." He glared across as his lawyer, who wondered briefly if the pounding in his chest meant he was going to die.

"My sources tell me the ship is to be searched upon arrival at Caracas, and they know what they're looking for." he continued.

"Shit!" exploded Warren, furious at this development.

"Precisely." Commented Westfield, "And it's going to hit the fan unless we act fast.

"What information have you got?" Asked Warren urgently, wondering how far the damage had spread.

"What I've given you. The port has been alerted for the ship to be searched on arrival. That's about it. I'm assuming that unless they find the ....cargo.... they'll have no link back to us."

"So we could be safe still." Gasped Ben, "If they don't find anything, we might be all right then." He continued eagerly. He wondered if he could suggest they tossed the drums overboard.

"Of course we can't afford to merely lose the merchandise. Quite apart from the enormous cost, our customers would slit our throats." Westfield spoke calmly but everyone knew he meant every word literally.

"So we need an alternative...." murmured Al.

"What we need is a solution. " Westfield stated. "Any ideas, gentlemen?" There were a couple of minutes of silence while everyone stared at the neat notepad in front of every place at the table. The paper was there for decoration - note taking was not encouraged at this sort of meeting.

Al Garcia drummed his fingers on the smooth mahogany surface, the sound breaking the silence and all eyes turned to him. For a while he didn't speak, obviously deep in thought. The drumming became louder as ideas took shape in his mind. It was an irritating sound but no one felt inclined to point that out to him. He was not a man to be angered. He had joined the Company soon after Randall had taken over. A thin rat-faced man, he was not popular among his co-workers, he was, however, extremely popular with the boss and never far from his side. He dressed immaculately, smelt of expensive cologne, but somehow he still looked like a cheap crook, a caricature of a thirties' gangster. It was not an image he was unaware of - in fact he courted it.

"Are they checking every ship coming in - or do they know which one to look for?" Al asked sharply, his rapid mind searching for a solution.

"We can't be sure - but my sources seemed to think they were looking for one specific ship." Randall had been expecting the first question to come from Al. He knew he could rely on him to think fast in a crisis.

"So we can't dock her anywhere else then - they'll be looking for that." Al continued drumming his fingers, his brow furrowed in concentration.

"What about some small South American port - those guys are pretty cheap to buy off?" Warren suggested not wishing to leave Al Garcia with a clear home run.

"Yeah, cheap is right." chimed in Charlie, anxious to make a contribution. He had no idea of any solution but he knew the others had a low opinion of him so he felt it necessary to say something.

"Yes they're cheap - and you get what you pay for - we couldn't trust any of them not to sell us out." Snapped Randall, dismissively.

"Yeah - we couldn't trust them." Added Charlie, unhelpfully. He gazed out of the window and across over the ocean. The headquarters building of Westfield Inc. situated near Miami Beach afforded panoramic ocean views. Charlie sat gazing at the scene as if hoping inspiration would leap out of the sparkling waves.

"OK, OK what if we don't dock to unload?" Al muttered half to himself as an idea gradually formed in his mind. "What if we send a boat out to meet it?"

"In the middle of the ocean? It would be spotted a mile off. No chance." Warren pointed out scornfully.

"What if it wasn't in the middle of the ocean? What if it had diverted closer inland, close to the Islands, maybe?" Al continued, ignoring the scorn in Warren's voice.

"What the hell for?" Randall was beginning to get interested but still couldn't quite see the full picture.

"Anything! I don't know - an engine fire maybe - who cares? Maybe the cook got sick, Captain's appendix burst, anything! We can sure as hell come up with something." He glared as Warren again countered him.

"We still need something to meet it - it would still be spotted." Warren pointed out obstinately, "We're no better off wherever the ship is. We've still got to get the stuff off and they're going to be watching for another ship."

"So we act fast. If it diverts with an emergency we can buy a bit of time - it ain't like it's being tailed! Sure they'll track it on radar so we send out something that they won't take notice of - a local fishing boat. Who the hell is going to take notice of one more native fishing boat." Al was growing more excited as the plan took shape.

"I like it! They bring it ashore...." Randall was already thinking ahead as to where they could hide a couple of drums.

"They wouldn't even need to bring it ashore." Interrupted Al, his mind racing now as he saw the answer more clearly, "There'd be less risk if they kept the stuff in a fishing net just offshore somewhere. It wouldn't be for long - those things are completely sealed - water tight ain't they?"

"Yes, yes you're right. Once the ship's docked and searched - they'll think they've been sold a dud and we divert another ship to bring the stuff in by the same method. Get the fishing boat to bring the stuff back up - transfer back onto another tanker and carry on with the original plan. It would just mean a slight delay on delivery - no big deal, just a switch in transport - no problem." Randall declared, delighted with the turn of events. It was a terrific idea he decided.

"Yeah." Charlie added dreamily "Like switching cars after a robbery - always a smart move..." his voice trailed off as he sat reminiscing.

The others ignored him.

"Which island?" asked Ben quietly, wanting to enter into the conversation and trying to redeem himself with the Boss. "My wife and I honeymooned in Antigua, it was... umm...very pleasant."

"No. Not Antigua. An associate of mine does a lot of business out of Antigua. I wouldn't want to go there." Randall stated quietly but firmly, his tone indicating an end to that option.

There was a few minutes silence as everyone considered the options. Ben wondered who Randall's "friend" might be but decided he would probably rather not know.

"One of the smaller islands then - there are plenty of them." Shrugged Warren.

"No - anywhere too small and anything out of the ordinary would be too obvious - and not one where they don't speak the right language!" added Randall as an afterthought.

"Barbados is away from the other islands - it sort of sticks out a bit, you know, away from the others...sort of...really." Ben mumbled, miserably, still not wanting to be involved, but ever eager to save his own skin.

"He's right Boss, Barbados would be okay. It's quite busy but still quiet enough, if you know what I mean." Al agreed, earning a grateful smile from Ben, which he naturally ignored.

"You'd have to be careful about bringing in a new fishing boat, might arouse suspicion among the locals." Warned Warren, although he had to admit it would work out very well, there were still a few problems to iron out.

"We could hire a local. Someone who knows the waters, and the tides and stuff like that." Al pointed out. "Some local schmuck who could earn themselves some extra cash by doing as they're told and not asking questions. It's a tourist place - there's bound to be locals for hire."

"Could we trust them?" Warren asked dubiously, they were talking about very valuable merchandise. "Some "local schmuck" might get greedy. They would have to be pretty sure what kind of organisation they're dealing with here. Who would you send to handle it? Are they watching us directly?"

Ben looked around fearfully, half expecting federal agents to leap out from behind the planters. Randall's opinion of him plummeted to new depths as he read the man's obvious thoughts.

"I don't know, but I'm not about to take chances. I can't send anyone from here. If one of my 'trusted right hand men' ..." he used the expression with heavy sarcasm, pausing he left the implied rebuke hanging in the air. The assembled group looked affronted, nonchalant or plain terrified according to their individual confidence in their own position. Randall scanned their expressions before continuing "as I was saying if anyone here suddenly leaves the country it might tip them off. No I'd need to send down a stranger. Someone totally unconnected with this Company. An expert of course...."

Randall smiled as the solution suddenly became crystal clear. "Oh yes, I think I know just the person to handle this. The guy

I'm thinking of would probably be very glad of a nice holiday on a quiet island in the sun. I'm sure he could pay a local fisherman handsomely to cover this little transaction - and I believe he is well versed in...shall we say, 'retirement plans', for our..." he paused and beamed at Al. "What was your expression Al, 'Local schmuck'? when the job is done."

Despite Randall's warm smile everyone present wondered briefly if the air conditioning had suddenly been turned a little too cold.

Chapter 2

Barbados - Late June - Andrew Kinloch gasped as he stepped from the plane onto the steps leading down to the tarmac runway at Grantly Adams Airport, Barbados. The heat felt as though he were stepping under a huge industrial dryer. The warm air felt so alien to him. Although Glasgow had been enjoying a relatively hot June when he had left that morning it was positively arctic compared to this tropical climate. He felt out of place in his smart suit as he surveyed his fellow passengers. The aircraft had been cool enough to warrant his jacket but now he felt over-dressed and self-conscious. "You're being met by a representative of your new workplace" he told himself sternly, resisting the temptation to take off the now stifling jacket. "You've got to look the part - first impressions and all that!" He paused at the top of the steps and looked around at what was to be his home for the next year. A young mother struggling with a baby and toddler as well as a number of bags paused beside him, more to catch her breath than admire the view.

"Can I offer you a hand Madam?" Gratefully the woman tried to extricate one of the bulging bags from her shoulder without dropping the sleeping baby. The toddler refused to let go of his mother's hand and howled his disapproval at the heat, the long journey and the strange man who appeared to be taking his mother's bags.

"Perhaps if I carried the wee one?" Andrew smiled, seeing the mother's hesitancy he added, "Oh don't worry I'm a doctor, I've handled many a baby" Smiling reassuringly he slung his own bag casually over his shoulder and gently took the sleeping infant. The toddler glared suspiciously at him as they slowly descended the steel steps. As they crossed the tarmac a young man in airline uniform hurried over.

"Daddy that man took Mummy's bag and our baby!" The toddler shouted accusingly, pointing at Andrew. Several nearby witnesses smiled at the scene as Andrew started frantically to explain.

With the thanks of both parents ringing in his ears, Andrew hurried towards the airport building. His cheeks were flaming as much from embarrassment as from the warmth of his unsuitable attire.

The airport itself was rather disappointing at first. It looked initially like any other small airport. A grey concrete building with large windows crowded with people anxiously scanning the incoming passengers for a glimpse of an awaited friend or relation, but there the similarity ended. A steel band was playing just outside the terminal. A pretty girl in a colourful costume was welcoming passengers with a glass of some sort of pink liquid and in the distance he could see palm trees swaying in the warm breeze.

Andrew continued across the runway towards the terminal building. He noticed an exotic sweet smell in the air, which he later learnt came from the sugar factories nearby. It was a strangely reassuring smell that brought back vague, but happy memories of making toffee as a child. He found himself subconsciously rubbing his fingers together as he remembered wiping his sticky hands on his mother's crisp apron.

"Welcome to Barbados Sir, would you care for a rum punch? Compliments of the airport" the girl's voice welcomed him as she handed him a glass and smiled warmly at him.

Andrew hesitated, it wouldn't do to arrive smelling of alcohol but the drink looked invitingly like fruit juice so he thanked the girl and gratefully accepted. He joined the slow moving line as it snaked towards the immigration desk, sipping his drink as he went. The light aroma of nutmeg drifted on the balmy air. It was not as innocuous as it had a first appeared and by the time he got to the desk he was feeling more relaxed. He completely forgot his decision to present a smarter appearance and slipped off the heavy jacket. To his surprise he even found himself tapping his feet to the music, discreetly of course - after all there were standards to maintain. The Island's magic was getting to him already. He smiled broadly at the immigration officer.

"Good afternoon Sir. Passport please. What is the purpose of your visit?"

"I'm a doctor, I've come to work at the Queen Elizabeth Hospital for a year. Do you know it perhaps?" He spoke with a gentle Scots burr but even so the official had no problem in understanding him.

"Oh yes Sir, we have only one main hospital. I'm sure you will be very happy there. It's a fine place. Thank you" He nodded politely and handed Andrew back his passport.

As he stood waiting for his luggage Andrew reflected for the hundredth time on his good fortune. When he had been offered a place in a state hospital in a third world country he had been expecting something quite different. It had been his senior tutor's suggestion. Dr Stuart had deliberately phrased the offer in those terms to gauge his reaction. Andrew had imagined a tiny hospital in the heart of some African country or maybe somewhere in India, certainly nothing like this. He had always wanted to travel, but medical school had taken all of his resources and to date he had not seen much of the world outside his beloved Scotland.

He stood reminiscing as he watched the endless stream of bags tumble through the flaps from the loading area and begin the slow journey along the conveyer belt winding around the baggage hall. The baggage handlers in their bright red jackets stood attentively beside their clients.

"I've just the two bags." He explained to his porter. The man nodded and together they watched the luggage procession.

Andrew Kinloch had always been determined to be a doctor. As a small boy he had had appendicitis and had never forgotten his initial fears until the family doctor, Dr Janet McIntyre had explained everything to him. She had talked to young Andrew like an adult, answering all his questions and allaying all his fears. He had thought, briefly, of marrying her when he grew up but, with the logical reasoning of a typical eight year old he worked out that she would probably be too old or perhaps dead by then, so he decided he had better become a doctor himself to replace her. He solemnly explained all this to her one day shortly after his operation. Janet had listened most carefully, showing all the proper respect for such sage reasoning, and said she quite understood. He had supposed when you got to her age, she was already in her mid twenties, you understood most things. It was a story Janet had reminded him of when she drove him to the airport that morning.

Now an incredibly ancient forty-five year old she had pointed out that she felt herself lucky to be still going strong!

He spotted one of his bags. "That's one of mine." he pointed it out to the waiting baggage handler. The man easily lifted the heavy bag onto a nearby trolley. "The other the same?" enquired the porter, searching the conveyor belt for a similar case.

"Just the same." Nodded Andrew as his thoughts returned to Scotland.

He smiled to himself as he remembered Janet. She was still gorgeous. Now happily married and mother to his young godson. He'd missed his opportunity. Perhaps he should have proposed to her while he had the chance all those years ago! Simultaneously he and the porter spotted his other bag, it was quickly retrieved and the pair headed off towards the exit.

Outside the customs hall Charmaine Harrison held up a board bearing Andrew's name. The hospital administrator, it was among her many duties to meet new arrivals at the airport. She watched as the passengers filed through and tried to guess which one was the doctor she was meeting. A young man smiled at her appreciatively and she smiled back encouragingly but he read the name on her board and walked on past. A young couple came along, arms entwined they walked dreamily by. A family group struggled by, their progress hampered by excess luggage and tired tearful children, she gave the mother a sympathetic smile. Finally she spotted another man alone. Tall, lean and fair-haired he searched the faces of the waiting crowd looking slightly at a loss. The porter stood beside him.

"Dr Kinloch?" She ventured, pronouncing the name "Kinlotch"

"Kinloch, like "lock" that's me, anyway it's Andrew" he smiled, "Miss Harrison?"

"Charmaine. Pleased to meet you. Did you have a pleasant flight?" Turning to the porter she pointed over to the car park. "I'm just over there."

They chatted politely as they walked across to Charmaine's car. The porter loaded the cases into the car and Andrew drew out his wallet. "I'm afraid I haven't any local currency..." he began but then realised he was talking to himself as Charmaine had already paid the man who'd quickly returned to the custom's hall to seek out his next customer. Andrew tried to protest.

"It's no problem. You can't buy local currency off the Island so I always come prepared when meeting people." She closed the boot down firmly and walked around to the car door.

"Are you tired? I could carry you directly to your apartment, or I could carry you along the scenic route and show you something of our island." Charmaine was busy unlocking the car door and didn't notice Andrew's rather startled expression. The local phrases would take some getting used to, he mused, as he pictured Charmaine 'carrying' him up the road - it was a faintly ludicrous if not unpleasant image to conjure!

"Well if you have the time I would really like a chance to see a bit more of the place. It's my first visit. He climbed into the passenger seat and looked around for his seat belt.

"You'll find all the islands vary a bit - but we like to think ours is the best!" Charmaine said proudly as she eased the car out of the car park and on to the busy road.

"I'm sure it is, I'm most impressed so far." He glanced across at Charmaine as he spoke. Something in his tone made her look sharply across at him, trying to interpret his remark but his blue eyes looked innocently back at her. To her annoyance she found herself blushing as she quickly averted her gaze back to the road.

"I mean," he added, "the scenery is truly beautiful - all of it!" He grinned at her and she had to laugh.

"I don't think you'll take long to settle in here!" she retorted laughingly. "Do I take it your speciality is surgery?" Seeing his puzzled expression she added innocently. "Well you certainly seem to be a pretty fast operator!" Within minutes of his arrival they were chatting like old friends. The combination of the rum punch and the friendly welcome making Andrew relaxed in his new colleague's company. He looked appreciatively around and gave a happy sigh. "This is good!"

As Charmaine drove and gave a running commentary on the surroundings Andrew discreetly studied Charmaine. She was certainly very easy to study. She had a golden complexion, not deeply tanned. He supposed that people who could sunbathe anytime probably didn't bother to. Her hair was long but swept up in a neat plait so he couldn't judge how long it was. He found himself wondering how it would look down around her shoulders. Deep brown eyes, a warm and friendly smile and an attractive face. She wore little make-up, it evidently wasn't necessary. She certainly seemed very at ease and confident, her soft, lilting accent describing the island clearly portrayed her love of her country.

"Your predecessor rented an apartment overlooking Dover beach. That's on the south coast. It's a bit lively around there but there's everything you'd need. It's very handy for the hospital too." She paused and pointed towards the glove compartment. "There's a map in there for you. It's a tourist thing. Shows all the main stuff."

Andrew reached in and unfolded the colourful map.

"You see Bridgetown there? Yes well Dover beach is further south. There are a couple of big hotels but mainly there are more apartments and guesthouses in that area. The west coast is quieter, very fancy hotels and some lovely houses. That's were all the celebrities stay!" She laughed, "It's very nice but very expensive!"

"I'll stick with the south then!" Replied Andrew. "Though I'd love a chance to see how the other half lives sometime." He looked at the map again. "What's up at the north?"

"Not a lot! It's largely undeveloped, lots of cliffs and caves very rugged...."

"Well I'm from Scotland - I'd probably like it." Andrew smiled.

"Funnily enough it's called 'Little Scotland' up there. You'll have to go and compare it with home." She continued with her commentary while Andrew continued visually travelling his guide.

She had an almost visible glow about her. The phrase 'golden girl' kept springing to his mind. She was slim but not excessively so. The curves were in all the right places, he concluded, using all his professional expertise. He guessed her to be about his age, maybe a bit younger even.

"You're very young to be a hospital administrator aren't you?" he asked during a pause in her narration.

"You're very young to be a doctor, aren't you?" She countered.

"We're both obviously brilliant to have got so far so quickly" Andrew laughed immodestly.

"Obviously quite brilliant!" Charmaine replied, matching his tone, "Actually my family have always been involved in the medical profession. Both my parents are doctors. I didn't like the idea but wanted to be involved in medicine in some way so I went to the University of the West Indies, studied business and economics and here I am. How about you?"

"Let's just say I was enticed into the medical profession by my love for an older woman!" He smiled as he thought of Janet McIntyre. She'd kill him if she heard herself being referred to as an "older woman"!

"Sounds intriguing!"

"I'll tell you about it sometime!" Andrew replied, trying to sound mysterious "I am very happy to be here though, this place is even more beautiful than I imagined. Of course I don't know what the job will be like yet but somehow...well I don't think a year in a tropical paradise will exactly kill me!"

Chapter 3

As Andrew and Charmaine drove away from the airport the American Airlines flight from Miami was just coming in to land. Brad Tucker had watched out of the aeroplane window as the runway came into sight. Like most newcomers to the Island he had stared at the amazing turquoise blue of the sea as the plane hugged the west coast on its approach to the airport. Unlike the other passengers he was more interested in what lay beneath the sparkling surface.

"Do you require a landing card Sir?" His attention was drawn away from the window by a soft female voice.

"I guess I'd better." he grinned as he took the proffered card. "Though I'd love to stay up here in the clouds with you Honey."

The flight attendant smiled as she shook her head as if to scold a naughty but loveable child and moved on. Brad started to fill out the form.

As a marine biologist he had originally planned to come to Barbados to complete his thesis on coral reefs and their marine life. He had intended a six-month term of study in the laboratory near the fishing village of Oistins. Recent events had changed his plans and he was looking forward to breaking the news to his host.

Having lived in Florida for most of his life Brad was accustomed to heat but he was also accustomed to air-conditioned planes and airports. The balmy tropical heat surprised him too but he revelled in it as he stepped from the plane onto the steps. The warm breeze ruffled his hair as he stood looking around. He was comfortably dressed in cut off denim shorts, a colourful lightweight cotton shirt. He looked every inch the happy holidaymaker. He winked appreciatively at the pretty girl serving the rum punch and, by nature less inhibited than the recently arrived doctor, he found himself swaying quite unselfconsciously to the music of the steel band.

Nathan Corbin, known to one and all as Corby, waited outside the customs hall for his friend Brad to appear. He didn't need the customary identifying sign, they were old friends. Nathan had met Brad when he had visited Miami the previous year. It was through the immediate friendship that had developed between the two men that Brad had secured a placement in Barbados.

A white Rolls Royce pulled up outside the airport. Everyone moved respectfully aside at allow it to park. "Looks like someone fancy is arriving." Thought Nathan. In contrast he remembered when he had arrived at the impressive laboratory in Miami. He had felt quite overwhelmed by its sophistication. It was a far cry from the small Oistins lab he was used to. Brad had been assigned to show him around and the two men had become firm friends, both sharing a love of marine life and ocean biology.

He watched appreciatively as a pretty girl strolled by. His thoughts automatically returning to his Miami trip. Brad had introduced him to his latest girlfriend, who in turn had thoughtfully brought a friend, and Nathan had introduced them all to the delights of imported Barbados rum. They had spent many a pleasant evening together and Nathan was looking forward to returning his friend's hospitality.

The birth of Nathan Corbin had been quite a surprise to his parents. Their other children were quite grown up when Marsha Corbin had discovered she was pregnant again. This turned out to be a considerable advantage to young Nathan as life was much easier for him than it had been for his older brothers and sister. The family had moved out of the small wooden Chattel house they had lived in when his siblings were babies. They now had a more modern concrete house with a nice garden and even a family car. His father was still just a poor fisherman but his brothers and sister contributed towards the family income and made sure Nathan had every advantage they could afford. He went to the local school and was encouraged to stay on and get his qualifications. He won a scholarship at the University and the whole family had looked on with enormous pride when he graduated. He was the family's big success and he knew he owed it all to them.

"Hey Corby! Great to see you man!" Brad shouted, as he walked out of the terminal doors leading from the Customs hall. Although it was crowded Nathan was tall enough to stand head and shoulders above the crowd and was easily spotted. "Hey you didn't have to go to all this trouble!" he pointed over to the waiting limousine. The crowd turned and stared, was he some sort of celebrity?

"Yeah right! Like that's for you!" Retorted Corby. Disappointed the crowd turned back towards the arrival hall.

"Brad! What kept you? That flight landed ages ago - didn't you want to get off?" Nathan shook his friend's hand warmly and helped him with his bags. "Cute flight attendants huh? I'm surprised you didn't just stay aboard for the trip home!"

"Yeah - like it's a real hardship to be here! Nah - Customs were a bit heavy with all the gear I've brought...but I got it covered - no sweat." Brad explained with a grin as the two men walked towards Corby's battered jeep. Badly in need of a paint job it was obviously intended for work rather than decoration, unlike the Rolls Royce that glided past them, the chauffeur's newly arrived niece sitting proudly in the back.

"You got it all through though? They didn't confiscate anything?" Corby asked quickly, anxious about the precious cargo of scientific equipment.

"Nah, like I said - no sweat. You know me with my boyish good looks I could charm my way round anyone. Now then, what's the plan?" He waited while Corby unlocked the jeep.

"I figured we could drop off your stuff at my place then maybe go out for a bite and visit a couple of beach bars. How does that sound?"

"Sounds good to me - I didn't eat much on the plane and boy am I looking forward to one of those flying fish sandwiches you keep promising me - it had better be worth the wait!"

"Trust me you'll love it!" Corby struggled to load the large, heavy cases into the back of the jeep. Carefully he wedged the equipment boxes so they couldn't shift too much and damage on the journey over the less than smooth Island roads. Brad casually tossed his hand luggage on top of the baggage. Corby winced as the flight bag bounced onto the boxes. "I hope it's packed well. What have you got in all this stuff?"

"I brought some new testing equipment with me. I've been working on some research into antidotes to fish venom. Thought you might be interested to see what we've got." Brad answered nonchalantly, as he climbed into the passenger seat beside Corby.

"Sounds interesting." Corby was instantly curious, "Okay if we swing by the lab first then to drop it off - I'd like to see what you've brought." Heavy import duties made new equipment all the more precious on the Island and Corby was very keen to check it out.

"Corby my friend, it can wait until tomorrow - you really are a fanatic! Give me a break! You know what they say about all work...." Brad laughed at his friend's enthusiasm.

"Okay, Okay I get the message, we'll pass by the lab, drop off the equipment....unopened," he added, seeing the warning look in Brad's eye, "and carry on from there."

They drove in companionable silence, Brad admired the local scenery, he didn't really give much thought to the equipment that he'd brought. He came from a wealthy background. Even at college if he wanted something new he bought it and now in the lab back home everything was state-of-the-art and he didn't have to worry about the cost of much. He was not an insensitive man but life had always been easy for him and he didn't possess Corby's sense of determined ambition. As they drove along his mind was more intent on dinner than lab equipment. The new gear Brad had brought, however, intrigued Corby.

"We could really do with a few replacements." Corby said, "Some of our stuff is pretty obsolete now." He glanced at his friend, "Maybe if we just unpack the cases..." he ventured tentatively to his friend, "just to check nothing got broken on the trip" he added quickly, trying to sound nonchalant.

"Corby, it's a good thing I'm here! You are in danger man - you are going to become a zealous old professor. Let me save you from yourself." Brad replied in mock seriousness.

"I may however need a couple of "nurses" to assist me in my desperate bid to save your sanity." he continued, "Know any good ones?" He rubbed his hands gleefully together in an imitation of a lecherous doctor, an image he conveyed with admirable accuracy.

Corby laughed. He knew when to admit defeat. There would be no work done today - he could see that.

"I guess I could come up with a couple of ladies to distract us - not that you need much distraction! We've got the most beautiful girls in the world here you know!" he boasted.

"Well lead on, I'm most anxious to meet some local dusky maidens! A bit of diversion from my heavy workload would be just about perfect right now!"

"You'd better watch out. Some of our girls are pretty special. You might just find yourself settling down here and never leaving the Island again!" Corby warned, as he pulled into the car park of the beach fronting the marine laboratory.

"I don't intend to ever settle down - not even here in paradise. When I die I aim to be as footloose and fancy free as I am today - and probably still as handsome! My ambition is to live a long, lecherous, wasteful life and end up shot by a jealous husband at the age of ninety-six"

Chapter 4

The waiter stole a quick glimpse at his watch as the enormous cake was being wheeled into the packed room. A chorus of voices joined together in the traditional birthday song. The crowd thronged forward. The waiter smiled. Time to go to work. He glanced around as dozens of his counterparts mingled surreptitiously among New York's finest, serving champagne and ensuring that the privileged didn't have to suffer the indignities of an empty glass.

"Champagne sir?" he quietly enquired as he approached a middle aged, silver haired man. The guest was in fact Mr Bertram T Leidermann. Head of Leidermann Industries. Bertram T Leidermann was a notorious recluse. He rarely ventured from his Long Island retreat and was always accompanied by at least one bodyguard. Tonight's outing was one of those rare occasions. It was the birthday party of one of his oldest friends, Jack Steinberg.

"Sure, sure, why not?" grinned Bert. The bodyguard at his side gave the waiter a cursory glance before both men turned back to the more entertaining spectacle before them. Jack was trying to blow out the candles ably assisted by a couple of most helpful young lady assistants whose dresses clearly demonstrated their more than adequate lung capacity. The girls bowed over the cake and the crowd jostled forward.

As Bert leaned forward for a better view the waiter stepped closer to replenish his glass. Lifting the silver salver slightly he deftly slipped the stiletto, up under the hapless partygoers ribs, piercing his red silk cummerbund which rapidly turned a deeper shade of crimson. The thin blade punctured the spleen before entering the heart. It was a neat and professional job. Skilfully the anonymous waiter retrieved the blade and melted back into the crowd. While the caterers had recruited the other waiters as casual labour he had been hired personally by the host. He didn't know why he'd been contracted to kill Jack's old friend, nor did he care. He assumed it was part of some sort of intimidation racket but he wasn't really interested. "Happy Birthday Jack" he thought as he slipped out through the bustling kitchen.

"Three cheers for Jack" a voice called. As the usual response resounded around the banquet room a couple of people noticed that Jack's old friend appeared to have passed out.

A couple of hours later the 'waiter' pleased with his evening's work was back at his apartment. Tony 'Smiler Baines carefully laid his shirts into a worn suitcase on his bed. Satisfied with his travel preparations he undressed and within minutes was enjoying a deep, untroubled sleep.

He had been named Anthony Charles Baines but for most of his life he had been known as Smiler. The name seemed incongruous considering his chosen profession but it did suit his face if not his personality. He was a chubby man, with sandy coloured hair and a ruddy complexion, and generally looked more like a salesman than a killer. He enjoyed his work and had no conscience about it at all. He had grown up in New York and had committed his first serious crime at the age of twelve when he stole his first car. After that he moved on through an early career of theft and auto crimes until he was seventeen when he shot and killed the manager of the liquor store he was robbing. He remembered standing over the bleeding, dying man and feeling and incredible sense of power - he didn't feel afraid or remorseful - he just felt powerful.

He had looked down at the man and smiled. Word had spread through the streets, naturally the story had become increasingly exaggerated with every telling, but the bottom line was the same - Tony Baines was tough - he could kill and laugh about it, from then he was known as Smiler. He had been a skinny kid then, just another skinny street kid; no one took much notice of him until then. After that night he changed - people noticed him, his peers treated him with awe and respect. It was a good feeling.

He woke before the alarm, showered and dressed quickly before getting down to the more serious business of preparing for his forthcoming trip. With pride he surveyed his collection of weapons. As a fine jeweller would sort through a collection of precious stones he picked over his arsenal, carefully selecting the right tools for his current assignment. Guns he dismissed instantly. Modern aircraft travel complicated their use. Curiously, for a man in his position he disliked guns. He found their action crude. Silencers were extremely effective but he felt cheated of the personal contact of the kill.

He gazed lovingly at his knife collection. Picking one up, he savoured its weighty appeal. It was a small bone handled flick knife. At first glance it appeared innocent enough. It was beautifully decorated. A real piece of art. He ran his fingers over the intricate carving. He easily found the familiar trigger mechanism cunningly concealed by an engraved rose. There was a faint clicking sound as the gleaming stiletto shot forward, instantly transforming the creamy beauty into black art.

For fifteen years he had honed his particular talent. He'd always preferred using a knife. He applied the blade silently with a surgical skill. His victims rarely had time to cry out before they died. He was long gone before anyone discovered the deed. He also had other methods of course, like a true professional he liked to give an extensive range of services, but the knife remained his favourite. He didn't only kill. Sometimes he just hurt people. He was frequently hired to "persuade" his victims to take certain actions. Sometimes, to his disappointment he didn't even have to harm the intended victim at all, they would submit voluntarily just by looking at him. His countenance was benign, even jovial, but his eyes were cold and totally devoid of human emotion.

Randall Westfield III had learnt of him through a business acquaintance and had been most impressed, he had kept in touch through a quite elaborate message system and had availed himself of his services on a couple of occasions. Now he was calling on him again.

Randall frequently breakfasted in a busy diner near his office. It was always crowded and strangers were forced to share tables. Randall always proclaimed to enjoy the menu. In reality he enjoyed the anonymity of the bustling restaurant. It was the perfect place for a clandestine rendezvous. The harassed waitress never remembered a face, unless they forgot to tip.

He was sitting awaiting his breakfast when Smiler slid into the seat opposite him. It was a narrow booth and both men sat centrally on the bench seat to discourage other diners. He didn't look up from his paper.

"When?" murmured Smiler, his eyes fixed on the laminated menu.

"Next week, Barbados. I'll need you for a couple of weeks, maybe three." Randall replied turning the page.

Smiler nodded slowly as if mentally debating the merits of waffles or eggs.

"It'll cost."

"No problem but it's got to be right."

Smiler allowed himself the luxury of shooting a scornful glance at his dining companion. For a brief second their eyes locked. Randall blanched visibly at the menace in his expression.

"If you don't think...." Smiler began, insulted at his expertise being questioned.

"Of course, of course." Soothed Randall. To his intense annoyance he found his hand trembled slightly as he turned another page. A detail not missed by the observant Smiler.

"Coffee?" enquired a passing waitress, pouring before she even heard a reply. "Yeah sure, be right there" she called over to the short order chef, who was yelling to attract her attention. The tension eased.

"Who?" queried Smiler, his pride satisfied by Randall's apparent nervousness.

"Your choice." Randall replied loftily, glad of a chance to regain some position of authority. He noted, with satisfaction, the brief look of surprise that passed Smiler's face.

"Interesting." Conceded Smiler.

"What'll it be?" enquired the waitress, brandishing her notepad. She noted that the next table needed more coffee.

"I'll have the special, eggs over easy. Toast not grits." He smiled at her and handed over the menu. Grateful for the conciseness of his order she nodded her appreciation and hurried off.

Randall rapidly explained what was required. Smiler was to take a Caribbean 'vacation'. Hire a local fisherman to meet a passing tanker, the SS Danzig, to offload a small cargo. Just a couple of drums, no big deal. He did not have to repeat the crucial details; Smiler had an excellent memory. He then had to wait before making the same arrangement in reverse. He was currently negotiating with another tanker to rendezvous a couple of weeks later. He would pass on further details when appropriate. Smiler's main priority was to locate the fisherman.

"You got anyone in mind?" enquired Smiler as he stirred his coffee.

"That's where you get your choice." Randall murmured smugly. He finished his coffee and folded his paper. The waitress was fast approaching bearing Smiler's breakfast. Randall looked at his folded newspaper and then glanced at the total stranger seated opposite him.

"You want this?" He enquired, offering the paper. The waitress reached their table.

"Yeah sure, why not? Thanks." Smiler took the paper with a brief nod of thanks. Randall didn't look back as he left although he mentally pictured Smiler deftly removing the thick envelope appropriately concealed in the sports pages.

"Enjoy your sport." he thought briefly as he strolled into his office.

Smiler poured himself another coffee as he recalled the scene at the diner. Thinking of the generous payment he hastily finished his breakfast and checked around his apartment before leaving. It was an impersonal place, he didn't bother with the usual detritus of life - he didn't like ornaments, he didn't need mementos of his trips. "Maybe this time it will be different," he thought "Maybe I'll bring back a little souvenir - I guess it wouldn't hurt." He gave a wry smile at his own sentimentality, it was an emotion quite alien to him, "Nah maybe not - nothing traceable, souvenirs are for suckers - what would I want with a plastic palm tree!" He was meticulous with his preparations; the apartment held no clue as to his destination, no travel agents' brochures to give any hint of his travel plans. The tickets were booked in the name of Howard Walker, naturally he had a false passport. He carried traveller's cheques in the same name to maintain his tourist image and plenty of cash. He did have one credit card in his new name but he wanted to avoid using it - credit card transactions were too traceable, if necessary he could always say he'd had his wallet stolen and pay by cash.

Opening his door he glanced down the corridor he noticed a neighbour heading toward him laden with groceries, ducking quickly back inside, he waited until she had passed before slipping noiselessly out. He didn't mix at with his neighbours. He'd lived in the apartment for many years but knew no one in the block and studiously avoided any contact. This was not considered unusual - a New York tenement is not renowned for its hospitality.

Out on the street he hailed a cab to JFK Airport; he'd booked a three-week package deal that included flights and hotel. Although he was being paid handsomely for the job he had taken the precaution of choosing a middle range hotel and an economy flight to be more in keeping with his tourist image. Once inside the cab he immediately opened his newspaper to indicate to the driver he was not inclined towards small talk, the driver merely shrugged and concentrated on his driving.

The airport was busy, force of habit made Smiler check behind himself occasionally, he was confident he was not being followed but in his trade it was considered healthier to be paranoid. He found the check-in desk and stood patiently waiting in line, a large family group in front of him haggled incessantly about their seat allocation but he didn't mind the delay. A patient man, he was used to long hours watching an intended victim and had developed waiting into an art. He was acutely aware of everyone and everything around him although to the onlooker he appeared to be just standing daydreaming, it was useful trick. Finally, the party in front seemed to have struck a satisfactory deal over their seating arrangements and moved on.

"Good morning Sir, I'm sorry for the delay. May I have your tickets and passport please?" The check in agent gave the usual line, half expecting a complaint from the traveller who had been standing so long in line.

"Morning, no trouble at all," he smiled broadly at young woman, "these things take time. I know you were doing your best - I guess you can't always please everyone!"

"What a pleasant man" thought the agent as she went through the usual formalities.

As the 'plane sped towards the Caribbean, Smiler broke one of his usual taboos and had a second scotch on the rocks. He wasn't actually starting his assignment today and he figured he was safe enough to relax now. He took a long swallow of his drink and reclining the seat, put on his headphones and stared intently at the movie, thus ensuring he was safe from unwanted interruptions while he mentally went over his forthcoming task.

Over the meal, maintaining his cover of the eager tourist, he chatted inconsequentially to the rather ample lady seated beside him. A native of Barbados, she was returning after a trip to the States to visit family.

"I don't mind telling you - I'll sure be glad to get back to the sunshine. New York is hot enough - too hot - but it don't get nuff nice sunshine, I guess 'cos a body can't hardly see the sky, let alone nice trees blowing about in a cool breeze. You bin to Barbados before?" She paused long enough to catch her breath and Smiler shook his head to indicate his answer.

"Well you see in Barbados you've always got the sea breeze - you ain't never too far from the sea - you can't be! 'Ceptin maybe downtown I guess, but usually you get that nice cool breeze - now just you mind you don't burn." She warned, glancing at his rather pale colouring, "People get burned real bad there - don't realise you see - 'cos of the breeze. Yup that can really get some people. You staying on the coast?" Not waiting for an answer she continued, "I guess you will be - everyone does. The people are real nice too. You'll be surprised especially coming from New York an' all - I swear I ain't never met such unfriendly folk as I did there. They sure are miserable - I was just standing in the market and talking to this guy in the line and he gave me such a look and then he made out like he didn't hear me! I declare I was shocked! I mean it don't cost to be friendly...." She broke off, suddenly embarrassed, "Hey I didn't mean...well that is to say, I'm real sure not all New Yorkers are unfriendly, I didn't mean... her voice trailed off as she, for once, became lost for words.

"Don't worry" Smiler reassured her, "I know just what you mean. I guess we're not renowned for our warmth. How's your lunch?" he enquired politely, changing the subject.

"Jes fine - I guess aeroplane food has improved a bit since I've been travelling..." She launched off into another long rambling speech about previous flights, Smiler looked attentive, smiling and nodding occasionally although in reality far from concentrating on her tedious monologue.

Thankfully after lunch the woman fell asleep and Smiler resumed his planning. The first move, he decided would be to hire a car, tour around a bit and get the feel of the island. Maybe find a couple of quick routes should he need to get away in a hurry. That was the problem with an island, he mused, you can't just drive away if a problem occurs. He thought back to his meeting with Westfield. He hadn't asked what was in the drums, and Westfield hadn't volunteered the information. Smiler had concluded it was probably drugs. Heroin or cocaine most likely. He shrugged; it made no difference to him. He really didn't care as long as he was paid. That was one of the reasons he was successful. He left curiosity to cats. Him, he had never been even remotely curious. If he was asked to kill someone, he did - he never asked why, he just did it. It was none of his concern what the reasons were. It was a philosophy much admired by his various employers.

Westfield had been particularly reticent about the job. This was not unusual in his line of work, but even so, Smiler got the impression that Westfield was exceptionally worried about this one. He recalled the scene in the diner, Westfield appeared almost nervous, which, although they had only met a couple of times previously, did not seem in character for the tough businessman Smiler knew him to be. This deal was obviously important to him. "Well he don't need to worry," thought Smiler immodestly, "he's got the best man for the job!" He smiled to himself as the 'plane started its descent.

"Well you're certainly looking forward to the next couple of weeks!" remarked the lady beside him, waking up and looking across at her travelling companion. "What a pleasant man, such a nice smile" she thought. "Planning your holiday? Don't worry - there's something for everyone here, I'm sure you'll be able to find plenty to smile about!"

"Oh I'm sure I will." Replied Smiler, "I'm real sure I will."

Chapter 5

The old lady shuffled around the small wooden chattel house, pausing to nod her head in respect to the large picture of Christ that adorned the plain wall. The lurid colours of the icon shone through the gloomy interior of the humble living room. The piercing blue eyes seemed to gaze down upon her as she polished the meagre furniture with a vigour belying her age. She listened intently to the ancient radio in the corner as she worked. Martha Richards always listened to the radio. Though she kept busy while she did so. "The devil makes work for idle hands" was one of her favourite sayings. All afternoon the radio blared out gospel music and hymns. Martha would join in loudly; calling a resounding "Amen" as each message to the Lord finished. In the mornings however the radio was tuned to the national station. She particularly enjoyed the daily obituary programme that listed deaths and funeral arrangements. The deceased name was announced, followed by a long list of family, close friends and good friends. "Close friend" of a male deceased generally being used as the accepted euphemism for mistress. She never missed an episode and if truth were known, she used the broadcasts for the basis of her weekly gossips in the market. The other government announcements she usually ignored, unless of course there was a severe weather warning, then the senior members of the family all took great interest. Barbados had not had a severe hurricane since the fifties but there had been a couple of close calls and with a son and grandson earning their living on the sea, the weather was all-important.

"Grandma why do you listen to that stuff? You know it only upsets you." A tall black youth entered the room and frowned as heard the mournful tones of the broadcaster.

"Today we say farewell to our dear brother..." The sombre voice stopped abruptly as the young man switched the small radio set off.

"Sweetboy, what you do that for? You knows I like that programme - you bad boy. You know I like to keep up to date with them things." Trying to get past the boy as he dodged around in front of the radio preventing her turning the programme back on, the old lady scolded her grandson. The battle of the radio stations was an ongoing saga.

"Don't you love me no more Grandma?" Sweetboy tried to look wounded, "Ain't I your precious Sweetboy?"

"Young fool, talking 'bout love and nonsense. What you knows 'bout love? Don't even love your old Grandma enough to let her listen to her radio!"

"Maybe I ought to move away. Go to America. Get me a fine job. Then you could listen to that radio all day 'cos you wouldn't be needing to cuss me out!" He said lightly.

"I never cuss. You wicked boy saying such things. The good Lord knows you is enough to make a saint swear but not me, no sir. Bad language is the devil's own. Your fool talk just makes me mad that's all. You ain't going to no America. You stay here with you family that needs you. Sides..." she paused, then mumbled "maybe you Grandma do love you.... not much sometimes though." She added defiantly, darting past him with surprising agility she managed to switch the set back on.

".... his wife Eugenie and their son, Matthew, his good friend Eloise and their daughter Catherine...." the mournful voice droned on. Martha paused wondering how much she'd missed. Sweetboy seized the opportunity to dart in front of her and switch the set off again.

Sweetboy Richards lived in the small house with his two brothers, one sister, parents and grandmother. The oldest of the children, he worked as a fisherman, usually with his father, but occasionally taking tourists out fishing. He was a good-looking young man of twenty-two with a willing smile and easy charm. His grandmother adored him despite the various troubles he managed to bring to the house.

"Grandma I swear you only listen to that cra...trash to hear if you name be called - in case sweet Jesus had called you and you hadn't noticed!" He laughed as he towered over her, defending the radio like a basketball player protects his goal. His grandmother was, like many Bajans fiercely religious and he knew just how to provoke her.

"Don't you be doing that! Don't you be taking our Lord's name in vain! You are a bad wicked boy - you ain't no "sweetboy" at all. No sir, not at all, we done named you wrong." Her scolding faded away to muttering as she realised that she was alone in the room. Her grandson had slipped past her and disappeared into the tiny kitchen.

"What you doing home at this time anyway boy? You supposed to be out with you daddy ain't you?" She called through to him, hoping they hadn't argued again. Recently Sweetboy and his father had been at each other's throats over just about everything.

"Daddy's gone down to Oistins to the fish market. We had a good catch early so he dropped me off." Sweetboy lied easily, knowing it wasn't worth upsetting her with the truth. She needn't know he hadn't bothered going out with his father that day. It would only get her mad at him. He just couldn't face fishing today so he'd told his father he had an errand to run for his grandmother. He knew she'd cover for him if asked - if only to keep the peace.

"And don't you go picking at that meal. You mummy didn't go getting that ready so as you'd spoil it before dinner." She called after him. Her daughter-in-law worked as a maid in one of the few hotels on the East Coast of the island near their home.

"Can I spoil it at dinner?" Grinned Sweetboy, coming back into the room, a large chunk of bread in his hand. Telltale traces of sweet potato pie around his lips demonstrated how much notice he'd taken of his Grandmother's words.

"You bad boy. Making fun of a weak old lady - you should be ashamed." Reaching up she cuffed him soundly around the ear.

"Ow! For a weak old lady you sure do pack a punch. Maybe we ought to enter you as a prize fighter!" He rubbed his ear laughingly. "Why don't you put some disco music on Grandma, I'll give you a dance." He twirled her around, the floorboards creaked ominously and a plaster Madonna on a shelf came perilously close to tumbling down.

"Put me down, you wicked boy, you'll be sending me to my Maker, then you'll hear my name called on that radio. Prize fighter, where you get this nonsense from boy? Now, talking of prizes - did you get my lotto ticket? You said you would." Martha Richards did the same numbers every week, she'd once won a small prize but she still dreamed of winning the big one.

"What you want to win the lotto for? You don't need no money, I always tell you I'm going to make it rich one day then we'll have all the money we need!" He grinned at her as he continued to dance around the room. "You'll have a new hat every week for church, you'll make all them old ladies crazy with jealousy - an' I'll drive you there myself in a big fancy car."

"You forgot again!" She ignored all his boasting; she'd heard it all a thousand times before. "I knowed you would. I just knowed it. Now put me down. I mean it Sweetboy; I'm getting real mad now. Anyway what's all this fool talk 'bout you making it rich? How you gonna do that - you answer me that! You never work at anything long enough." she grumbled, slapping his arm in a vain attempt to break free of his firm grasp.

Sweetboy gently dropped her into her favourite chair and smiled down at her. Teasingly he checked his pockets as if unaware of their contents before drawing out the promised ticket.

"Here's your tickets Grandma, I didn't forget, and I am going to make it - you'll see. I'm not going to waste my life away in that old boat." He said with a sudden grim determination in his voice as he handed over the precious ticket.

"That's honest work! Didn't sweet Jesus choose the fishermen to follow Him? It's a good honest job for a man." The old lady cried, alarmed by his tone, "There's no shame in honest work!"

"There's no money in it either!" he retorted, "Catching flying fish all day and selling at the roadside - there's no real money in that." He looked angrily around the wooden house with its shabby furnishings and worn flooring.

"There's enough! It kept your Daddy didn't it? Please Sweetboy, I worry for you. Don't be getting no ideas about big money - that's fool talk - don't be looking for no trouble." Her eyes filled as she looked at her young grandson. Why couldn't he be satisfied like his father was?

"Look at this place Grandma! It's a dump. There's got to be better than this out there. I just..." he broke off, frustrated, trying to find the right words.

"It not a dump! It's clean and it's paid for. There's many out there with worse I can tell you. The Lord says, "Blessed be the poor".... ain't no shame in being poor not if you's clean and pure and and....." She stopped abruptly and slumped down in the chair, clutching at her heart. Then putting her hands over her face she peeped through her fingers to gauge his reaction.

Sweetboy was instantly contrite, he hadn't meant to upset her, it was just that life was so frustrating at times. He knew there was nothing wrong with her heart. He also knew there was no point trying to convince her of his argument.

"Hey now, don't you go worrying about me. I ain't looking for no trouble, you'll see, things will work out. Ain't I always been lucky? Maybe we'll both win the lotto. Here I'll even put that terrible radio show back on for you - give you some names to gossip about down the market"

"I'm sure I don't know what you mean. I just like to know if anyone I know has been taken so as I can make sure and pay my respects." Martha sniffed indignantly, recovering miraculously from her heart attack, "Anyway, one of us has got to listen for them hurricane warnings - you never do."

"Grandma you know we ain't had a real hurricane since before I was born, they always miss us, see even the Island is lucky!" He laughed at her and, blowing her a kiss, he sauntered out the door.

"You mind you is home for dinner, and don't you get into trouble - you wicked boy!" She was wasting her breath, Sweetboy was long gone, along the road to meet up with his friends and bemoan their lack of funds.

Sweetboy strolled along the dusty lane. Hands thrust in his pockets, kicking at loose stones in his way. "There's got to be more than this." he thought to himself, "I'm gonna have to find a way to change things." He knew a couple of his friends sold the odd joint to the tourists, they made good money, but he didn't know their supplier, and he wasn't sure he'd want to get involved with anything like that. It would break his grandma's heart if he got caught. "Maybe if I was real careful," he reasoned, "Maybe just made enough to set myself up in something else, something legitimate, something worthwhile, something with a bit of respect - anything but selling flying fish!"

"You'll see Grandma." He muttered "They'll all see. One day I'm going to make some real money. I ain't gonna grow old in no chattel house."

Chapter 6

Andrew Kinloch reported for his first day at the Queen Elizabeth Hospital, Bridgetown, with mixed feelings. On the one hand, he reassured himself, he'd had the finest training in the Western world. He had passed all his exams with flying colours, and was generally considered to be a fine doctor. Then again, he thought with some trepidation, he had never worked outside of Britain and his only knowledge of tropical diseases was what he had studied in textbooks. He knew very little about the hospital he was coming to, nor for that matter, about the people with whom he would be working.

He walked in through the large glass doors into the reception area where he was due to report at 8.00 am a little early. Glancing around he found his immediate impressions were that the hospital was much the same as the one he had left. He knew it had 600 beds, a 24-hour casualty unit and that it was state owned and administrated. That much he'd gleaned from the information he'd been sent. He walked up to the front desk where two receptionists were seated. They looked up with open curiosity at the young man in the pristine white coat. Andrew's attention was distracted at that moment as he caught sight of Charmaine walking across the foyer carrying a large manila folder. His eyes lit up at the sight of a familiar face, especially hers. She smiled across at Andrew and came over.

"Charmaine!" he called as she approached. The two receptionists exchanged knowing looks. Charmaine noticing the quick exchange winced inwardly. "No prizes for guessing the topic of gossip today!" she thought with a wry smile. "It'll be all round the canteen by lunchtime!" She gave Andrew a brief frown and swiftly directed her glance over to the desk then back to Andrew.

"Good morning Dr Kinloch. All set for your first day?" she enquired formally, trying to suppress a grin at the receptionists' obvious interest.

"Good morning Miss Harrison. Yes, thank you - I'm all ready and keen to start." Andrew sensed that hospital etiquette had been breached in some way and answered her in an equally formal tone.

"Good, glad to hear it. If you'll follow me I'll show you the way to Dr. Jones' office." She turned and led the way through the building. Dressed in a tailored suit she looked smart and efficient. Her golden skin glowed against the peach linen of her short sleeved jacket. The skirt was just above the knee affording a glimpse of her shapely legs. Low-heeled cream court shoes matched her cream blouse. Discreet jewellery and make-up completed the picture admirably. Andrew tried to appear subtle in his study but his open admiration shone like a beacon from his eager face.

"Did I say the wrong thing?" He asked as soon as they were out of earshot of the desk.

"No, not really. It's just it's a small place and...well you know how quickly people get the wrong idea!" To her annoyance, Charmaine found herself blushing.

"Sorry. I wouldn't want to get your boyfriend jealous or anything." Andrew answered quickly, enjoying her discomfort and fishing for information.

"As it happens I don't have a boyfriend at the moment. I...." she stammered.

Andrew grinned happily and bit back the obvious reply.

"Do you think we could get back to a more professional level here, Dr Kinloch? I am supposed to be showing you around. I don't think you've actually noticed anything yet!" Charmaine retorted archly.

"On the contrary Miss Harrison, believe me I've been paying rapt attention!"

Together they walked through the corridors of the hospital, Andrew carefully looking around and trying to familiarise himself with the place. Like many state hospitals it was clean but slightly shabby, the floors gleamed but Andrew noticed the walls could do with a coat of paint. Having come directly from an inner city National Health Hospital, Andrew found the decor oddly comforting. "Home from home" he murmured as they walked briskly along.

"Did you say something?" Queried Charmaine, glancing across at him. He looked very different today in his spotless white coat and his stethoscope draped casually around his neck. A marked contrast to the rather anxious looking tourist she had collected from the airport only a couple of days before.

"No, just thinking aloud." Andrew smiled at her, "What's Dr Jones like? Has he been here long? I had a letter of introduction but it didn't say much."

"Obviously not." Charmaine grinned, "He is a she! She is a lady doctor, and actually considered to be the finest doctor on the island." She paused, waiting for his reaction.

"Sorry - didn't mean to be sexist! Actually the finest doctor I know back home is a lady and, if it's not again being sexist to point it out, a damn attractive one as well." He smiled warmly as he thought of Janet McIntyre, he even found himself feeling a little homesick as he imagined her busy doing her rounds in his small Scottish home town.

Charmaine saw his expression and irrationally felt a slight pang of jealousy. "Well I'm not sure if you will feel quite the same way about our Dr Lois Jones, she's probably a little older than your lady doctor." She said briskly, then immediately felt guilty and rather ashamed at her rather childish reaction. The truth was she liked Lois Jones, she was indeed an excellent doctor and also a thoroughly pleasant person, much admired and liked by her staff, Charmaine hadn't meant to sound even faintly critical of her.

"Actually she is a lovely lady, in every respect, very warm and caring, and very down to earth. She'd been here for years and has worked her way to the top, which hasn't always been easy - even in medicine - there are still many who think it's a man's world!" She smiled at Andrew as she spoke to show she was only teasing, much to his relief.

"I look forward to meeting this paragon! I considered myself honoured, as a mere male, to be allowed into her presence!" He answered in a mock humble tone.

"You'd better believe it - she eats junior doctors for breakfast! Anyway here we are." She knocked at a door that bore the lady in question's nameplate and paused for a response. Andrew straightened his tie and squared his shoulders as he prepared to meet his new boss.

"Come" called a voice through the door and Andrew found himself being ushered into Dr. Jones' office. Charmaine introduced him and, with a brief smile at Andrew, excused herself and left.

Dr. Jones rose from her desk and shook his hand firmly.

"Welcome to the Queen Elizabeth, Dr Kinloch. I hope you will be very happy here - please take a seat." She pronounced his name perfectly he noticed, the first person to do so since his arrival.

For a few moments the two sat opposite the desk mentally assessing each other. Lois Jones was a small black woman, he judged her to be in her mid fifties, short grey hair neatly arranged in a soft, and casual style and a kindly looking face. He warmed to her instantly, she had bright eyes and small half glasses that he noticed kept slipping down her delicate nose. He noticed the photographs on her desk, two showed young people dressed in cap and gown, obviously graduation pictures of her children, judging by the close family resemblance. Another silver frame held a family group, he recognised the doctor, the two children, probably not much younger than he was himself, and a large quite stern looking man standing proudly at the back - obviously her husband. They made an attractive group.

Lois discreetly evaluated the young man seated opposite her; she had noticed the exchange of smiles between him and Charmaine. "I hope he's not going to be one of those hospital Romeo's!" She thought briefly, "That's all we need - all the nurses falling in love with the new young doctor!" He didn't look the Casanova type though, she mused, attractive enough to be sure, but he looked more like the boy next door type than a smooth charmer. To his credit he looked keen enough, eager yet slightly apprehensive - a good sign, she always thought. She disliked the "seen it all before" type of doctor who thought because they'd come to a small island they had a better, more sophisticated knowledge.

"So Dr. Kinloch, have you seen much of our hospital yet?" She had a soft voice with an unmistakable air of authority to it.

"Not yet - but I'm looking forward to it. From what I saw as I came in, it looks much like the hospital I left in Glasgow, but I'm sure it will be very different."

"Oh I think you'll find us very similar to what you've been used to, and our patients I expect will have much the same sort of complaints as yours back home."

Andrew nodded and smiled, thinking she was probably very wrong, but certainly not about to contradict her.

"I have been revising my knowledge of typhoid and hepatitis, those were the main vaccinations I was instructed to have before I came so I imagine that is one of the main areas of concern here." He said, hoping to impress her with his background knowledge.

"I must commend you on your precautionary actions," she replied, smiling at his eager enthusiasm, "but actually, I'm quite relieved to say we haven't had any cases of either of these diseases for very many years. I know some of the other islands have though, and I'm afraid the various health authorities tend to recommend the vaccinations for anyone visiting the Caribbean - I'm sure they think all the islands are the same - although really such precautions are not in fact necessary for Barbados."

"Oh, er...good." Andrew tried to summon up the right response to this news, which wasn't easy when recalled how stiff and sore his arm had been after his typhoid jab and the longs hours he'd spent reading up on the treatment of both typhoid and hepatitis.

"Well never mind, I'm sure you'll agree - extra research is never wasted. Now, shall we take a tour around the hospital?" She rose to her feet and walked around to the door, Andrew courteously opened it for her and together they started their tour of the hospital.

As they walked around the hospital Dr Jones pointed out the various wards and departments, Andrew listened intently, trying to remember as much as possible, while keeping up with the energetic pace of his new employer.

Touring the wards, Andrew found Lois Jones had been very accurate in her suggestion that most of the patients were indeed suffering from the same sort of complaints as his previous ones had - there was not an exotic tropical disease in sight.

"Well you were right Doctor. I haven't seen anything that unusual so far - perhaps I had rather a romantic idea of dealing with strange tropical maladies!" Andrew commented sheepishly.

Lois Jones laughed, she found herself really warming to this honest and immensely likeable young doctor.

"As a matter of fact, we did have an outbreak about six months ago of a relatively mild tropical disease - Dengue fever. Are you familiar with it?"

"Ah Dengue fever, um...er...yes, ah Dengue fever." Andrew racked his brains as he struggled to remember what he had learnt of Dengue fever, giving up, he shrugged his shoulders, disappointed at not having a comprehensive answer to his first medical question. "To be honest I really don't know much about it, I do recall a few vague details, we certainly covered it in medical school but I've never actually come across a case personally. I couldn't guarantee I'd recognise it, isn't it a bit like flu? Sorry."

"No need to be sorry - it's not that common in Scotland I shouldn't think! It's a viral disease, transmitted by mosquitoes, characterised by headache, fever, pain in the joints and skin rash. As you said, it's a bit like flu, and, like flu, not usually that serious. Having said that it can be fatal, generally in cases involving the vulnerable. The very old, or the very young and anyone with an existing medical condition. So it's not something to be dismissed lightly. As I said we last had an outbreak about six months ago so we shouldn't have another for quite a while, it's not that rife - but worth watching out for. When it does flare up we try to contain it fairly rapidly. Right now, to start off I'm afraid I'm rather throwing you in at the deep end as we are a bit short-staffed in casualty, but your colleague, Dr Griffin will brief you and advise you if you should find anything you're unfamiliar with - though I don't expect you'll have any problems. I'll just finish the general tour with you then we'll head on down to casualty."

An hour later they found themselves at the entrance to the busy casualty department. The scene was one of bustling activity and again Andrew was struck by the similarity of the hospital he had left to this one.

"The main problems we have here are the typical accidents, fall cuts, abrasions, that sort of thing. We also get quite a few victims of sunburn, which can be quite dangerous, a lot of people are caught out by our climate...." She broke off as they entered the department to be greeted by a rather harassed looking doctor. "Ah Mike, there you are, I'd like you to meet your new colleague - Andrew Kinloch. Dr Kinloch - Dr. Griffin. Dr Kinloch will be joining us for a while and I'm starting him here in casualty."

"Great! Pleased to meet you." Michael Griffin pumped Andrew's hand enthusiastically. Mike Griffin was an Englishman who had come to Barbados on a similar assignment to Andrew but had decided to stay and had been at the hospital for a number of years. He had married one of the nurses at the same hospital and now considered the island to be his permanent home.

"We could certainly do with an extra pair of hands here today." he continued.

"Problems?" Queried Lois quickly, if they needed her, she would stay on herself and give a hand.

"No, not really, just lots of minor accidents - nothing too serious but time-consuming and the waiting room is filling up." Turning to Andrew he added, "Have you done much casualty work?" They walked towards the first cubicle as they spoke.

"I did six months, from September last year to February this year in Glasgow General, though we didn't have much call for sunburn remedies! Our main occupation was setting the limbs of people who had fallen on the ice - I don't expect you have that problem! At least he could say that with a degree of confidence he thought laughingly as Mike Griffin pulled back the curtain of the cubicle. A young man sat up on the examining bed, obviously in pain; he was clutching his leg and moaning.

"What seems to be the problem here?" Mike asked, glancing at the man's notes. The patient was dressed very smartly in a crisp white shirt and neat red bow tie. "A very formal attire," thought Andrew quizzically, "for such a young man."

"Well Doc, the thing is, I works in the Hilton - in the bar, I was unloading the ice from the machine when the bag split - the ice went everywhere - I skids on it and I think I bust me leg - it sure hurts bad!" He sank back against the pillows, his face shining with a mixture of heat and exertion.

"It's not all bad news - we happen to have an expert in this field with us today." Lois hid a wry smile; "I'll leave this gentleman in your hands, Doctor." She said smoothly as she turned and left the cubicle.

Chapter 7

Brad Tucker found his first day of work in Barbados altogether less stressful. It began with him and Nathan unpacking and examining the various pieces of lab equipment he had brought with him. Corby, although he tried to appear nonchalant, was as excited as a child on Christmas morning opening presents, while Brad looked on with the amused, indulgent smile of a wealthy parent. "Corby my friend," he thought, happily, "You are in for a real surprise!

The Barbados Institute of Marine Biology, situated at the fishing village of Oistins was set back off the road, its entrance partially obscured by a beautiful Flamboyant tree. Tall trees fringed the car park in front of the building, providing cool, shady parking for the staff. The building itself was a typical example of island architecture. Concrete breezeblock construction; single story with a bright orange tiled roof and whitewashed walls, giving it a faintly Spanish look. Large windows with vertically slatted glass made full use of the ocean breeze while ornate wrought iron "burglar bars" covering each window enabled them to be kept permanently open without any security risk.

"I like your 'air-conditioning' Corby my friend." Exclaimed Brad, leaning back and enjoying the through breeze.

"Huh? Oh yeah, well it's a lot cheaper." Explained Corby, hardly glancing up form his fervent unpacking. "Course we have to have one room electrically air-conditioned. The one with the equipment and samples and stuff but on the whole we do pretty well."

"You'll have to show me later." Yawned Brad, "When you can drag yourself away that is."

"You won't find that room a yawn I can tell you." Corby exclaimed proudly, "We've got samples of marine life from all around the world. We might be small but..." he laughed, "like the old saying goes, we're small but perfectly formed."

"Glad to hear it!" Replied Brad calmly. "I've always tried to reassure you Corby - size isn't everything!"

The lab was partly funded by the Barbados Government, it also received financial support in the form of a grant from the European Economic Community, but the staff who worked there were all too aware how precarious public finding could be. Brad had done the rounds trying to obtain a grant from the US Government towards the running costs. The Institute had been founded originally to investigate the science of marine zoo toxicology, the study of poisonous and venomous marine animals, and it offered advice to hospitals around the world.

"You can mock..." started Corby.

"Thank you!" Interrupted Brad.

"I'll have you know we're pretty proud of ourselves here. We get requests from everywhere for info on marine poisons and venom. Though recently we're getting more and more involved in pollution and contaminants." he paused thoughtfully, "I guess that's just the way the world's heading."

"That's why they've got heroes like us!" Exclaimed Brad. "Come on let's get this lot unpacked then you can show me the nerve centre of this mighty establishment."

Later that morning Brad and Corby sat enjoying a cup of coffee in the small staff rest area of the lab. The lounge contained a coffee machine, a few uncomfortable plastic chairs and a Formica topped table. It was obvious the Institute was not about to waste its precious funds on the unnecessary luxuries and the room did not seem, upon first impression, to be the most attractive of amenities for leisure time. It did however, boast the most magnificent view of the beach and the sparkling Caribbean Sea from its large picture windows which transformed it into a veritable oasis, where one could sit, quite contented, for hours.

"So, what are you working on at the moment?" enquired Brad casually, as he sipped his coffee. He was watching a girl on the beach applying sun lotion, ordinarily he would have been looking for an excuse to go out and offer her a hand - literally - but today the news he was about to impart far outweighed such trivial matters.

"Actually the QEH..." Corby began then laughed as he noticed Brad's quizzical expression. "Sorry, I was forgetting you're not from around these parts. The QEH is our state hospital, The Queen Elizabeth. We work with them quite a bit. I'll take you over sometime and introduce you."

"Sounds good to me - plenty of nurses. I do like a woman in uniform! Then again I quite like them out of uniform, or in a bikini, or out of a bikini, or..." he pretended to give the matter serious consideration.

"Yeah, Yeah, I get the picture. Anyway as I was saying. The QEH..." he was again interrupted.

"The Queen Elizabeth Hospital, you see I am paying attention. On the ball me you know. Not easily distracted or anything."

"Will you shut up and listen. Do you want to hear this or not. A simple nod of the head will do." He paused and Brad solemnly nodded his head.

"Sorry professor." He muttered, grinning at his friend.

"Anyway. The Q...the hospital passed on an interesting fax yesterday from a British hospital. It was regarding an English woman, recently returned from a Caribbean cruise, who developed an unusual ulcer in her leg, which is not responding to treatment. Apparently they'd faxed the QEH really as a shot in the dark to see if they could offer any help. They passed it to us as it sounded like our department. It would be pretty handy to be able to help a London hospital. Might help with the funding." Nathan said casually, watching his friend surreptitiously, he expected him to find a case like this quite irresistible.

"Had she been bitten or stung" As expected Brad rose to the bait, he mentally ran through the possibilities. In cases such as this, his work was much like that of a forensic scientist.

"Not that she could recall, so it obviously wasn't an instant type of injury." Corby gave out the information sparingly, testing his friend's knowledge.

"Any scratches or welts?" Brad's concise questions demonstrated the way his mind was analysing the problem. He thought carefully of the various cases he'd been called upon to assist with in the past.

"Just a small scratch on her calf, just above the ankle - hardly noticeable." Corby grinned as he watched his friend working out the puzzle.

"How are they treating it?" The jocular manner was gone; Brad assumed his role as a serious scientist.

"The ulceration started to spread so they've put a full plaster cast on the leg, from the knee down, to immobilise it." Corby knew his friend would find that snippet of information interesting - the game was nearly over.

"Wow - that's a bit drastic!" As Corby had guessed Brad realised immediately how serious the ulceration was as soon as he heard the lengths to which the British doctors had gone in order to bring it under control.

"They had to be on the safe side until they knew what they were dealing with." Corby began to look smug. "Okay hotshot - times up - what do you reckon?"

"Coral cut." Brad stated firmly, "Got to be - does that check out?" He sat back and waited for confirmation of his diagnosis.

"Yeah - you got it." Corby was not really surprised, coral poisoning was one of the more common complaints they were called in to deal with it could cause varying amounts of difficulty, but in some unfortunate cases a violent reaction did occur. It was good to know Brad hadn't lost his touch though. "Turns out after the doctor suggested it to her last night, upon my advice of course, she did remember getting a little scratch while snorkelling over a reef, apparently it was so trivial she'd forgotten about it!"

"The great Nathan Corbin saves the day!" Diagnosis over, the clowning Brad returned.

"I know - it gets tough sometimes, always being the hero! They wanted me to play superman you know - but I didn't like wearing tights!"

"That's not what I've heard! What did you suggest? Is the wound responding?" The treatment - and its effect - would confirm their suspicions.

"It's early days yet, but I reckon a few days of kaolin poultices, dressing of magnesium sulphate in glycerine solution and a course of antibiotics and she'll be fine." Corby shrugged and tried to look modest - he failed!

"It proves one thing though - we need more research in this field. People need to be better educated about the dangers of apparently innocuous marine life - that woman could have had a major problem." This was one topic that even Brad felt strongly about, his face grew more solemn as he contemplated the unknown woman's possible fate.

"Yeah but like - we don't want to scare off the tourists." warned Corby, a native Bajan, he was well aware of the possible consequences of scare mongering.

"I'm not saying we tell people they can't go swimming! I just think they should be aware of possible dangers, and how to treat little problems so they don't become major problems - it makes sense! Look with proper treatment that coral cut would have been nothing at all - it should never have got that far!" Brad argued.

"Which is why we're trying to get our project here more funding. I want to get as comprehensive collection as possible of various marine venom and poisons. Each sample catalogued, and identified with all possible treatments and antidotes. Eventually I want to produce a complete paper on the subject, worldwide publication so every tiny hospital knows what to do when a patient presents with unusual symptoms. You can't expect some doctor in the middle of England or inland USA for that matter to recognise instantly a tropical poison...." Corby warmed to his subject with the fanatical zeal of a religious convert.

"Hey, hey, steady on - this is me you're talking to, remember? I'm on your side! Which brings me to another little matter...." he paused, trying to look disappointed while suppressing a grin.

"We didn't get the grant." Corby said flatly. He'd been half-expecting a negative response from the US government, obtaining public funding was always a difficult task, and getting funds for a foreign country, doubly so. He'd resigned himself to disappointment when Brad hadn't mentioned it earlier.

"We did! Actually it was the expert powers of persuasion by yours truly which secured for us..." he paused again keeping Corby in cruel suspense, and savouring his moment of triumph. "...three years of government funding from the good ole U S of A. My powers and the minor detail that the congressman got stung on the ass by a jellyfish while scuba diving." He added, grinning broadly as he remembered the Congressman in question, pompous type, the jellyfish had the worst of the incident! Actually he had no idea where the jellyfish had stung the man but it made for a better story.

"You bastard! Why didn't you tell me sooner - how could you keep that to yourself? Three years! That's fantastic - man you are ace - you really are. Three years! Wow! What did you do with the Congressman's ass - kiss it better?" Nathan was practically dancing around the room.

"Professional secret - I got the grant though, didn't I? I couldn't tell you sooner - I've only been here a day - I was just waiting for the right moment! Thought I'd let you sweat for a while! Anyway,

I'm afraid it's not all good news." he hesitated, as if loathe to part with bad news.

"What? Tell me!" Corby looked worried, he figured there had to be a catch somewhere.

"It means I've got to hang out in this little tropical paradise for three years! Your love life is going to take a serious down turn when the local ladies see me - you won't stand a chance! Reckon you can go without for that long!" He leant back in his chair and laughed, now the news was out he felt great - what an assignment - three years in Barbados!

"You're staying? That's great - and don't worry, if anyone is going to lose out in the dating stakes - it sure ain't gonna be me! You'd better start looking out for those cold showers - you're gonna need them! Right now - when do we start? Now - of course - but where? Do they expect monthly reports or results as they come through? Maybe we ought to map out a plan of action? How about if we start by cataloguing all the stuff we've got coming in at the moment. I've had some new reports from that Australian lab - the one in Melbourne, you know it? They've had some great results on antidotes for stonefish stings. Have you seen the reports? It was a great piece of work! They've got this antivenin..."

"Time out!" Brad raised his arms in horror. "You don't have to go crazy! We've got three years! I suggest we start today's research into marine life with a nice seafood lunch, where we can calmly and rationally discuss the implications of our forthcoming financial arrangements - in other words - let's eat first!" He rose to his feet and, with one last, wistful, look out at the girl on the beach, headed for the door.

Corby jumped up, still full of anticipation for the forthcoming project and unable to drag his mind back to more mundane matters.

"Okay I'll give you that - I guess you deserve it. By the way did I mention we're getting some pretty good results on our work on ciguatoxic fish - Why do they turn from edible to toxic?

Is it just what they feed on? Apparently the liver can become engorged...."

Brad raised both hands in mock surrender. "Way too much detail Corby! Like I really need to know all that just before a fish dinner. Maybe I'll order pasta!"

Chapter 8

Smiler awoke early, the sunlight streamed through the curtains promising another beautiful day. The room was light and airy. There were heavy curtains at the window to block out the sunshine for guests wishing to sleep late. Smiler had deliberately left them open, preferring to have only the lightweight voiles that not only allowed in light, they allowed in sound as well. There was no chance of anyone sneaking in through the patio doors of the room in the still of the night. As ever, meticulous about his personal safety, Smiler thought of everything. The room itself was typical enough, twin double beds, a couple of comfortable chairs, small table, satellite television. It was on the ground floor and had a small private patio that opened onto a grassy area a few feet from the hotel pool. Once the job was over he'd be able to relax and really enjoy his vacation he thought to himself as he lay in bed, listening to the soft hum of the air conditioner and planning his day ahead.

Frowning slightly, he recalled his journey from the airport, the taxi had followed the main route across the island, along a broad highway and then travelling up the main west coast road to his hotel. He knew this area to be considered the more affluent part of the island from his guidebook, but even so he noted the abject poverty of the local people.

The fancy hotels contrasted sharply with the randomly interspersed wooden chattel houses. To most visitors this gave the island its own unique charm, but to Smiler, who had an inbred contempt of poverty, stemming from his own background, it was an unpleasant reminder of his past.

The ragged children playing along the streets brought back painful memories of his own childhood playing in the slums of New York, hanging around the street corners, glaring resentfully at the occasional expensive car as it passed quickly through. He remembered how he'd jeered at the rich folk as they drove past, they obviously thought they were being terribly chic driving through the slums - he hated them all. His expression grew hard as he recalled the misery of his life then; angry with himself for bringing to mind a time he had long struggled to forget.

Totally blind to the vast discrepancy between the two cultures. He didn't see that the kids here were genuinely happy. They laughed as they waved at the passing cars and grinned at the tourists. These visitors were their livelihood, and they were certainly not resented. Smiler saw none of this, he saw only poverty and it disgusted him.

"Shouldn't be a problem to hire some local beach bum for the job - these guys will do anything for a US dollar." He thought contemptuously, as he rose and headed for the shower.

"Just so long as they don't get greedy - still I can soon put them straight on that one." He grinned to himself, he enjoyed being a bully, he looked forward to flashing the cash around and anticipated the eagerness of the local youth he would employ to respect him for it. Respect - that was what it was all about, what he'd always craved. Respect and fear, and now he'd got it. It was a good feeling.

He dressed carefully in the uniform of the tourist, flowery shirt and lightweight shorts. With his usual attention to detail he carefully applied a strong sun lotion, he couldn't afford to be laid up with sunburn. The cargo ship would be at the planned rendezvous point within a week, so time was of the essence and he was well aware of the importance of timing.

Smiler had pre-booked a moke from a local car hire for the duration of his visit and went down to the reception area to collect it and arrange his visitor's driving permit. He sauntered casually through the wide reception area. The walls were painted plain white, abstract paintings in pastel shades vaguely suggested coastal scenes with their scattered seashells and waving ferns. Large comfortable chairs were dotted around with cane tables strategically placed around them. Each table held a vase of beautiful tropical flowers that provided a splash of colour against the cool white walls. A rack on the wall near the reception desk held a multitude of brightly coloured brochures advertising the island's many attractions, and copies of the local free magazine 'The Visitor' were piled high on the counter.

Keeping up his charade of the carefree visitor he went through the usual formalities at the desk, smiling cheerfully at the young receptionist.

"Are you going out to explore the island today Sir?" She enquired as she handed over the car keys and a map of the island.

"I expect so - I haven't really made any plans." he replied, airily, he didn't want to engage in small talk, always an intensely private man, an occupational hazard, he supposed. He loathed discussing his plans even when they were totally innocent, but he realised the necessity of maintaining his casual image, so he smiled at the receptionist, encouraging her to continue.

"Well it's pretty hard to get lost here. This is a map showing some of the main areas of attraction, which might help you to plan your route. Everywhere you go you'll see bus stops and they all say one of two things, either "To City" or "Out of City". If you follow the "To City" signs you'll find yourself in Bridgetown fairly quickly, and then you just follow the west coast road back here - it's easy really!" she said brightly, tracing the route on the map with her finger to make the directions even clearer.

"Thanks, I'll remember that." He walked off before she had time to say more and headed into the restaurant for breakfast. The restaurant overlooked the beach and many of the tables were outside on the wide, shady veranda, he requested a table nearest the beach, pointing out a corner table, and sat at an angle to the view, partly facing the sea, but also able to see anyone approaching. The table had the added advantage of keeping the other diners at a safe distance. He ordered breakfast and sat examining the map while he waited for his meal.

"Planning a trip around the island Sir?" A waiter asked, filling his glass with iced water. Smiler glanced at him briefly, his quick reflexes weighing the man up and deciding he was just what he appeared to be - an ordinary waiter. As usual his professionalism kept him alert. He smiled as he recalled his own last job. Waiters could be dangerous people to ignore.

"I might, I haven't really decided." He didn't look up again; the man was obviously insignificant and unnecessary for his plans. The waiter continued unabashed.

"It's a good day for it. You could maybe have a run over the east coast, it's really pretty over there - but don't swim there, man those currents will drag you off so fast, you'll be half way cross the ocean before you know it!"

"Thank you - I'll bear that in mind." He replied shortly, continuing to study the map.

"Well if you need anything, just you let me know - you have a good day now!" The waiter added cheerfully as he carried on around the tables.

"Planning a trip out today Sir?" The waitress enquired, as she brought his breakfast. She too looked exactly what she was, a local girl earning a decent living in the hotel trade, nothing unusual about her.

"I'm thinking about it." He almost snarled at the girl, but managed to check himself in time. It wouldn't do to arouse suspicion, but what was it with this place? Didn't anyone mind their own business? In New York you could go a month without speaking to anyone - here everyone seemed interested in his actions, or was he being paranoid again?

"That's nice. I'm sure you'll enjoy it. Have you thought of where you want to go? I could recommend a route if you like. What sort of thing are you interested in?" She looked over his shoulder at the map.

"Nothing special, I might just drive around for a while." He folded the map and nodding dismissively to the girl, picked up his fork to start on his breakfast.

"Well if there's anything I can help you with, just you let me know." She smiled as she walked away.

A short while later Smiler left the hotel and headed his hired moke towards Bridgetown, the island's capital. He drove along the coast road, past the oil refinery and along the main highway towards the town centre. As he neared the harbour he noticed a huge cruise ship had docked, a long line of taxis waited for the tourists to disembark.

"More fat cats coming to mingle with the peasants!" He thought scornfully, his memory again flashing back to his early days. He forced his mind back to the matter in hand and concentrated on his driving. Although the traffic was much slower than back home, he found he had to concentrate on driving on the left.

He parked in the town's only multi story car park, and quickly found the steps down to a small shopping mall through which he found himself on the streets of Bridgetown. A colourful sight greeted him; the streets were teeming with life. Old ladies sat along the pavement in front of trays of fruit, selling mangoes, pineapples, and other more exotic fruits - some of which he didn't even recognise. Pushing through the crowds he walked along a small backstreet through an open market. Men wielding lethal looking machetes with an expert skill even he was forced to admire, lopped the tops off coconuts and offered refreshing drinks to passers-by. Stallholders selling sunglasses, cheap jewellery and a myriad of souvenirs called to him as he passed, and everywhere dozens of taxi drivers offered to drive him "Back to the ship mister?" "Tour the island, mister?" It was a kaleidoscope of colour and noise and for a man with such keenly attuned senses - a complete nightmare. Thankfully he ducked into a small rum shop and, with a surprising stroke of luck, found a quiet corner of the bar.

"Banks." He ordered, noticing a poster advertising the local brew. The barman opened a large cooler and brought out a bottle of beer, deftly knocking off the cap on a convenient opener crudely nailed to the side of the counter, he slide the bottle over.

"You wanna glass, man?" he enquired casually, as he mixed a strange looking concoction into a large demi-john. It was the first batch of the day's rum punch, ready for the lunchtime trade.

"It's fine like this." He decided to take a chance, hoards of tourists milling around afforded him the opportunity to gain a bit of local knowledge, he would never be remembered among so many similar clients. The small bar was dimly lit, quite a contrast to the bright sunshine outside, he found it took a couple of seconds for his eyes to adjust to the gloom, a point worth remembering he thought.

"Sure is busy around here, you must do a good trade." he commented, keeping an eye on the door. Outside the cacophony continued. The relative peace inside the bar became all the more welcoming.

"S'Wednesday" the man shrugged, continuing his preparations, obviously expecting a rush at any time.

"Wednesday?" echoed Smiler, not understanding any significance to the day. Was Wednesday perhaps some sort of public holiday? Surely not every Wednesday?

"Wednesday - cruise ship day. Big money day." Explained the barman, finally satisfied with the recipe he was making, he gave the jar one last vigorous shake and placed it on a rather precarious looking shelf behind him.

"So it's not always like this?" Smiler mentally filed the information away, realising immediately if he ever needed to lose himself in a crowd - Wednesday in Bridgetown was the day to do it.

"Well - I guess it's always fairly busy in town, cepting Saturday afternoon - shops close up lunchtime Saturday - but Wednesday is our really crazy day. It's early yet, but you wait, couple of hours, this place will be jumping." He grinned and Smiler was startled to notice a gold lion somehow attached to the man's front tooth.

"Bought this tooth with the takings of one Wednesday!" he boasted proudly, thrusting his face closer for Smiler's approval.

"Looks great." Muttered Smiler, trying to summon up the appropriate enthusiasm, which was so obviously expected.

"Don't it though! That's my sign you see. Leo! That's me - the lion - and this...." he made a grand sweeping gesture around the rather dingy bar, "this is Leo's place. You can get these at a pretty good price at the jewellers up in Da Costa's mall. You tell 'em Leo sent you - you'll get a discount! You off the ship?" He added, eyeing Smiler's holiday garb, obviously a tourist, he surmised.

Smiler toyed briefly with the idea of saying he was on a cruise, but swiftly dismissed it, he may want to return and it wouldn't help if he were caught out in a lie, the truth was simpler.

"No, I'm staying at a hotel up the road a way, I'm here for a couple of weeks." He replied casually, swallowing his beer appreciatively, the flavour was surprisingly good he decided, and thankfully very cold.

"Well you sure picked the wrong day to visit town mister!" Leo grinned again and the emblem glinted briefly through the gloom. "You visit on a Wednesday you'll likely get swallowed up in the crowd! Hey - but, no sweat man, you're still safe, know what I mean. Bajans like tourists! 'Course you gotta be a bit careful. Ain't everyone here is a native - if you catch my drift. Some of those other islands, they've got some pretty mean folks, not like us, and some of them come over to our patch, but mainly Barbados is OK, like I said - no sweat!" His patriotic pride shone as brightly as his dental work.

"Honey! Honey look at this cute little rum shop - isn't it just the sweetest thing you ever saw? Honey - come on I wanna drink." An enormous woman wearing a lurid shorts and shirt set squeezed into the suddenly tiny room, dragging a profusely sweating, equally enormous man reluctantly behind her.

"Babe - it ain't even air conditioned!" he protested, looking around dubiously, obviously not impressed by the surroundings, "Why don't we go to one of those nice hotels we saw from the ship?"

"'Cos they ain't authentic! Those places look the same everywhere - I want a genuine authentic Barbados rum shop where we can have a real local speciality. Now - what shall we have?" She demanded loudly, ignoring her husband's protestations and peering up at the chalkboard on the wall.

"Got any Budweiser?" Asked thc man hopefully.

Chapter 9

Andrew was eagerly anticipating his first visit to a Barbados beach. He looked around enthusiastically as Charmaine's car pulled into the small beachfront car park. The beach was quiet as it was still early. A couple of beach vendors were busy setting up their stalls selling colourful wraps and sarongs. A uniformed policeman sauntered casually along patrolling the area, pausing to chat with the stallholders. A few local people enjoyed an early morning swim avoiding the fierce heat of the day. Although usually an early riser Andrew found the time difference between his homeland and Barbados meant he was awake even earlier than usual and he took advantage of the fact to get a good position on the beach. Weekends being the busiest time in the casualty department of the hospital Andrew was given a day off mid week, this meant he had started work on a Tuesday and had the following day off to spend on the beach - not an unpleasant start to his new job!

Charmaine worked a more conventional five-day week and so was dropping him at the beach on her way to the hospital.

"Do you not fancy joining me for a quick lunch maybe?" Andrew asked as they drew into the sandy car park. "There's surely a beach bar or restaurant nearby?"

"I'd love to, but I'm afraid I can't. Oh there are plenty of restaurants and beach bars, that's not the problem. I only get an hour and you'll find there's no such thing as a 'quick' lunch on this island. I should imagine the waiter would be insulted if you suggested such a thing!"

"Perhaps we could arrange to go out for dinner sometime then?" He suggested.

"Perhaps - sometime." she murmured. There was a moment's silence as they both contemplated the idea. It held mutual appeal. "I expect I'll see you at work sometime. Anyway," she continued briskly, "you'll be ready for home before lunch. You don't want to go overdoing it on your first day. You don't mind getting a taxi back?"

"Fine. I appreciate you bringing... "carrying" me down here - I love your language! I'll get a cab back, I'll just stay for a couple of hours."

"Watch that sun. That breeze can fool you, you know." She looked at him again, noting his fair complexion. "You're a bit too lily white for this place! Be careful! I mean it."

"Trust me - I'm a doctor" he laughed at her, then seeing her wry grin he hastened to reassure her, "Look, joking apart - I do know the dangers of sunburn. I'm not stupid you know. I'll be fine, go on with you. Go run the hospital. Minister to the sick - aid the afflicted - all that good stuff! I'll be thinking of you while I'm lying on this tropical beach, sipping a cold beer and watching the bikinis. I'll be checking each girl thoroughly for malignant melanomas - I promise!" he vowed solemnly, a twinkle in his eye clearly showed how serious his intentions were.

"You're an inspiration to mankind, aren't you? Such a dedicated doctor. It's a wonder we ever managed without you!" Charmaine matched his tone. "Go on, get on with that bikini health check! I'll catch up with you later." She waved at him as he got out the car. Seconds later she was on her way through the busy morning traffic on her way to work. Andrew was left with the calm tranquillity of the early morning beach.

He walked along the water's edge marvelling at the colours of the sparkling sea, its blues and turquoises changing as the gentle currents zigzagged through it. He was startled as a shoal of flying fish leapt from the water near enough to the shore for him to clearly see their scales glinting iridescently in the early sun. He selected a sunny spot near the end of the beach and stretched out on a towel for a spell of sunbathing. Remembering Charmaine's warning Andrew reapplied the sun lotion and lay back in the sun.

"Women!" he thought "Surely she didn't really think he would get sunburn! Any first year medical student could tell you the dangers of excess sun!" He checked his watch, nearly 9.30, no problem, he'd have about a quarter of an hour then move under the shade of a palm tree, maybe have another stroll up the beach, a cold drink perhaps? Contemplating such relaxing activities he fell into a deep sleep, the combination of jet lag and his first day at the hospital catching up with him.

"Sir? Excuse me Sir?" The policeman looked faintly embarrassed, as he tried to wake the soundly sleeping man. He was not supposed to hassle the tourists but any fool could see this man was getting burnt, and burnt bad. He cursed himself for not noticing him on his earlier trip along the beach. He made a regular patrol along the beach, checking trade permits, making sure the beach vendors didn't harass the tourists, and generally making sure everything was fine and everyone was happy.

Andrew grunted in his sleep and eventually opened one eye. He squinted up at the policeman and wondered briefly where on earth he was. Suddenly realisation dawned and he sat up and looked quickly at his watch, 12 o 'clock damn! He had been asleep for over two hours! Thanking the policeman, and reassuring him that he was grateful he had been disturbed, he began to hurriedly gather his things together. He paused and looked down at his legs, they were only very slightly pink but he had a strong suspicion that they would be lobster red and painful by evening. He sat on his beach towel and considered his next move, probably his best bet would be to take a cool shower and apply lots of after-sun. Then again he could perhaps have a quick swim first and hope the salt water would cool his parched skin.

"Good morning Sir." A deep and cheerful voice interrupted his thoughts. Andrew felt his hand being vigorously shaken by a large black hand.

"Allow me to introduce myself" the man continued, "I am the beach doctor and I am here to do you a great service."

Andrew looked up; an extremely tall native man was standing over him. The man was wearing shorts and a faded tee shirt. An extremely battered coconut leaf hat was thrust on his head. He looked rather like a modern day Man Friday with Andrew cast as a rather bemused Robinson Crusoe.

"You see my friend, you are, what we here in the tropics call - sunburned. Do not worry! This is paradise. No one should worry in paradise. You see I have the cure..." he paused for breath and reached into a scruffy looking carrier bag he was carrying. Andrew looked quite alarmed as the "Beach doctor" produced a quite lethal looking knife. My God! Thought Andrew, surely that was a bit drastic for simple sunburn. For a second he thought he was going to be robbed but, noticing the policeman in the background obviously unconcerned and if anything quite encouraging the man's actions, he relaxed slightly. He continued watching in quite silent amazement as the man reached further into the bag and produced a strange looking green leaf. Deftly slicing the leaf lengthways down its smooth surface he opened it out and produced a quite revolting looking green slime. He scraped the slime into an empty rum bottle and commenced on another leaf.

"What on earth are you doing?" Andrew asked, incredulously.

"You'll see my friend, this is the healing plant. Trust me I'm a doctor -" Andrew smiled as he heard his own favourite phrase being quoted to him, "well... a kind of doctor...of sorts - a beach doctor. This bottle will be a great comfort to you tonight when the skin starts to burn. Yes my friend - you'll be glad you met me today. For only ten dollars I - the beach doctor - will cure you!"

He continued with his task, slitting open leaves with an expertise worthy of a real surgeon.

Andrew grinned, so that was it. He should have known. He almost felt sorry for the guy - he was going to feel pretty sick himself when Andrew revealed that he was in fact a bone fide doctor! He would have to take his quack remedy elsewhere! Leaning forward he spoke quietly to the man but was unable to keep a hint of smugness from entering his voice as he softly advised his new "friend" of his identity.

"Actually I do hate to disappoint you...but I am a doctor - a real one! So I'm afraid..." He started to pack away the now rather redundant sun lotion and fold up his towel, expecting the disappointed beach vendor to realise his mistake and leave. To his surprise the sales pitch didn't waver for a second.

"That's great! Then I don't need to tell you how good this stuff is. This is the real McCoy you know - pure vitamin E - Aloe Vera fresh from the plant! How many bottles you want?" He rummaged noisily in the bag and produced more empty rum bottles.

"I don't think you understand me! I am a doctor. I do know the remedy for sunburn and although I appreciate the merits of vitamin E I also appreciate the merits of basic hygiene and I'm afraid those bottles don't look to me to be entirely sanitary. Now - if you'll excuse me, I intend to go home, take a cool shower and apply a more technically advanced substance than slime from an old bottle." Andrew rather pompously dismissed the man. Rising to his feet he picked up his beach towel and bag and gingerly donning a shirt, he headed towards the taxi rank.

"Hey no sweat man! Good luck with your remedy. I'll be here again tomorrow when you change your mind! Have a good day now - you hear?" The beach doctor called cheerfully after him not at all perturbed by his intended patient's refusal of treatment.

As he sat in the back of the taxi taking him home Andrew smiled to himself as he recalled his conversation with the so-called "beach doctor". What a charlatan! It really was quite amazing! He wondered how many people the man took in.

"You look a happy man!" Commented the taxi driver, glancing in the rear view mirror. "Had a good morning?"

"Very entertaining actually! That beach is really beautiful. I expect it's very popular with the tourists. What was it called again?" Andrew had already decided he'd want to return to the area again. It was exactly what he'd been looking forward to, with its white sand and swaying palm trees.

"That was Accra beach. Yeah it's great. I like it myself. Course it all depends what you want. Accra beach gets quite busy. Lots of beach trade there. You can buy just about anything you want for a holiday, and the water's safe. You can walk out for miles and not need to worry about no current or nothing but some people like the quieter beaches up on the west coast. I could take you to one if you like. No problem." He twisted around in his seat and looked back at Andrew briefly before returning his gaze to the road.

"Thanks - maybe another day. I think I've had enough sun for today - besides there's no rush I'm not here on holiday. I'm working here, so there's plenty of time to explore." Andrew was already beginning to feel the telltale prickle of his skin as the sunburn deepened. He was desperately hoping he wouldn't look too red for work the next day - which would be embarrassing

"Yeah? You working here? What you do?" As if reading his mind, the taxi driver asked about Andrew's work. Andrew felt faintly embarrassed explaining he was a doctor when he was already displaying signs of ignorance of the sun, perhaps the driver hadn't noticed.

"I'm a doctor. Working at the Queen Elizabeth Hospital actually. I'm here for a year. I've only just arrived." He added, sinking a little lower in the seat, out of the driver's clear view.

"Good job, you'll like it there. What part you working in? You living in those staff quarter places or you got yourself an apartment? I could show you a couple of places if you like. No problem. You'll maybe need some wheels too. I know a guy works down the garage. He could fix you up with a cheap rental - no problem. Could you manage with a moke? I guess you'd want something more than that though huh? Though I guess if you're in the hospital you won't be making no house calls. Doctors don't make many house calls anyway. Do they do that where you come from?" The driver cheerfully honked his horn to let another taxi out of a side road, "My Man!" he called over to the other driver and received a similar reply.

Andrew wondered which question he should answer first - if any! What was with this guy? Was he just being friendly? Or was he on the make? He'd spent long enough in an inner city to be wary of a con artist. This guy seemed genuine enough, just a bit nosy perhaps.

"I'm getting an apartment. I hope to take one over from the doctor I replaced, but it's not ready yet so I'm staying in staff quarters for now. It's quite nice really. As for the car... well I'll have to think that one over. I've not been here long and I'm still getting my bearings - maybe later." He replied cautiously, still unsure of the driver's intentions.

"Well I'll give you my number, anything you decide you need - just you call me - I'm sure I can fix you up - no problem! That sure is some accent you got. Where you from? Some place in England? My wife's family are in England - Leeds. You know it? We're supposed to be going to see them sometime. Maybe when the kids are older. You married? Got any kids? I guess you're a bit young for all that. Still no time like the present. Maybe you'll settle down here. Me, I love kids, big family man me. How about you?" The driver again twisted around to Andrew briefly, the car lurched alarmingly before he twisted back, honking his horn and waving at the other taxis on the road. There was no sign of road rage. He was just happily acknowledging the other cars. It was all very strange.

"I'm from Scotland, and no, I'm not married and I don't have any kids..." Andrew began to feel slightly nervous. Should this man be out on the streets?

"Least ways none that you know about, huh?" laughed the driver, again turning around to grin at Andrew and narrowly avoiding a moke heading towards them.

Andrew sat back in alarm and tried to surreptitiously fasten his seat belt. It had no buckle. He clung to the broken strap and wondered about the driver. Was he some kind of nut? The taxi driver from hell? The driver carried on blissfully unaware of his passenger's growing misgivings.

"Scotland huh? Can't say as I know it. We've got a Scotland here you know. Little Scotland. It's up north - I don't get there much. It's real quiet, not much trade. Sometimes take the kids up on a Sunday for a picnic. I could take you there if you like - do you want go for a scenic trip? We could go now if you like, won't take long, what do you say? No problem you know." Again he turned around in his seat and looked questioningly at Andrew.

"Perhaps some other time." Andrew murmured weakly, wondering if he would survive the journey that he was on before he contemplated another.

"Yeah you look like you need to get home a cool off. You got a bit burnt didn't you? Got any aloe? We could stop at a beach and pick you up some. They sell it all along - it'd be no problem. We could get you a beach doctor. You wanna stop?" He called over his shoulder, much to Andrew's relief; at least he was looking in vaguely the right direction.

"I'll be just fine thanks - like you say here - no problem!" Andrew wondered if the inhabitants of the island were all taking some sort of drug. Happy pills perhaps? He saw to his great relief that they were almost at the hospital.

"That's it man! You're getting the hang of the language now! No problem! That's what we say - and ain't it the truth?" He pulled up to the curb and stopped the meter. Handing over a battered card he proudly announced.

"This is my card. You want anything you just call. Ask for Errol. If I'm not there I'll get back to you - like I said...."

"I know" interrupted Andrew, grinning with a mixture of relief and amusement, "No problem!"

Chapter 10

Leaving Bridgetown to the Cruise ship invaders, Smiler drove out of the other side of the city and along the south coast before heading up towards the east coast. He intended to hire the services of an east coast fisherman if possible. He had already ascertained this to be the quieter part of the island which suited his plans. His immediate problem was finding the right person for the job. Reaching the east coast road he drove slowly along looking out for a bar or rum shop, seeking out a local meeting place.

Ignoring the majestic scenery of the ocean crashing against the huge boulders dotted along the coast, Smiler noticed a motley gang of youths hanging around outside a small bar. Could be perfect, he decided and pulled over. Reaching for his straw hat he sauntered over to the group.

"Hey man, you want a cold beer? This is the place! Hey Sandra - customer for you!" One of the youths grinned as he shouted into the gloom of the bar, where a woman stood drying glasses.

"Great idea - sure is hot!" Smiler strolled past the youth and into the bar, it was noticeably similar to the one he'd just left behind in Bridgetown, a good omen he decided. He bought the customary local brew and, again declining a glass, he sipped from the bottle as he wandered back outside where he stood ostensibly admiring the ocean view.

"Day off?" He sat down on a convenient wooden bench and opened the conversation.

"Not enough work man, you know how it is - times is tough. Still," the self appointed spokesman of the group shrugged, "We get by - no problem." He sat down on the bench and looked with open curiosity at the stranger.

"Ain't it the truth - still it looks like a good place to be getting by - at least you got the view!" He gestured towards the beach and raised his beer bottle in salute.

"Yeah - best view in the world - but you can't eat it!" There was no bitterness in the boy's voice as he replied, more a casual acceptance of the situation.

"Well let me get the beers then - at least we can drink to it!" Turning to the bar he called, "Three more beers please Sandra. So what do you do? You guys all from round here?"

"Yeah around and about. We get the odd work at the hotels, bit of bar work, bit of work showing the tourists around. Anything really, sometimes supplying the visitors with..." he paused, eyeing the man up carefully - he didn't look like a cop. He was definitely American, and, most importantly, looked like he had a bit of cash. "...well some of the visitors like a good smoke - if you catch my idea, we can usually supply the goods." He looked meaningfully at Smiler.

Smiler suppressed a grin - perfect! Short of money and not afraid of breaking the law - it was too easy really. He took another long swallow of his beer and gazed out at the breaking waves, carefully showing no reaction to the boy's veiled offer. He didn't want to appear eager for their help in any way. Sandra came out with a tray of beers, Smiler opened his wallet and thumbed though the wad of bills as if looking for the right notes, he handed over a couple of bills of local currency.

"This should cover it - keep the change." He smiled at the girl and watched appreciatively as she walked back into the bar - he didn't want the boys getting the wrong idea about him wanting their company.

"Hey thanks man! Anytime you want a guide to show you around - you just call. Right guys?" The spokesman glanced around at his friends, the image of the bulging wallet firmly fixed in his mind.

"Sure thing!" They chorused, grinning at their benefactor as they sat around on the sandy grass enjoying the cool beer.

"Hey no sweat - I'm on vacation. I came out here alone, an impulse thing really but sometimes it's good to have a drink with the guys, you know?" He leant back against the peeling paint of the wooden shack and stretched out his legs. Nodding towards the ocean he nonchalantly enquired.

"Looks pretty rough out there. What's the fishing like?" He was pretty confident at least of the assembled group would be into fishing.

"Great man! Snapper, grouper, even barracuda - you can catch anything out there. You wanna fish?" One of the boys asked eagerly - the guy obviously had money to spare.

Smiler pretended to consider the idea. "Maybe, know anyone with a boat?"

One of the group stood up, a tall young man with an open friendly face, he shook hands with Smiler and introduced himself.

"They call me Sweetboy, I got a boat - and I know where the best fishing is. You interested? I can take you anytime - no problem." he said eagerly.

"I might be interested - depends really, how big is the boat?" Smiler replied, still not revealing his interest.

"A good size - just right really." Sweetboy was cautious about the size of the boat - not knowing what the man wanted he was afraid he'd say the wrong thing.

"Fishing boat?" Smiler continued his casual probing.

"Yeah, but it's clean and comfortable - reliable too." Sweetboy added an unexpected note of pride in his voice - he'd never been overly proud of the craft before but if his new found friend wanted a good boat then his was the best.

Smiler stood up and stretched as if growing bored with the conversation, he wandered towards the shore away from the rest of the group, Sweetboy practically dancing at his side like a puppy eager for a treat.

"How many does it take to crew it? I don't like crowds." Smiler spoke quietly.

"No problem man - just you and me if you like - whatever you say." Sweetboy picked up on the man's change of attitude and it both puzzled and intrigued him.

Keeping his back to the group Smiler pulled his wallet, noting with satisfaction how Sweetboy's eyes grew wider at the sight of so much money.

"Like I say, I don't like crowds - I like my privacy - do you understand me?" Smiler's voice took on a softly menacing tone.

"Yes sir, I understand - no problem. You want privacy - you got it - no problem. Yes sir." Sweetboy nodded his head vigorously, his eyes never leaving the wallet; he'd never seen so much cash.

"Tell me er..." he paused and looked questioningly at the tall youth.

"Sweetboy." Sweetboy interjected quickly.

"Ah yes...Sweetboy, unusual name, would you like to earn a great deal of money? I'm talking real money here, you understand?" He watched him closely, noting the variety of emotions that flitted briefly across the boy's face, fear, greed, curiosity - it was all there, the boy was an open book.

Sweetboy swallowed nervously, alarm bells were ringing in his head but he ignored them. His grandmother's words earlier that day about fishing being honest work resounded in his memory - something told him this man was not interested in the catch of the day!

"Don't get me wrong Sweetboy, I'm no rich fool - I don't throw my money around and I can guarantee you one thing - I will not be cheated." Taking off his sunglasses he looked directly into Sweetboy's eyes, despite the warm sunshine Sweetboy felt a sudden chill.

"Yes Sir, I mean - no Sir - I mean I wouldn't cheat you, no way man, not me - you can rely on me. No problem! What do you want though?" He looked apprehensively at the man, a few possibilities crept into his mind, what could be worth "real money"- and how much exactly was "real money". He half regretted getting into this conversation yet was excited by this unexpected opportunity.

"Nothing difficult. I only need you and your boat, I just want to go on a little fishing trip, nothing to concern you at all." Smiler said almost soothingly, he didn't want to scare the youth off completely.

"Right - a fishing trip" Sweetboy muttered, still at a loss, the guy was being a bit mysterious about a simple fishing trip.

"I might be netting quite a catch though - maybe quite a weight - think you can handle that?" Smiler continued. He knew he'd need a winch and lifting equipment.

"I'm sure I can." Sweetboy replied, with more confidence than he felt. Summoning up his courage he asked as casually as he could, "er...exactly what sort of catch are you after, I mean like rod fishing or what? Like I can arrange anything..." he added quickly, "No problem, just...well...what stuff would you need?"

"Before we continue I want to be absolutely sure I can trust you - you understand that our conversation is strictly confidential?" He spoke quietly and Sweetboy had to lean forward to catch the words.

"Yes Sir! Ain't nobody's business 'cepting you and me, you can trust me, Sir." Sweetboy hastily assured him, checking over his shoulder quickly to make sure none of his friends had wandered close enough to hear them.

"We'll discuss the details later, but I want some nets - new ones - I'll pay for them, and I'll need a marker buoy and some sort of winch to haul the nets aboard. You got all that? After we've done you get to keep the new nets too." he added as an afterthought, it would convince the boy he was genuinely "fishing" and also serve as an added bonus to clinch the deal.

"Oh sure." Sweetboy looked relieved, "That's no problem - I got all that stuff - got good nets too...." seeing the look in Smiler's eye he continued rapidly, "but if you want new ones, that's just fine. The winch and stuff - no problem. This is a proper fishing boat you know, not just some dinky tourist thing - no Sir - this is the real thing. You can rely on me - with my boat you could catch a whale and haul it aboard."

"Good - looks like I've got me the best man for the job then, now for the financial arrangements...." he peeled off a few hundred dollar bills, Sweetboy licked his lips, his palms felt sweaty. This was it - his chance to make some money at last.

"Where is this boat?" Smiler glanced around, as if expecting to see it pulled up on the shore somewhere.

"Up by Cattlewash, you know, at Bathsheba? Everyone knows Bathsheba. It's not far, but um...." Sweetboy hesitated, his father had the boat, he was still out with it, Sweetboy hadn't given a thought as to how he was actually going to get hold of it - or what he was going to tell his father!

"A problem?" Smiler asked, sharply.

"No Sir. No, Sir, not at all but...it's not here at the moment - but I can get it - real quick. It's out with the fishing you see. We might not have time today before it gets dark...." Sweetboy's voice trailed off miserably, he was losing his one big chance, this man didn't look the type to be kept waiting, then a thought occurred. "Less of course you're thinking of night fishing - that's real good you know - yeah night fishing - good stuff." He looked hopefully at his potential customer.

Smiler looked benevolently at the boy, he was obviously scared of him - which was just the way Smiler liked things, passing over the bank notes he spoke softly.

"Good idea. I think night fishing would be just perfect - not tonight though - I'll be in touch." He nodded over to the group by the bar; "As far as that lot are concerned we didn't make any arrangements because you haven't got a boat today, ok? You don't tell them nothing else, understand? Like I said - I'll be in touch in the next couple of days, now here is a ...retainer, you understand? This money is to keep you going for the next couple of days - make whatever arrangements you have to - discreetly! I've got a few of my own to deal with and then I'll come and let you know when I want you, it'll be a night soon so make sure that boat is ready."

Sweetboy gulped there was no mistaking the danger in this man. Every instinct was screaming at him to give the money back and run but the mental image of his parents' chattel house appeared in his mind and he firmly pushed his doubts away.

"I'll be right here Sir, yes Sir. I'll be right here - I ain't going no place till I hears from you. I'll be right here - no problem I swear it!"

Smiler grinned, it was too easy. "Just as long as we understand each other - and Sweetboy," He leaned over and lowered his voice to almost a whisper, "you'd better be here waiting when I get back...don't fuck with me cos I'll find you and next time you go fishing - you go as bait."

Chapter 11

Captain Ivan Chojecki frowned as he assessed the instructions he'd received from Miami. Suddenly he let rip with a colourful stream of expletives in a variety of languages. The seaman at the helm winced. He'd understood a couple of them and it didn't take a linguist to translate the rest.

"Get Obelenski!" He commanded he strode over and grabbed the helm. "Well go on you fool. What are you waiting for?" The seaman bolted. Quickly he located the first officer Nick Obelenski who hurried to the bridge. They were both back within minutes. The Captain's mood had not improved.

"My cabin" he barked, striding out the small bridge towards his cabin. Nick and the seaman exchanged glances then Nick shrugged and followed him.

"Come on you lazy bastard - do you think I've got all day?" The Captain's voice bellowed back at them and Nick increased his pace.

The seaman shrugged and returned his attention to the ship's instruments. He had no idea what had incurred his Captain's wrath but it didn't usually take much. His Slavonic temper was legendary. It was probably nothing to worry about. Despite the tempest in the Captain's cabin The SS Danzig continued calmly on its course to Venezuela.

Reaching the cabin Ivan waited impatiently for Nick to clear the door before slamming it shut behind him. Ivan paced up and down the tiny cabin like a caged animal cursing under his breath. Nick watched and waited for his old friend to calm down and explain the problem. He lived this scene a thousand times before. The older man continued to pace. He was a big man, tall and broad shouldered. His craggy weather-beaten face making him appear older than his years. He had an unruly shock of hair that had turned a lively salt and pepper in recent years, piercing dark eyes and a huge bushy moustache that had not yet turned the colour of his hair. Its sheer size and blackness making it look almost like a comical false disguise. Nick suppressed a grin at the way Ivan's muttering was making his moustache shake - it looked like it would fall off at any moment.

"What the hell have you got to laugh about - Damn fool!" Ivan yelled suddenly, catching Nick's expression. "This is bloody serious, you know?"

"Actually no I don't." Commented Nick mildly, "You haven't made any sense yet - I was just waiting." He was the perfect foil to his Captain. As narrow as the Captain was broad and as calm as he was fiery. They made a good team.

"They're waiting for us in Caracas." Ivan stated shortly.

"Who?" Nick asked quickly.

"The bloody welcome wagon - who'd you think?" Ivan screamed. "The cops, port authorities, I don't know, they're on to us!" He slumped down in a chair. "We're in the shit!"

Nick sank down into another chair and digested the news. The two men sat staring into space for a couple of minutes. They both pictured the innocent looking oil drums lashed to the deck. The SS Danzig was a standard tramp ship with a cargo of general merchandise. It was packed with a variety of containers, which made it the perfect vessel for the smuggler.

"I knew it seemed too good to be true" murmured Nick. "Easy money they said. Should have known." He frowned as he remembered being approached by the stranger at the dock. He remembered, partly, the night they'd got roaring drunk on the generous advance they'd received. He smiled fleetingly as he recalled Ivan singing his way through his repertoire of incomprehensible Polish drinking songs. They'd got through some vodka that night. Now, some weeks later, he was beginning to feel sick.

"How's your health?" Replied Ivan abruptly, carefully looking over his colleague as an idea formulated in his mind.

"Fine thanks, any reason why it shouldn't be?" Nick replied cautiously, startled by his Captain's apparent ability to mind read.

"You're about to have appendicitis that's why!" Ivan replied. "We've got to divert the ship. Into the Islands they've told me. We need an emergency. We've got to divert and drop off the cargo." He jumped to his feet and again began pacing around.

"Won't we be searched wherever we divert?" Ivan rose and tried to follow him to discuss it but gave up and addressed himself to the back of the Captain's head. He jumped as Ivan suddenly spun around.

"That's why we need an emergency - to buy a bit of time." he roared. "For God's sake man, work with me on this one."

"Okay, okay so we buy some time, then what? We've still got to dock. Won't we be searched then?" Nick argued.

"We're not going to dock. That's why I need your appendix.... oh not really, don't panic!" he added with a sudden grin seeing his colleague's expression. "You just collapse with the belly ache and I'll do the rest. It's not like we've got a real doctor aboard. We can check it out with the medical book. Then we get close enough to get you taken off and while you create a diversion a fishing boat is going to rendezvous with us and take off the drums."

"What about the crew?" ventured Nick, checking for any flaws in the plan.

"I've thought of that. I figured maybe they could have a bit of unexpected shore leave. Kind of making the most of the situation, you see? I'll offer to be the one who stays aboard." he laughed,

"Naturally I'll be too worried about my pal to go drinking all that rum! The sacrifices I make. You see I'll be doing all the hard work, you just have to collapse in a heap!"

"Why me?" Nick ventured, although he had to admit it was a sound enough plan.

"Well, unless you've any other ideas. My medical knowledge isn't that extensive and I should imagine an appendicitis is probably the easiest thing to fake. I know all the more obvious symptoms and anyway we can check the rest when we look it up. We don't want to bring anyone else in on this now do we?" He paused while his companion shook his head, acknowledging the truth of that statement, then continued with a sudden smile, "I am no longer in possession of my appendix, which makes it pretty tough to complain about and anyway...." his smile broadened into a wide grin; "...you look sick!" He roared with humour as he surveyed his old friend. It was true, Nick Obelenski, did not look a well man. Actually he was remarkably fit but the truth was belied by his appearance. He was of average height, but thin to a point of appearing gaunt, fair haired with pale blue eyes and a complexion so pale he looked anaemic. It would not be any real problem to convince anyone he was at death's door ... and knocking.

The two men finalised their arrangements and Nick went below to prepare for his sudden onset of ill health. Ivan returned to his charts and calculated the optimum position to warrant a diversion inland. A few hours later the Barbados Coast guard received a distress call from the cargo ship SS Danzig.

"Barbados Coast Guard, this is the SS Danzig, request assistance for marine emergency." The radio operator, with his worried Captain at his side, sent out the distress call. The operator, unaware of the contrived nature of his superior officer's collapse was genuinely concerned and greatly relieved when a prompt reply was heard.

"SS Danzig, this is the Barbados Coast guard, please state nature of emergency."

"Medical. We have a crewmember with severe symptoms. Request permission to anchor off local waters and seek medical assistance."

"Are quarantine restrictions advisable?"

"Negative. Symptoms suggest appendicitis."

"Do you want a doctor transferred aboard?" Suggested the Coast Guard. The radio operator looked up at the captain.

"No, don't waste time. Get him into hospital where they can operate safely." he answered shortly.

"Negative, Coast Guard. The Captain requests that the patient be taken ashore for possible surgery."

"Permission granted. Please stand by for co-ordinates. We will arrange a launch to rendezvous with you and collect patient. He will be transferred directly to the Queen Elizabeth Hospital for emergency treatment."

"Ok then. I'll leave you to sort out the details." Ivan looked relieved as he spoke to the radio operator. "I'll go down and check on Nick. Call me when we're close enough."

The Captain went below to assure his first officer that help was on hand. For such a sick man the patient gave a surprisingly strong handshake upon hearing the news.

Chapter 12

Andrew stared in the mirror dejectedly. His nose was beginning to peel and the rest of his face still remained a distinctive lobster red. Hearing the men's room door open behind him he began vigorously washing his hands.

"Don't tell me." Mike said cheerfully seeing his colleagues over-tanned face. "You fell asleep on the beach!" He laughed heartily and slapped Andrew on the back. Andrew yelped in pain.

"Oh God! Sorry - I was forgetting how painful it can be. Got anything for it?" He continued more sympathetically.

Silently Andrew reached into his pocket and drew out a variety of after-sun products. Lining them up along the sink he surveyed them glumly.

"I think I've bought just about everything the pharmacy had - for all the good it's done me!" He looked up at his reflection again and winced as much from embarrassment as pain. "I missed lunch to go and get this lot. Now I'm sore and starving!"

"There's probably a hot-dog cart out front. Why don't you nip out quick?" Mike suggested, picking up one of the bottles, he read the label. "What's in this lot anyway? I'm surprised there wasn't a beach doctor about. They're usually pretty sharp."

"Oh there was a so called 'Beach doctor' all right!" Forgetting his hunger Andrew laughed, despite the pain it caused him.

"Oh good so you're fixed up with some Aloe then." Mike said happily, shaking his head he put back the more commercial remedy. "Well that should sort it out then." He looked closer at Andrew's parched skin. "It's usually very fast - when did you last apply it?"

"You're kidding right? You don't mean that filthy old stuff in those dirty bottles works?" Andrew asked incredulously. "I thought it was a tourist trap!" he wailed.

"It's pure Aloe Vera!" Mike shook his head, laughing at Andrew's pained expression. "Didn't they teach you anything in that med school? Wait here I'll see what's in the staff fridge." Still chuckling to himself he left the room. He returned a couple of minutes later bearing an old rum bottle.

"You're in luck, one of the nurses had some left - here you go." He handed the bottle to Andrew who stared at it suspiciously.

"This isn't some sort of 'get the new doctor' gag is it?" he asked eyeing the unsanitary looking 'cure'. "I won't end up with a bright blue face or something?"

"God forbid that I could do anything to make you look stupid!" Mike roared with mirth, "Look at yourself! You look like a traffic light stuck on red!"

Andrew gingerly applied the cool clear liquid. It felt wonderful! The burning pain disappeared immediately.

"Oh that's great!" He groaned. "God that's wonderful. That feels fantastic. Ooh Mike you're brilliant."

"Steady on old chap." Mike said looking at the door. "Anyone walking by is going to get the wrong idea about you!" He chuckled. "More to the point - they might start to wonder about me!"

Andrew laughed. "That's reminds me. Where's the best place around here for a really romantic dinner. I want somewhere really special." He began applying the liquid to his arms.

"Well that's very kind and all that but I have to say you're not really my type. I'm a married man you know." Mike replied, pretending to consider the offer.

"Not you, you pillock." Andrew retorted. "I want to take Charmaine out. I want to really impress her."

"A second ago I was brilliant!" Protested Mike, looking at Andrew's crimson face he continued. "Well if you really want to impress the lady I suggest you go somewhere pretty dark! Candlelight I think, mind you if the glow of the candles doesn't make her swoon the warmth from your skin probably will!"

A few hours later Andrew and Charmaine were driving in a taxi along the west coast road heading for a quiet dinner. He had pre-arranged with the driver not to mention their destination, as he wanted to surprise her. He was determined to at least act sophisticated - even if he didn't look it.

"Carambola!" smiled Charmaine; "I'm most impressed. How did you know about this place?"

"Mike told me it would be dark! That is to say Mike recommended the food here." Andrew amended quickly. Charmaine suppressed a smile.

"How is the sunburn?" She enquired gently.

"Better now thanks!" Laughed Andrew as he courteously helped her out of the car. Together they walked into the candlelit restaurant. Taking a small torch the Maitre'D showed them down a small flight of steps to a platform built on the side of a shallow cliff overlooking the sea. There was a single table beautifully laid with crisp linen, sparkling crystal and fragrant fresh flowers. A delicate glass lamp protecting the flame from the sea breeze provided the only light.

"That's two I owe you Mike!" Thought Andrew as he surveyed the scene. Seating the couple and handing them their menus the Maitre'D discreetly left. The glow of the lamp circled the table but beyond that was darkness except for a single spotlight under the platform which shone into the sea below them. They sat in contented silence looking out at the tranquil Caribbean Sea for a few moments until a waiter arrived bearing a pitcher of iced water.

"Good evening Sir, Madam. My name is William. Our chef sends his compliments. His recommendation for this evening is seafood soup, followed by Chateaubriand. Perhaps you may care to consider that? May I get you something from the bar?" he enquired as he deftly removed the linen napkins from the water glasses and draped them over their laps.

"Charmaine?" Enquired Andrew, "What do you recommend? I'd like something tropical and exotic." Mentally he added "and perhaps something to drink too!" as he looked across at Charmaine. She raised her eyebrows at him, reading his thoughts perfectly. She looked radiant in a white off the shoulder lace dress decorated with a single fresh hibiscus bloom. Andrew stared into her eyes, the waiter stared tactfully out to sea.

"Did you try rum punch at the airport?" She asked remembering the first time they met and his relaxed attitude in the car.

"Oh yes, that was great. I'll have one of those. Thank you." he said to the waiter.

"Well I'll have a Yellow Bird then." Charmaine replied smiling at the waiter. He left as quietly as he'd arrived, returning moments later with their drinks.

"That looks nice. What's in it?" Asked Andrew as he watched Charmaine sipping her drink.

"It's based on orange juice, naturally there's rum and it's topped with Galliano Liqueur. Would like to try it?"

"Thanks." He took a sip and they discussed the merits of the various Bajan cocktails. The waiter stood patiently nearby.

"Would you like a few minutes more to decide?" He asked, looking at their folded menus. Andrew realised with a start that he hadn't even glanced at it yet.

"I think we'd better have just a wee while longer if you don't mind." he replied, looking questioningly at Charmaine who nodded her agreement. "I expect we'll be ready for another of these excellent cocktails by then also." he added as the waiter smiled and left.

"Certainly Sir, I'll be back in a few minutes." He grinned as he walked back up the narrow steps. "Honeymooners!" he thought.

Andrew and Charmaine sipped their drinks and read the menu. Remembering he'd missed lunch Andrew suddenly realised he was famished. The menu was excellent but, despite his hunger, Andrew found it hard to make a choice from the exotic array. The waiter reappeared and they settled on the chef's recommendation. Andrew carefully perused the excellent wine list having first ascertained Charmaine's preference and chose a wine that he hoped would impress her.

"That rum punch is very refreshing isn't it?" Commented Andrew, draining his second glass. "Bit like a sort of fruit cocktail I suppose." Charmaine sipped more cautiously at her drink.

"They can be a bit deceptive, you know." She warned.

"Oh don't you worry about me. I'm a Scot! We know how to handle a dram or two!" Andrew beamed at her. He was beginning to relax more. The glow of the lamp seemed to envelop them both in their own cosy world. They watched in awe as a Manta Ray drifted sedately through their private floodlit sea. Charmaine pointed out the spiky black sea eggs nestling on the sandy ocean bed. The waiter came and brought the first course of seafood soup. Andrew was slightly perturbed to find a whole baby octopus floating on the surface but since it didn't seem to bother Charmaine he didn't comment. Over their meal Charmaine told him all about the island and Andrew told her all about Scotland.

"I haven't forgotten you have a Scotland here." Andrew mentioned, "Do you think you could perhaps show it to me sometime? Just so as I don't get homesick. I think a wee trip would set my heart at rest."

"Well Doctor if that's your professional opinion, how could I refuse?" Agreed Charmaine. "Next time we're both off I'll take you on a tour around the island."

"Sounds perfect!" Said Andrew; "I'll hold you to that!"

The main course was equally delicious and, Andrew gratefully acknowledged, completely devoid of baby octopus. They finished their wine and declining a dessert they sat lingering over coffee and brandy. Andrew paid the bill but they didn't move. Neither wanting the evening to end. Eventually they took one last lingering look at their private oasis and headed up the narrow steps to the waiting taxi.

"Do you know Mike got me some of that Aloe Vera today and it actually worked? No, really it did!" Andrew stressed. "I know it sounds crazy but it's good stuff. I canna feel my sunburn at all!"

"Really?" Asked Charmaine, dryly "And me a native Bajan and I didn't know that!" She laughed. "Actually Andrew I'd be surprised if you could feel anything. You do sound a little... mellow?"

"I feel mellow!" Andrew exclaimed, happily. "I feel wonderful. Aloe Vera, rum punch and you, the most beautiful girl in the world!" He sighed, "I think I must be the mellowest man in the world!"

"I don't think I've ever been compared to a bottle of Aloe before!" Laughed Charmaine. "By the way, did you enjoy your dinner?"

"It was great! Actually," he leaned forward and whispered to her. "To tell you a secret I missed lunch today because I was hoping to cure my sunburn before my hot date tonight. I really wanted to make a good impression." He gave her a conspiratorial wink. "Of course that's just between us you understand?"

"Don't worry your secret's safe with me!" She leaned forward and spoke to the driver. "I think we'll drop him off first driver. Perhaps you could wait while I make sure he gets safely in. Rum punch!" she added by way of explanation.

"No problem!" Grinned the taxi driver, he'd seen it all before.

Charmaine turned back to Andrew who was slowly sliding down the seat. "So you missed lunch and then had two rum punches on an empty stomach?" She shook her head, no wonder he was 'mellow'!

"Not a problem!" Rallied Andrew, "Remember I'm a Scot. I belong to Glasgow! Actually I know a song about that!"

Chapter 13

For two days Sweetboy hung around the small bar as if passionately enamoured with the barmaid. He raced down there first thing every morning and stayed until late every evening. Resisting his instincts he had been very cautious about the money. He knew he couldn't risk suddenly appearing to have spare cash, as it would arouse suspicion among his friends so the hundred dollar bills were still hidden away. Sitting on the wooden bench outside the bar he dreamed of what he would do with the promised "real money" when it arrived. He still wasn't exactly sure what he would be required to do - but he was pretty sure it wouldn't be fishing. Probably a smuggling job he decided, import duties were high on the island and people sometimes came up with various ways of avoiding them.

He wasn't overly worried about the risk. Ever optimistic, he figured no one would stop a fishing boat, and besides - hadn't he always been lucky? This was obviously just what he had always known was waiting for him - opportunity!

"Sweetboy - ain't you got no fishing with you daddy?" Sandra called to him as she bustled around the small bar.

"Nah, got me a couple of days off - figured I'd come down here and keep you company - I knows how you always had a soft spot for me." he laughed back. Sandra was several years older than he, married with four children was, she had known Sweetboy all his life.

"Woman would have to have a soft head to get involved with you! Your poor daddy working all them hours to keep a lazy son." She scolded, "bout time you got you a conscience! How is your Grandma? You tell she I was asking for she. Your mummy well? She still at that hotel? Your mummy and daddy work so hard and there's you done sitting all day.... what you grinning for boy?" She interrupted her lecture when she noticed the effect it was having on the boy. He was laughing openly at her tirade.

"Sandra you sound like Grandma! She's fine, still listening to that radio show, waiting for she name be called! I do work you know - I go out on the boat. As a matter of fact I...." he stopped abruptly as he heard a car approaching, it passed by and he sighed, he hoped the man hadn't changed his mind.

"You what? What you doing? You sure look like you're up to something. Why you keep watching that road? You waiting on something?" Sandra peered at him suspiciously, she liked Sweetboy - everyone did, but he was easily led and she worried about him.

"Nothin' I ain't watching for no-one and I ain't up to nothin' I just having a couple of days off that's all - ain't nothin' wrong with that is there?" he spoke sullenly; Sandra had a big mouth he decided. He wanted to walk away but he didn't dare. Suppose he missed the man, he might ask someone else - it didn't bear thinking about.

"I jes' thought the others might be coming down, thought I'd meet them here." he mumbled, scuffing the ground under the bench with his bare feet and staring downwards to avoid eye contact. "A man had no privacy round here"

"Since when any of them deadbeat friends of yours had them a car? They's lucky if they can afford to ride the bus! I declare I..."

The 'phone ringing in a back room mercifully distracted Sandra and she hurried off, Sweetboy slumped down on the wooden bench kicking despondently at the ground. "They'll see" he muttered,

"I'm going to make it big then they'll all change their tune. When I get me some real money - then we'll see who gets the respect round here." He sat up suddenly as a car pulled up - it was him! The main man - Mr Opportunity himself!

Smiler looked around, the place looked deserted; the boy was alone - what a stroke of luck. This was going even better than he'd hoped.

"Get in quick" he ordered sharply, leaning over and opening the passenger door.

"Yes Sir!" Sweetboy jumped eagerly to his feet and into the car. Without waiting for the door to be closed, Smiler drove off before anyone saw him. When Sandra reappeared a minute later there was no trace of him.

They drove in silence for a couple of minutes, and then Smiler pulled into a parking area by the side of the road and switched off the engine.

Smiler broke the silence, his casual tone gone, replaced by a sharp, no-nonsense manner. "You haven't mentioned our little arrangements to anyone I assume?" He enquired sharply, searching the boy's face for signs of deceit.

"No Sir! No way Sir, I ain't mentioned nothing to nobody Sir, not me Sir. Like I said before discreet - that's me Sir." Sweetboy swallowed nervously, his face beaded with sweat, the alarm bells were still ringing shrilly in his head but he steadfastly ignored them. This was it - his big chance.

Smiler noted the boy's discomfort with pleasure - he was clearly terrified of him - perfect. He felt pretty sure the boy wasn't lying - "He wouldn't have the guts!" he thought, scornfully.

"Well son," Smiler continued, his manner appearing to soften, he felt like a cat playing with a mouse, allowing it to think it was safe briefly, before pouncing again for the kill. "I think it's about time we took our little trip - tonight about midnight. I think a bit of night fishing is just what I need right now. Ok? - you got the stuff ready?"

"Yes Sir! Like you said - new nets - good strong ones. And the boat's all ready - ready and waiting - like I said. Yes Sir." Sweetboy babbled eagerly. "Midnight" he thought, relieved that he wouldn't have to ask his father if he could borrow the boat during the day - maybe his father didn't even have to know he'd taken it.

"Uh Sir?" Sweetboy hesitated, not wishing to incur the man's wrath, "I was jes wondering - not that it matters you understand - like it's no problem or anything - I was jes' well ...curious...like - well that is to say - would we be back by morning? Like I say - it ain't no problem or nothing - it's jes' that if we is back by morning when they goes out fishing - my daddy that is - well no-one would ever even know we'd been out in her - I mean - well it's my boat an all - it's jes that my daddy takes her out most mornings. I mean I could tell him he couldn't have her - no sweat there but, like you said, it's more - well private like - if he don't need to know." Sweetboy stammered.

Smiler gave him a patronising, yet reassuring smile. "I think that's an excellent idea er...Sweetboy, we'll be back in plenty of time, probably only be out for a couple of hours - like you say - no-one need ever know we'd been out." he paused, weighing up how much information Sweetboy would need to know to make any arrangements, against the security of keeping the boy entirely in the dark. He felt pretty confident of the boy's fearful discretion.

"I can trust you, can't I?" he spoke softly; Sweetboy had to lean closer to catch his words. The boy swallowed nervously. "Oh yes Sir! You knows it!" This was it - details of his big chance.

"Right." Smiler said decisively, ""We'll meet at midnight tonight at...where did you say the boat is moored - Bathsheba wasn't it?" He paused while Sweetboy again nodded vigorously, confirming Smiler's excellent memory. "Then we go out for a couple of hours and when I've netted my 'catch' we'll stop in a quiet bay for a while, so I'll need you to check out a suitable area - then return home. If you do a good job tonight I'll want to make the same arrangement for a couple of weeks time - so you get to double your fee." He watched as the boy's face grew animated with delight at the prospect of doubling his already generous financial agreement.

"Oh I'll do a good job - don't you worry about that. I'm the best there is - you'll see!" Sweetboy grinned with relief, it didn't sound too bad, in fact it sounded pretty good - easy money!

A few hours later the two unlikely companions were headed out into the inky black night on the old but quite sea-worthy "Bathsheba Beauty", a rather optimistic name for a boat, which although moored at Bathsheba, could hardly be called a beauty.

"Head around towards Bridgetown." Smiler commanded his hired "skipper" quite enjoying the change of scene. If Sweetboy thought it an odd choice of fishing site, he wisely kept his views to himself. "Keep at least 5 miles out - we don't want to attract attention from the shore - don't go within sight of land."

As they neared Bridgetown Sweetboy saw the lights of a tanker in the distance. "Sir - there's a cargo ship ahead - do you want me to go out further so as they don't see us?" He asked, already steering the small craft away from the lights, anticipating his Boss's need for privacy.

"No, that's quite all right - that's a friend of mine - I want to meet up with him. Head towards it - but not directly - go around the back and then casually approach - wouldn't want it to look like we were deliberately meeting up with her - know what I mean?" His eyes scanned the horizon, reassured by the pre-arranged system of lights, which identified the ship as the correct vessel. "Keep it quiet and dark though, I don't want to attract attention." He produced a torch from his pocket and flashed a series of lights towards the ship. Seconds later they saw a similar message returned.

They approached the cargo ship and came alongside a few feet away from a small lantern that appeared to be hanging over the side. Smiler waited patiently, Sweetboy looked mystified until a net suddenly appeared over the side of the ship and something was lowered towards the deck of the small fishing vessel.

"Grab a hold" whispered Smiler urgently, as he guided the swinging net towards the centre of the deck. Together they manoeuvred the net until it landed with a heavy thud on the deck; the small boat rocked alarmingly and sank lower in the water from the weight of its unexpected additional cargo. Smiler swiftly unhooked the load and again flashing the torch to signal the unseen donor, he curtly instructed Sweetboy to pull away. In the moonlight Sweetboy could just about make out the shape of two 45-gallon drums - "Drugs!" he thought, "Must be millions of dollars of drugs in there - wow!" His heart pounded as he realised what he'd become involved in - no wonder he was being paid so well - "Sweet Jesus - drugs!"

Smiler too looked at the drums - he hadn't been told what he was collecting, such information was obviously on a "need to know" basis and he certainly hadn't asked. He too assumed his cargo was drugs, although he had no qualms about them - it was just another job. "You have picked out a suitably quiet bay like I told you, haven't you?" He asked Sweetboy nonchalantly, who was still shaking from his discovery of his "catch".

"Yes Sir" squeaked Sweetboy, then coughed to clear his voice, "I mean...yes Sir, Skeete's bay, it's overlooked by cliffs, very quiet, won't take long to get there...." his voice trailed off, overwhelmed by the enormity of the chain of events.

"Good then we'll lower these drums over the side with your winch and mark their position with a buoy. In two weeks I'll want you to come and pick them up and return them to my friend. I guess you could say we're just doing a bit of baby-sitting - no harm in that now is there?" It was a rhetorical question. Sweetboy was shaking too much to be able to provide an answer.

Chapter 14

With the usual resilience of youth, Sweetboy's awe of his knowledge lasted a mere 24 hours. Excitement replaced his initial horror as an overwhelming range of possibilities opened up to him. He lay in bed; the sea breeze caused the old wooden Chattel house to groan and creak, gently rocking throughout the balmy night, a combination that had sent him to sleep for the past 22 years. Tonight though sleep eluded him as his mind buzzed with the incredible opportunity fate had brought his way.

He had no idea of the value of what he assumed to be a huge amount of drugs, not that he was entirely confident on the variety of narcotic involved but he figured it had to be pretty substantial. "Must be about a trillion dollars worth!" he mused, "An I'm the only one who can get it - me Sweetboy Richards, fisherman and... drug baron!" He thought dramatically, savouring his newfound importance. "I could jes' go, haul me up a drum and help myself!" He chuckled gleefully to himself, then sobering quickly, he thought of the ominous stranger.

He realised immediately the perils of such actions; the guy was not to be messed with. "Still," he mentally argued with himself, "I guess he might not miss just a little bit - a fella wouldn't need much, some of that stuff is really worth big money, maybe jes help myself to a little bit..." He wondered how the stuff would be packed. Perhaps in small quantities, individually wrapped in little polythene bags? He remembered seeing something like that on a detective show on the TV once. Maybe it was just kind of loose in the drum?

His imagination ran riot as he visualised the drums, filled with white powder, ready to bring him instant wealth. He pictured himself driving around the island in a big fancy car, of course he'd have to tell everyone he'd won the lotto, couldn't tell anyone how smart he'd been, how he'd outwitted an American drug smuggling ring. Disturbingly the stranger's face filled his mind again, Sweetboy knew he'd get himself killed if he got caught - it was a hopeless idea...but the chance...this might be his only chance to make it really big. All night the argument raged within him. What should hc do? At 3.00 a.m. he'd decided to go to the police and explain how he thought he was being hired to go night fishing. Then he pictured the police Inspector questioning him.

"So you're telling me you thought this guy was giving you several hundred dollars to go night fishing? You think we going to believe that? What you take me for? No boy - you in big trouble - real big trouble."

The image faded as fast as his honest resolve, it was too late - they'd never believe him. Drug smugglers were very severely dealt with in Barbados; even tourists had learnt that - to their cost. A local boy wouldn't stand a chance - they'd lock him up and throw away the key he decided. No, that wasn't the answer. Next he resolved to do just what he'd been hired to do, retrieve the drums, take his payment and walk away. That was it. That was the best way...and then what? His busy imagination again took hold; he saw himself in the future, becoming just like his father before him - just another poor fisherman - no prospects - no hope for a less mundane future. At least he'd have a future, his conscience argued, which is more than he'd have if the stranger thought he'd double crossed him. Round and round his thoughts went. Endless scenarios flashed through his tired brain until at last, nearing dawn, he fell asleep, no nearer to any solution.

Sweetboy, dressed in the latest fashion, his gold jewellery glinting in the sunshine, was driving down Spring Garden

Highway in a huge white Mercedes Benz convertible. Everyone was waving and calling out to him, his heart swelled as he saw the respect and admiration in their eyes. He was truly king of the road at last. He heard his father calling him and turned to wave at him.

"Sweetboy! Sweetboy - how many time I gotta call you, man?" It was strange, his father sounded angry, surely he liked the car? Maybe he wanted a ride - yes, that was probably it. Sweetboy carefully steered the car over to the side of the road.

"Sweetboy! What's a body got to do to get through to you - damn fool child!" His father's voice resounded in his semi conscious brain.

"OK Daddy - I'll give you a ride." Sweetboy mumbled, "No need to shout - there's plenty of room." He flung his arm out expansively to demonstrate the vast area of leather seating. "Ouch" His arm made contact with the wooden bedroom wall, what was a wall doing in his new car? He wondered sleepily, then groaned as he realised it had all been a wonderful dream, except, unfortunately, his father calling him - that was no dream - more like a nightmare, he sighed.

"Sweetboy you is even dumber than I thought. You lazy good for nothing son of a ... what you talkin' about - give me ride? I'm been giving you a free ride all you life! You ain't worked for days 'bout time you got up off you lazy ass and did some honest work my boy...." his voice ranted on but Sweetboy tuned him out, still thinking about the beautiful white car, and it could be his - it was there for the taking... "Ouch!" Sweetboy was brought sharply back to reality as his father cuffed him soundly around the head.

"You listening to me? Don't you go ignoring me boy - I'm warning you. When you going to make something of yourself?" His father stood over him, shaking with anger and frustration at his son's reluctance to grow up and take some responsibility for his life.

Sweetboy sat up, swinging his legs over the side of the bed, he sat rubbing his ear, sulkily staring down at the floor.

"I'm gonna' make it - you wait and see - I's just waitin' for the right opportunity...." he began before his father interrupted him, sick of hearing Sweetboy's usual refrain.

"Hah! Opportunity! That's all we hears from you! Opportunity! You couldn't even spell it - well I can and let me tell you it's spelt W.O.R.K. that's how you gets opportunities - you damn well work for them. Now stop this fool talk and get dressed - you ain't hangin' round no Sandra's bar today - not if you wants to eat you ain't..." still scolding he turned and strode out the room, pausing to hug a worried looking Martha Richards who had overheard the tirade and now stood anxiously waiting in the tiny living room.

"He's young, Courtney, he'll grow up jes' try and be a bit patient. You were that age too remember?" She pleaded her beloved grandson's case, trying to calm her angry son.

"I knows it Mom, I knows it, but at his age I was already married with a family - I was already growed up - I look out for them don't I? He jes' seems to think it's all going to land right in his lap - I jes' can't get through to him...I don't know..." he sighed deeply, his anger waning to be replaced by disappointment. "I was so proud when I had me a son, where did I go wrong Mom?"

"Give him time, he'll settle down an' anyway I said you was too young to be married didn't I? Makin' me a Grandma at forty - this is God's punishment!" she smiled at him, Courtney knew what it cost her to make a religious joke, he smiled back.

"I guess you's right Mom, you always tells me He works in mysterious ways. Yeah I guess maybe that boy'll grow up one day - I jes' hope I live long enough to see it." He sighed and started out for the door. "Tell him I'll see him down at the boat, maybe a walk will cool me down a bit - no sense in spending the day fighting with him, Bye Mom." He walked out the door, down the dusty road towards the sea. Martha watched as he walked away, he looked so like his son, they even walked the same, only in his very early forties he could easily be taken for the boy's brother. She sighed - if only they thought the same way, she thought sadly.

From the door of his bedroom Sweetboy watched his grandmother. He'd overheard their conversation and now felt really guilty as he saw the expression on his grandmother's face. He knew what she was thinking, well he'd show her, he thought determinedly, he'd make her proud of him yet. Tonight he'd do a little night fishing of his own and he'd net himself a fortune.

Chapter 15

His decision made, Sweetboy strode down towards the sea with a spring in his step, surprising his father with his enthusiasm for the day's work. Together they fished throughout the morning, netting a good haul. It seemed even the fish caught their exuberance and leapt into the nets like happy lemmings leaping to their fate. Martha Richards was relieved to find them both in high spirits when they returned home and happily joined them in gutting the fish and preparing it for market.

"Well, it does a body good to see you two." She declared joyfully, as the three of them sat outside busy with the catch. "You see Sweetboy, fishing ain't really a bad way to earn a crust now is it?" The baleful eyes of the dead fish offered a mute protest. Expertly she sliced the head off a red snapper and flipping it over, sliced down the belly and gutted it cleanly in a matter of seconds, tossing it into a bucket she reached for another.

"No I guess you're right Grandma, as a matter of fact...." he paused, trying to sound casual and reached over for another fish. "I thought 'bout what you done told me this morning Daddy, and you's right. I gotta work, I was thinkin' of maybe taking her out again tonight, maybe getting a catch for the early market at Oistins - yeah..." he pretended to consider the idea, "I likes a bit of night fishing - it's cooler and I need a bit of quiet to think a few things over." His two companions exchanged glances over his head, surprised and slightly sceptical at the youth's sudden passion for honest labour. Sweetboy bent to concentrate on his task, keeping his eyes carefully lowered so they wouldn't see the excitement shining in his eyes.

"What's all this then? You keepin' something from us boy?" Courtney grinned at his son, who looked up sharply, his heart beating faster - did they suspect something?

"What do you mean? I ain't keepin' nothing - what you mean?" He stammered nervously swallowing and carefully avoiding eye contact with his father.

"Well I was thinkin' maybe you's in love or something - you keep disappearing an' now all of a sudden you wants to work hard - there ain't nothin' you wants to tell us hey?" Courtney teased his son, enjoying the boy's discomfort, maybe this was what they'd all been waiting for, the lad was finally going to grow up, nothing like love to make a man ambitious.

Sweetboy sighed with relief, "Thank God!" he thought, "Well that's just great - let them think it." He pretended to look affronted, "Maybe, maybe not, maybe I jes' want to spend a bit of time alone that's all - I thought you wanted me to work." He added defiantly. "I could always go back to hanging around that bar if that's what you wants!"

Courtney and Martha grinned at each other, so that was it. Martha shot a warning look at her son.

"Now Courtney don't you go giving the boy a hard time - if he wants to work nights then good luck to him. The Lord be praised that the boy wants to get on. I knowed he would, like I said didn't the Lord Jesus call upon the fishermen to follow him? 'Cast out your nets' He said, it's good honest work and we should be proud. I knows I is." She nodded her head, defying her son to make light of the boy's ambition.

"Yes Mom, I knows it... jes' as long as it's only them waves what are rocking that boat tonight!" He added, suppressing a grin.

"Courtney Richards I is ashamed of you! What is going on in that mind of yours? You ain't too old for me to take a strap to yet, you know!" Martha Richards stood up and strode indignantly into the house to wash her hands and begin work on the lunch. The two men exchanged grins like a couple of guilty schoolboy co-conspirators. Courtney experienced a great lifting of spirit as he felt closer to his son than he had been in many months.

The moon shone brightly through the balmy air as Sweetboy headed once again out into the night. He felt nervous, yet exhilarated by his intended task. After all it wasn't really stealing, he reassured himself. Well not from honest men anyway. Wasn't there a saying 'You can't cheat an honest man'? Well then he surely wasn't dealing with honest men so in a way they deserved to be cheated a little, and he wasn't going to take much. He rationalised his decision all the way to Skeete's Bay, still wondering in what form the drugs would be.

Reaching the Bay, Sweetboy removed the lobster pot marker buoy from the nets and attached them to the boat's winch. The winch strained as the heavy drums were slowly hauled aboard, the moon dancing dully off the wet drums. Carefully he positioned them in the very centre of the deck so their immense weight wouldn't unbalance the small craft. He stood in eager anticipation staring at his magnificent 'catch'. The drums looked reassuringly ordinary.

He examined them carefully trying to find a way to open them without disturbing the paintwork and leaving any signs they'd been tampered with. He tried to insert a screwdriver under the lid of one of them but to no avail, the surface was completely sealed. Thoughtfully he ran his fingers around the rim. "There has to be a way." He repeated again and again, the whispered mantra failing to calm his pounding heart.

Finally he found a series of clamp screws just under the rim. Crouching down he laboriously unscrewed each one, making sure he didn't chip the paintwork with the screwdriver as he worked. It seemed an unending task. "Just be patient Sweetboy, be real real careful." It was a lengthy task. Finally all the screws were out. He stood up, grasped the lid either side and tried to lift it off. It didn't move. He paused, "Sweet Jesus! What is holding this down?"

He tried to insert the screwdriver under the small opening he'd just created by removing the clamp screws. The sealed flange of the lid gave slightly. He was in! Triumphantly he grasped the lid, convinced this time he'd broken some invisible seal. Gradually he came to realise it was the lid itself which was sealing the drum down, it was unnaturally heavy. It appeared to be lined with lead or something very like it. Puzzled he carefully worked the screwdriver around the entire rim, slowly and carefully. He dare not risk scratching the paint. He could see that the lid was no longer attached except by its own weight. Sweetboy's muscular body honed by years of lifting heavy nets strained as he lifted the lid and laid it carefully upon the deck his breath coming in short gasps.

The boat creaked gently on the turning tide. The dull gunmetal grey of the lid shimmered coldly in the moonlight. It was lined with solid lead, at least two inches thick by Sweetboy's reckoning. "Perhaps that's what you need to protect the stuff." He thought, shrugging as he turned back to the more important task of retrieving the drugs. He peered into the drum, then stepped back sharply, nearly falling backwards over the upturned lid beside him. He leant forward again to examine the contents, a frown crossing his puzzled face. No sachets of white powder, no sign of powder at all, instead a large, bright orange ball appeared to be suspended from a series of springs attached to the drum. The sides of the drum were also thickly lined with lead. He stood staring at it in silent disbelief. His dream was disintegrating along with his nerve.

"No, maybe this was how serious drugs are packed." He countered, his hopes rising momentarily. "How the hell should I know any different." He was beginning to feel a cold dread creeping through his body. Something was very wrong here. "Look you've come this far, stay cool, Sweetboy." He told himself sternly, "It ain't gonna bite, just have a closer look." Tentatively he reached into the drum and touched the orange ball. Strangely it felt warm. Did drugs feel warm? He shrugged, "Guess they do" he thought. Reaching for his fishing knife he prodded at the surface of the ball. It was heavily covered with a lurid waxy coating. Carefully he sliced through the coating and raised it slightly with the tip of the knife, trying to decipher what lay below. It certainly wasn't loose powder, although it did have a slightly powdery feel to it. He poked his finger under the waxy surface; he couldn't make out what it was. He made the hole a bit bigger and managed to get another finger under the surface. It felt warm, almost like warm metal, but with that strange, slightly dusty, feel to it. He leant over the drum and using his jacket as a cover over his head to hide the light he shone a small torch into the hole in the waxy surface. Rubbing his fingers against the surface he looked carefully at the powdery residue on his fingertips. They were covered with a grey film. It just didn't make any sense. Switching off the torch he sat back on the deck and wondered what to do. Sweat beaded his brow; he wiped his face with his hands. His heart was pounding and the feeling of cold dread that had filled him earlier escalated into a rising panic. "It's not drugs" his mind screamed, over and over the message repeated until he could almost hear it aloud. Then a horrifying thought occurred to him - what was bigger than drugs?

In trepidation he drew closer to the drum again mesmerised like a moth drawn to suicide by a flame. Dispensing with the precaution of masking the torchlight he shone the beam into the drum. Picked out in the fierce light Sweetboy could understand the letters but make no sense of the words stamped across the ball. 'DANGER - HIGHLY TOXIC TRANSURANIC ELEMENT' "Sweet Jesus! What could it be? It must be something real terrible! Christ I've touched it!" In blind panic he reached over the side of the boat and began vigorously washing his hands in the inky black sea. He remembered the heavy gloves he had aboard to haul rope with, fumbling in panic he pulled them on and tried to patch up the waxy surface to conceal the hole he'd made. "It don't look too bad," he thought, calming himself a little. "You'd have to look pretty close to see the repair, maybe it would be okay after all." Quickly he hauled the heavy lid back into place, the adrenaline coursing through his veins giving him inhuman strength. Frantically he replaced the clamp screws; his hands were shaking as he tried to fit them back. With a metallic clang one of the screws fell out of his trembling fingers and rolled towards the open gap in the deck rails where the nets came through. Desperately he dived across for it, his gloved hands unable to grasp the spiralling screw. With a small splash it fell into the sea. He lay across the deck staring down into the water in despair. Would they notice? Did it matter if one of the clamps was missing? What had he done? Terror-stricken he leapt to his feet and gathered the net around the drums. Winching them up he inched them back over the side and lowered them back into the innocent ocean, re-attaching the marker buoy before heading home as if all the demons in hell were chasing him.

As the drums sank slowly back to the bottom of the sea the salt water started to seep through the tiny gap made by the missing seal. An invisible, insidious killer violating the clear crystal waters of the Caribbean.

Chapter 16

It took two days for the first victim to be washed onto the shoreline. The delicate pink hue of the Snapper's scales turned a putrid white. Its eyeballs were missing. By midday there were a dozen more. By nightfall the shoreline was littered with the ghostly carcasses.

The Department of Tourism was called upon to act. The Saga of the East Coast began. For such a laid back island the problem was treated with the utmost urgency. Tourism was all-important naturally but there was also the question of food safety. Fish was the staple diet of many people and if some new form of disease was taking hold it was of grave concern. It was a problem that could not be ignored. The Minister called upon Barbados Institute of Marine Biology to investigate the problem and hopefully find a rapid solution.

Technicians from the Institute visited the beach. Wearing protective clothing they gathered as many samples as they felt the laboratory could reasonably handle. They swept the beach to remove the debris. Paradise was temporarily regained. The Barbados Coast Guard stepped up patrols of the area in case someone was dumping some sort of pollutant off the coast. Despite all attempts to play down any publicity of the problem the local newspapers were full of accounts of the unusual occurrence.

Reporting of the phenomenon varied considerably according to the type of publication. Some papers blamed the Government, hinting darkly at secret deals to allow waste to be pumped into the sea from unknown origins. An allegation hotly denied. Others blamed a new form of mutant marine virus developing from a breakdown of the ozone layer. Readers were encouraged to write in with their own suggestions. The whole episode was blown out of all proportions as increasingly bizarre speculations hit the press. As a small island with little crime and few major incidents anything unusual gripped the imagination of the news hungry population.

"This is Marvo Mainwaring reporting for the Barbados Broadcasting Channel." The outside reporter began her street interview. "We're here on the streets of our Capital getting the public opinion of this inexplicable phenonomen." She smiled for the camera and looked around at the gathered audience. A large local woman lunged forward from the crowd.

"Madam what is your opinion?" The woman didn't need to be asked twice. Grabbing the microphone she bellowed into the camera. "Sodom and Gomorra! Like the good Book says... it's all there in Genesis. You jes read chapter 19. God warned us all. " The sound man winced as the tirade hit his ears. Frantically he gestured to the presenter who tried in vain to calm the vitriolic address. "That Calypso contest gets lewder every year. It's a disgrace! That's what it is. Downright shameful! This is God's message..." The presenter wrested the microphone back. "Thank you Madam. Back to the studio I think."

A local man wrote in to a national newspaper swearing he'd seen an alien spacecraft hovering out to sea sending down gamma rays. However he also mentioned he'd discussed the whole thing with Elvis as they walked home from the rum shop so this theory didn't carry much weight!

The Director of the Barbados Institute of Marine Biology, Paul Scobie, summoned Nathan Corbin to his office. A quiet man, Canadian by birth, Paul had first visited Barbados some thirty years earlier. Like so many before him he had fallen in love with Island and remained ever since. He was one of the founder members of the Institute and was extremely proud of how the tiny laboratory had grown to be an establishment commanding worldwide respect. Despite having lived for thirty years in the tropics Paul Scobie was as pale as the day he arrived. His pale colouring and once auburn, now white, hair meant he burnt very quickly. He always wore a broad rimmed hat and was careful not to venture out in the middle of the day unless fully protected from harmful rays. Unfortunately his colouring tended to make him look more like a newly arrived tourist than an adopted native making Bridgetown on cruise ship days a place to avoid.

While awaiting the arrival of his two junior colleagues Paul scanned the local press for the latest reports of the escalating problem. Now nearing retirement age he had hoped to bow out of his working life quietly and discreetly. He sighed as he read the increasingly ridiculous nature of some of the reports. His lips pursed with disapproval as he read with increasing dismay. He hated any sort of fuss. Colleagues had joked that he was entirely suited to marine life, as he was a bit of a cold fish himself. This was not entirely true; it was just that he enjoyed a tranquil life.

Shunning any sort of excitement he was happiest when enjoying the cool stillness of the huge aquarium, where he spent as much time as his duties allowed. He had been widowed some ten years previously but despite this fact was in a habit of discussing any difficulties with his late wife as though she were still around to listen. Sitting at his desk, the newspapers spread across it he shook his head and addressed the empty room.

"Well I just don't know, Shirley, what a load of nonsense." He adjusted his half moon glasses and peered at the colour picture of a dead kingfish graphically displayed on the front cover of the paper. Barbados newspapers occasionally had some trouble printing colour pictures. Often slightly blurred, they had a curious 3D effect causing the reader to suspect they should be examined through two-tone glasses. "Simply ridiculous some of these stories. Why do they bother printing them? That's what I want to know. This sort of thing can turn the place upside down," he continued with a faint shudder, "You mark my words Shirley, they'll be newspaper men camped on the doorstep, all sorts of comings and goings. Dreadful business. Simply dreadful."

Brad and Corby arrived at the office. The door was slightly ajar and hearing a voice they decided to wait. A minute passed but still they only heard one voice.

"Who's he talking to?" whispered Brad, peering into the office. As far as he could tell the man was alone. "Is he on the phone?"

"No it's all right, he's talking to his wife." replied Corby equally softly. "I should have warned you, he is a bit eccentric."

"I guess it is a bit strange to be talking to your wife these days. Where is she? Hiding under the desk?" Brad laughed.

"She's dead. She's been dead for years."

"Don't you think someone ought to tell him!!!" His laughter turned into a polite cough as he saw his new boss look up and notice them.

"Ah, Nathan and er...Mr Tucker isn't it? Yes, yes well I'm afraid you seem to be joining us at a most unfortunate time. Yes, most unfortunate, all those fish...dreadful, quite dreadful." he shook his head sadly, as he looked down again at the cover story on the paper. The unfortunate kingfish appeared to be staring glassy-eyed back at him. He folded the paper and started again with a more brisk tone.

"Yes, well, no sense dwelling on that sort of publicity. Absolute nonsense from what I've seen. Gentlemen it's up to us to solve this particular little puzzle and with the utmost urgency. This sort of thing is very bad for tourism you know." He warned, well aware of the importance of his last statement. "Now I want you two to put aside your current project...yes I know how important it is to you..." he interjected noticing Nathan's expression, and knowing of the man's enthusiasm, "but I'm afraid this has to take priority. I truly believe you two are the best we've got and I know I can rely on your dedication as well as your discretion in handling this case. I think it would be best if we turn the whole thing over to you two alone, thus avoiding any possible 'leaks' to certain aspects of the Press. You may be approached by journalists and the like, but I want to make it quite plain.... he paused, and taking off his glasses, looked directly at the two men to emphasis his point.

"I don't want to read of any speculation originating from this establishment. Until we are fully confident of any findings, and I do mean completely sure, of the cause of this phenonomen we do not discuss this outside of these four walls. Please keep me appraised of your progress." He nodded in dismissal, rising to his feet to shake hands with the two men. Picking up a large tub of fish food, he headed back to the sanctuary of his beloved aquarium, mentally composing a brief statement for the Press.

"The research into the current situation regarding the East Coast is being handled exclusively by our two foremost experts in the field of marine biology. No further statement will be issued until the full result of their research is available."

Smiler Baines sipped thoughtfully from his breakfast cup of coffee as he read the release in the local paper. The whole business regarding the East Coast, and its dying fish, had begun shortly after his precious cargo had been deposited there. The matter of the increased Coast Guard patrols was an added complication he could well do without too. Smiler frowned as he mentally pictured young Sweetboy, his nervousness and his pathetic gratitude for the cash. Surely the young fool hadn't interfered with the drums? Would the contents have this effect on marine life? Then he realised he wasn't entirely sure what the contents were, and whether they could be the cause of the current crisis. There were however two things he was sure about, he decided grimly. Sweetboy had better not be involved in all this and that Tony "Smiler" Baines did not believe in coincidence.

Chapter 17

Sweetboy woke in the early hours of the morning with the sudden realisation that he was not a well man. He'd been feeling slightly queasy for a couple of days but put it down to a guilty conscience! This was more than pangs of guilt. His stomach was churning and he felt overwhelmingly nauseous. Leaping to his feet he barely made it to the tiny bathroom at the back of the wooden house before he was violently sick. When the terrible retching finally subsided he staggered to his feet and over to the wash basin to rinse his mouth and face with cold water.

Fumbling in the dark for the taps he felt a sharp pain through his finger. Cursing the fool who'd left something sharp in the sink, he reached for the pull cord and winced as the bright light flooded the room making his head throb unbearably. He squinted, with half open eyes, into the sink, looking for the cause of the pain in his fingers. The sink was empty. Puzzled, he looked down at his fingers - his eyes widened with horror - his headache momentarily forgotten, he stared at the open sores which covered the tips of two fingers of each hand. The wounds looked like burns, raw and blistered and excruciatingly painful. He looked up, his blood ran cold in his veins as he saw his reflection in the mirror above the sink, his face was similarly marked, a streak of red slashed an angry weal across his upper forehead.

Shocked he gripped the wash basin and pain shot through him as his fingers again contacted with the cold surface. Another wave of nausea hit him and he dropped to the floor. He was still lying on the floor, semi-conscious and racked with pain when his father found him a couple of hours later.

As the ambulance screamed its way towards the chattel house the inhabitants each reacted in a different way. Sweetboy too sick and too scared to care much about anything lay on the sofa and wondered if he was dying. His mother, Janet, held his hand and tried to talk soothingly to her ailing son. The years fell away and she murmured gently to him as she had when he had had the usual childhood maladies.

"Come on now my precious Sweetboy. You ain't too big to give your Mother a hug now are you?" She softly crooned.

"Aw Mum, I feel real bad. What do you think I got?" Sweetboy whispered fearfully, "I ain't a bad boy am I Mum?"

"Course you're not. You're gonna be fine you see. We'll get you fixed up real quick you see." She rocked him slowly in her arms and prayed that the ambulance would be swift.

His father hovered anxiously in the background, usually a strong, practical man, this was a situation he was unable to deal with, he couldn't fix it, so he was at a complete lose as to what he should do. The younger children watched with undisguised curiosity at the drama unfolding before them. His youngest sister, Bethany-Ann, who was only six, cried as she saw her hero looking so ill.

Martha Richards, ever practical, set about looking for a clean pair of pyjamas, no one ever wore pyjamas of course, but there was always one set ready for emergencies. Then she set about cleaning Sweetboy's bedroom to try and rid the house of the nauseating odour. Lifting the corner of the mattress to strip the bed, she stooped to pick up a small bundle that had been concealed there. Glancing back through the open door she briefly caught the eye of her prostrate grandson, for a fraction of a second their eyes locked, Sweetboy gave her a look of silent pleading and shook his head almost imperceptibly. Smoothly she slipped the bundle into the pocket of her dressing gown and was rewarded with a brief, grateful smile from Sweetboy.

"Dear Lord, please don't let it be drugs" she offered up a silent prayer as she carried on with her vigorous cleaning, glad to have something to keep her occupied.

The ambulance duly arrived and the unfortunate Sweetboy was gently loaded into the back. Leaving Martha in charge of the younger children, his parents went along with him, calling last minute instructions as they went. Suddenly the house fell silent. The younger children looked to Martha for guidance. Briskly she allayed their fears.

"No sense in a carrying on, you knows how that boy is. He'll bounce right back - don't he always? Ain't he always been the lucky one - ain't that what he tells we? Now come on now enough of all that, time to get breakfast. Bethany -Ann you got you reading book ready for school? Well where is it? Come on now child - there's things to be done...." Deliberately bustling around to distract the children, and possibly to keep her own mind occupied, Martha started getting the household ready for the daily routine of work and school. Outside a beautiful sunrise streaked the sky with pink and gold heralding another glorious day.

In his now familiar hotel room, Smiler lay awake watching the sunrise through the filmy voile curtains. He contemplated his next move. Would he have to notify Miami? The increased Coast Guard patrols could prove to be a problem. Frowning he sat up in bed and reached for the 'phone. He had taken Sweetboy's number, everyone on the island had a telephone, even in the lowliest of Chattel houses it was considered a necessity. He had also, reluctantly, given Sweetboy a means of contacting him - with strict instructions it was for emergency use only. He hoped the boy himself would answer the 'phone, but was ready with a plausible story if he didn't.

"Hello?" A cautious female voice answered the 'phone on the first ring, Martha was anxiously waiting for news.

"Oh - good morning. I'm sorry to be ringing so early but I was hoping to get hold of Sweetboy before he went out fishing for the day, is he available please?" Smiler spoke casually, yet politely despite hating having to speak to a third party. The fewer people who knew of their connection the better.

"Sweetboy won't be going no fishing, no Sir, he's sick, taken real bad he is. The ambulance done been and carried him to hospital. Who did you say was calling?" Martha asked, recognising an American accent and wondering whom it could be.

"Oh he won't know me - I was just given his name in the bar here, as someone who might be able to take me out sea fishing one day. No problem, I'm really sorry to have disturbed you. Please don't bother him. I hope he's better soon. Goodbye." He hung up quickly before she had chance to question him further.

Cursing, he paced around the hotel room. It was obvious what had happened - the boy had sampled the merchandise. He sat down at the small table and ran his hands through his hair. Well that settled it - he would have to contact Miami. The boy was ill - an overdose? It could be that the stuff was contaminated in some way - maybe Miami should be warned of that possibility? He had really screwed up on this job. He tried to think of a way of salvaging the situation. It was no good; he had to seek instructions from higher authority. Reaching for the phone he dialled an overseas number. He had memorised the number previously, as ever meticulous in covering his tracks.

There was a brief pause while the 'phone was answered with a curt "Yes". Smiler's reply was equally curt, "Phone me" then he hung up and waited for Mr Westfield to return his call on a more secure line. Minutes later the phone rang again,

"What the hell do you want? This is not the arranged time!" Westfield started, angry at the deviation away from the planned schedule. He hated being disturbed early in the morning at the best of times.

"We have a problem." Smiler stated flatly, knowing there was more than his reputation at stake here. His life could depend on how he handles this call.

"I don't want to hear that - I thought you were the best! What problem?" Westfield's voice grew dangerously quiet. He was already under pressure from his South American customer; he couldn't afford any delays.

"It appears our messenger may have sampled the merchandise, don't worry..." he added quickly, hearing a sharp intake of breath, "I'll take care of him." He paused and waited for the inevitable explosion, he didn't wait long.

"What the hell are you talking about?" It didn't make any sense - the guy was supposed to be a poor fisherman, what the hell would he want with plutonium?

"I know, I know, I thought he was...I was sure he was... controllable but I guess he got greedy. But he's sick - real sick - are you sure the stuff's okay. Maybe he's tested it for you and saved you some hassle..." his voice trailed off as he tried desperately to find some saving grace in the mess. He held the phone slightly away from his ear as a stream of expletives shot through the airwaves. Finally the tirade eased off and Mr Westfield's voice again went very quiet.

"I'll repeat - what are you talking about?" Sweat beaded his brow, how the hell was he going to explain this to his customer. What was that damn fool in Barbados doing?

"The...drugs" even knowing the line was secure, Smiler felt anxious saying the word, "I think he's taken some of them" He winced as another angry tirade began.

"THERE ARE NO DRUGS - DO YOU HEAR ME YOU MORON! WHAT THE HELL ARE YOU TALKING ABOUT?!!" Randell Westfield was about ready to explode with anger.

"What's in the drums then?" Asked Smiler in genuine bewilderment, any thoughts of security forgotten.

"Plutonium you asshole! Who mentioned drugs? Did you tell some kid there was a ton of drugs and then expect him not to go after them? For Christ's sake - I thought you were a professional!" Even as he was berating Smiler, Randall's mind was weighing up the options.

"Ok - there's no point in going over past mistakes, we've got to contain the damage...."

"Don't worry I've got the co-ordinates of the bay. I know exactly where they are. I'll get someone else to bring them back up..." interjected Smiler, still trying to remedy the situation, realising, at last, the seriousness of the situation.

"Forget it - it's too late." snapped Randall, "I'll have to send in a team of experts. Your job is over - no wait - I'll need you to contain the damage there. How many people know of this? Can you clean up down there - effectively?" The last word was said with heavy sarcasm and Smiler realised immediately he was being given a chance to redeem himself.

"Consider it done. I mean it - I accept I screwed up - I didn't know what was involved but I can assure you - I'll put it right. There will be no witnesses here - I guarantee it." He said grimly.

"Right -there'd better not be. Your job now is simply damage control. Forget all about the drums - as far as you're concerned they no longer exist. Just make sure when you leave the island no one else knows they ever existed. Do I make myself clear?" Randall acted fast to cover his tracks, he'd have to get an expert team in to retrieve the drums - that would cost him, but the main thing now was to prevent the break down in plans from ruining him entirely. "Keep me posted - and Mr Baines, try and get it right this time." He hung up.

Courtney and Janet Richards called home from the hospital. Sweetboy was in an isolation room undergoing tests to try and determine the cause of his illness. Martha Richards replaced the 'phone after speaking to them, her heart heavy, what was that boy mixed up in? She remembered the bundle she'd found, digging around in her pocket she pulled it out. It was a bundle of hundred dollar bills and a picture postcard. Where did he get hold of that sort of money? Totally puzzled she looked at the card, it was a picture of one of the fancy west coast hotels, turning it over she read.

"Dear Fred,

Having a great time, this is my hotel. I'm in room 101 which is right at the front. I'm thinking of hiring a local fisherman soon to go and catch me some of them flying fish. See you soon, Howard.

It made no sense she decided, and thrust it back in her pocket. The post card was stamped and addressed to a New York address, probably Sweetboy was supposed to have posted it, she shrugged, "Guess he forgot - typical!" If Smiler Baines could have seen her he would have felt some measure of satisfaction, his way of giving Sweetboy a method of contacting him worked at least. It meant nothing to anyone else.

Chapter 18

Following his conversation with Smiler, Randall Westfield paced angrily around his tastefully decorated bedroom. Snatching up the tiny mobile phone from which he'd first received the urgent message to call Smiler he felt an urge to throw it against the elegant oak lined walls. Reason took over and he realised nothing would be gained from such a childish act, anyway, he shrugged, it was too valuable a piece of communication equipment. Very few people knew the number; it was always with him and was the latest model technology could offer. Randall had invested heavily in hi-tech equipment, in his line of business he needed to be able to communicate with as little danger of being overheard as possible. He had a secure phone at home and at work, both were constantly being tested by his security firm and currently both were being proved highly effective against eavesdroppers - whatever their motive.

Time to face the music he decided, quickly he called Al and arranged to meet him at the office early, before anyone else arrived. An hour later the two men were again seated at the oval conference table, their faces clearly betraying the seriousness of the situation.

"Right I'll leave you to start checking out specialist teams to retrieve the goods - we can only assume if the seal has been broken there's a chance of contamination...." He broke off as he realised he hadn't checked that with Smiler, God how stupid! "Christ this thing gets worse! Okay I'll try and get back to our contact in Barbados, I don't expect any leak will be detectable this soon but I'll check it out. Meanwhile..." he paused and grimaced with distaste, "...meanwhile, I'll inform our clients of a small delay. You'd better arrange for extra security here - you know how these Latin types can get." It was a pretty lame attempt to make light of a gravely worrying situation - a situation Al appreciated fully.

Al rose to his feet. Ignoring the niceties of adjourning a meeting he left abruptly, there was no time to be wasted. After he left Randall sat for a long time just staring at the phone. He got up and walked around the conference room, waiting for some sort of inspiration to strike. He was already under pressure from his South American clients. They had not taken kindly to the original two-week delay caused by the diversion. Although their language was always most courteous it was obvious they didn't trust him - they were in a delicate political situation and they couldn't afford to trust anyone. The only question was ...how strongly would they react to a delay? Well, there was only one way to find out...

Javier Cardenas took the call in his personal office in the penthouse suite of the magnificent skyscraper that towered above the streets of Quitto. The opulence of his surroundings was in stark contrast to the poverty on the streets that bordered the building. Quitto was a city of contrasts; the poorest people in the world eked out a meagre existence, yet the City had some of the most lavish churches, filled with riches beyond compare. It was a unique place, the temperature remained constant every day, year around, temperate enough during the day but, due to the high altitude, dropping considerably at night. The people too, contrasted each other depending on their place in the social stratum. The poor dressed in bright, colourful peasant garb, wearing several layers to accommodate the changing temperatures. The businessmen of the City wore sharp, sombre looking suits, well tailored and obviously expensive.

Javier sat at his huge mahogany desk, over six feet in any direction it did not appear over sized in the spacious, almost palatial room. It was an impressive, yet startling office. Impressive because it boasted a magnificent view of the hills in the distance, the lush greenery of the jungle terrain framed in huge picture windows. Startling because a life-size replica of Christ's Crucifixion dominated the room. It was incredibly life-like, the crown of thorns appeared to be pressing into real flesh, the agonised expression caused discomfort in even the most stalwart atheist. Like many South Americans, Javier was a devout Catholic; his wife attended Mass every morning to pray for her husband's soul. Javier himself didn't go that far but he had made certain of maintaining good relations with the local Catholic priest so that, should an emergency arise, he would have time to confess of his sins before he came before his Maker.

He listened with quiet respect to Randall Westfield abject apology for the delay in delivering the promised merchandise. His expression hardly changed but a close observer would have noticed a small vein throbbed in his neck, revealing his emotions were not quite as in check as his demeanour would indicate. Finally he spoke, his voice quiet and calm but with an unmistakable edge of menace to his tone.

"Mr Westfield, I do hope this is not a deliberate ploy to alter the financial arrangement?"

"Certainly not. I assure you Signor Cardenas it is merely an unfortunate delay - nothing more. I'm sure I don't need to justify my extra security arrangements to an astute businessman like yourself.... after all I know you appreciate the delicacy of this situation. Naturally I cannot be too careful and if this should incur a small delay...well surely that is a small price to pay for the knowledge that the goods are quite safe and - shall we say - unnoticed?" Although it went against his nature to have to placate the man, Westfield was a shrewd enough businessman to know when a little ego massaging was necessary.

"You compliment me Mr Westfield, but perhaps I'm not such an astute business man after all. This is the second time I have been told of a delay - perhaps my judgement was less than sound when I chose my supplier. I was under the impression I was dealing with an expert - it may now appear I may have been wrong." He replied smoothly, his tone still courteous.

Westfield struggled to maintain his composure, where did this guy get off? However he persevered, there was more than money at stake here.

"Signor Cardenas, I repeat, this is only a slight delay, nothing serious, let us not be hasty here..."

"Mr Westfield," interrupted Javier, his impatience growing, "... hasty is precisely what I want to be. I cannot afford these constant delays; there is a most important schedule involved here. If you do not feel able to keep your part of the bargain perhaps I should reconsider my options."

"There is no way you'd be able to get another shipment within your time scale - you must know that." Westfield played his trump card.

"You're telling me I have no choice but let me tell you, if you cross me you may find yourself with very limited options yourself." Javier's voice was soft but the threat was obvious. Westfield felt suddenly cold as he realised the implications of his words.

"I understand, believe me, Signor Cardenas. I will resolve this - you have my personal guarantee." He said with as much dignity he could muster.

"I was under the impression I had that already." The connection was severed.

"Well?" Al had come into the room as Randall replaced the receiver.

"It's not good - but I think he'll stay with it - though we can't hold him much longer. You've increased security?" He looked up at Al who nodded his head briefly.

"We need to handle this very carefully - I'm not sure how far I can trust those guys - the sooner this deal is over the better."

Ironically enough, a few thousand miles away, Javier Cardenas was echoing his words.

Chapter 19

"So how's the night shift working out then Andrew?" Enquired Mike as the two doctors enjoyed a break together. It was Andrew's third night on duty. "I hear you enjoy working with the day staff better, or is it just one certain hospital administrator?" As Charmaine had predicted gossip was rife in the small hospital about her and the new doctor.

"Can you blame me?" grinned Andrew. Charmaine had been wonderfully understanding about his rum punch capacity. They had lunched together in the canteen the following day. "To be honest it's quite nice to have a bit of time off during the day though. I did just drop by at 5 o'clock yesterday, just to see if I was needed you understand!"

"Of course nothing to do with our Charmaine finishing at 5?" Mike continued, "You don't have to explain to me - I've been there remember? I was only going to be here a year myself - that was ten years ago! I still haven't heard the full version of that dinner." He teased, Andrew had been very reticent about the evening. "I know you liked the place, and I happen to know Miss Charmaine Harrison received an enormous bouquet the following day..." Andrew raised his eyebrows questioningly. "my wife knows the hospital florist, you don't get away with much around here! Come on give me the sordid details."

"It was fine, just fine. As for the night shift." interrupted Andrew, changing the subject quickly, Mike grinned, no doubt he'd get the details eventually, Andrew continued rapidly, and "To be honest it's much the same as night shift back home I keep expecting something more unusual. Maybe some sort of tropical illness. So far all I've seen is the usual. Drunk drivers and domestic accidents. Though I have to say - you get a nicer drunk here than you do in Glasgow!"

"Perhaps it's the rum. Maybe we ought to write a paper on it! I'll even offer to do the research myself. Mind you I've seen my fair share of punchy drunks here you know, whatever they're drunk on. You've just been lucky so far. " Mike helped himself to another coffee. "Anyway you had a bit of excitement the other night didn't you? I thought for a while there one of us was going to get a sea voyage - well out to the deep water harbour anyway!" He laughed, recalling the previous night's call from the Coast Guard.

"Oh yeah. How could I forget - that was very dramatic!" Andrew replied, smiling at the incident. "All prepared for an emergency appendectomy and the patient dashes to the men's room as soon as he arrives. Turns out he was constipated! I examined him of course; did I not tell you I'm a fine doctor? But that's all it was!"

"Apparently they diverted a ship as well! Must be the most expensive case of constipation in history!" Mike laughed.

"I bet his boss took the news well!" Andrew commented, sipping his coffee and picturing the ship's captain receiving the news.

"Seemingly he was quite good about it, they stayed off shore for 24 hours to make sure all's well." Mike replied. He'd seen the captain when he'd arrived to check on his crewmember.

"Didn't trust my diagnosis huh?" Andrew, who was quite confident of his analysis of the situation, wasn't worried by any lingering doubts.

"I think it's more a case of justifying the diversion. Diverting a ship just for a short spell in the men's room probably wouldn't go down too well with the ship's owners. A 24 hour medical emergency - well - you could put that down to an intestinal blockage couldn't you!"

"Call it what you like- it amounts to the same thing..." Andrew shrugged, then jumped to his feet as the distant sound of an ambulance arriving disturbed the quiet. "Here we go again. Heads or tails?" He tossed a coin to see who'd get the new patient. "Don't bother, there's another one. Like buses aren't they? You wait for ages then two come along together. Shall I be getting the first?"

"Sure why not" shrugged Mike, "But if it's a lovely young girl needing a bit of mouth to mouth I may claim seniority!"

"And you a happily married man!"

The two men hurried over to the entrance in time to see the ambulances pull up. A young black man, in obvious discomfort was being unloaded, an older couple, presumably his parents, hovered anxiously in the background. Mike went straight past them with a brief smile and met the second ambulance.

"Ok what have we got?" Andrew asked the ambulance driver, as he walked alongside the gurney heading towards the casualty unit.

"Patient collapsed at home, severe vomiting, general non-specific symptoms. Not much to go on really" The ambulance driver hadn't been able to pin point the problem as the symptoms were too vague. Leaving the patient to the care of the hospital, he went back to the waiting ambulance to commence the rather unpleasant clean up job that was required.

"Are you related to this gentleman?" he asked the couple accompanying the patient.

"Yes sir, we his parents. What ails the boy doctor?" Janet asked, wiping away a tear, her son looked so desperately ill.

"Well I'm not sure yet but we'll soon find out. Perhaps you could just give the nurse here a few details, medical history and the like. Has he ever had anything like this before?" Seeing them shake their heads he turned to the nurse standing nearby.

"Please find out what you can from them and see if you can track down any previous notes. Let me know would you? Thanks." Turning back to the parents he continued, "The nurse here will show you to somewhere a bit more quiet to sort out the details while I get your son more comfortable. Don't worry you'll be with him soon."

"Sir, Do you know where you are?" Andrew asked, the boy was laying with his eyes closed, moaning quietly, but he was conscious.

"Hospital" Sweetboy murmured.

Andrew checked the boy's vital signs as he spoke. Noticing the lesion on the young man's face he discreetly donned surgical gloves and indicated for the nurses to do the same. Turning away from the boy he murmured to a nearby nurse. "Could you check the HIV register please nurse, thank you." She hurried off. "Can you tell me your name?" asked Andrew turning back to the boy.

"Sweetboy. Doc you gotta help me - please I feel real bad." His voice a bare whisper, Sweetboy struggled to answer before another wave of nausea swept over him. A nurse deftly placed a bowl near his face.

"OK now er.... Sweet boy...." Andrew shrugged, well he'd call him whatever he wanted, "Don't worry - you're in the right place. Now I want you to try and tell me as much as possible - Nurse, could you set up a saline drip please, this patient is becoming dehydrated."

The nurse quickly set up the drip, and replaced the bowl with another. Carefully she cleaned the boy's face, cautiously avoiding the obviously painful lesion.

Sweetboy mumbled to himself, grateful he was getting some medical attention but too terrified to be coherent enough to help the doctor.

"Doc I feel so bad - am I gonna die? You gotta help me." he gasped before falling back onto the pillow. "I don't know what's wrong with me - I ain't done nothing. I ain't - I swear. Am I gonna die?" He repeated, his voice rising in panic.

"Of course you're not going to die. We'll soon sort you out. Ok nurse, let's get him stable first." Andrew could see he wasn't going to get much sense from his patient until he was calmer.

"Put him in an isolation room please, full protection, I don't want anyone going in without mask and gloves until we know what we're dealing with. Could you arrange for full blood screen, including films, full bio tests, checking vital signs every...." he paused and looked at his patient, how serious was this? "okay every thirty minutes for now. I'm going to consult with Dr Griffin, call me immediately if he deteriorates at all." As he left the cubicle the nurse who'd gone to check records returned.

"Doctor, he's not on any register. The only previous notes are from Casualty five years ago when he got a fishhook in his finger. Parents can think of no reason for his condition. No one else in the family is ill and he seemed perfectly well yesterday. Although his mother did say he has been off his food for a day or so. She said that was very unusual. She asked me to tell you she sure it's not caused by what he's eaten 'cos he's hardly eaten a thing. His parents thought he was in love!" She smiled.

"Thanks nurse. I'm afraid he's more than just love-sick!" He smiled back at her. "Though I do agree with his mother about the food poisoning. He doesn't have the other more obvious symptoms. I'll come and have a word with them in a minute."

"I'll let them know, doctor." She headed back to the waiting room and Sweetboy's anxious parents.

"Dr. Griffin, I wonder if you could spare me a minutes please?" Andrew asked Mike, he was in another cubicle where a young white woman, in party clothes, was clutching her arm in obvious pain.

"Could you take this patient around to x-ray please nurse?" Mike asked, turning to the girl he added, "Don't worry - shouldn't be too long and that pain killer should kick in quite soon." Leaving the cubicle he turned to Andrew,

"Poor kid, she's from the British hockey squad, they only arrived yesterday and she slips over at the welcoming disco! Welcome to Barbados! I'm pretty sure she's broken her arm - what have you got?"

"I'm not sure, young guy, local fisherman, collapses at home. Severe vomiting, his blood pressure is fairly normal, but he's obviously unwell. There are just no specific symptoms that I can put a label to. He does have an open lesion to his forehead - could be a burn - I can't get through to him to ask. He's in quite a panic though."

"AIDS?" Mike queried, thinking of the lesion.

"Could be - not on the hospital register though. The lesion could be unrelated. Could it be Dengue fever?" Knowing of the recent outbreak, Andrew was aware of the possibility.

"Doesn't sound like it. What have you done?" Mike's mind went through the options open to them.

"Well I've ordered all the usual tests, blood films to look for parasites in case it's a tropical disease and all the usual. I've set up a drip to stabilise him - he was getting pretty dehydrated. I guess we'll have to see what the tests show."

"Well you wanted something unusual. Now's your chance! I'll come and take a look in a minute. I'd better go and have a word with the hockey coach first, I hope she wasn't their star player!"

Andrew walked back to the cubicle where Sweetboy lay. The boy had fallen asleep, exhausted by the previous few hours. He stood for a few minutes looking down at the young man. "I wonder what you've picked up?" He thought to himself, "Probably just some local bug - oh well, time will tell." He turned and walked back to the waiting room where Sweetboy's parents were anxiously awaiting news. Maybe they could shed a little light on his Caribbean mystery.

Chapter 20

Despite his busy night at work Andrew found it hard to sleep the following day. Two issues were uppermost in his mind. His growing feelings for Charmaine and the strange case of the young fisherman. He knew which one he'd rather concentrate on but his professional dedication intruded on such thoughts. His room had heavy black-out curtains and air-conditioning designed to help night shift workers sleep but despite this he lay awake staring into the blackness as the thoughts chased around his head.

He was still staying in staff quarters at the hospital. It was a comfortable room and naturally very convenient for work but he was looking forward to having the privacy of his own place. He'd arranged to take over his predecessor's apartment that afternoon so he rose and showered quickly. Dressing casually he threw back the curtains and winced as the bright sunshine filled the room. His eyes quickly adjusted and he wasted no time in packing and preparing to move out.

Checking his watch he rang through to Charmaine's office.

"Administration, Charmaine speaking. Good afternoon." As a medical man Andrew knew it was not physically possible for his heart to flip when he heard her voice - but it did.

"Hi, it's me." He said quietly.

"Andrew!" The delight in her voice was obvious. Her colleagues in the office exchanged knowing looks. No prizes for guessing her feelings.

"How's the packing going?" She asked, turning away from her laughing friends and lowering her voice.

"Nearly done. There wasn't much to pack really." Andrew replied looking across at his suitcases open on the bed. "I'll have to get some shopping though. I know it's not far from here but it's not so handy for the staff canteen. I guess I'm going to have to get used to my own cooking again!"

"It'll do you good to fend for yourself. You men are hopeless sometimes!" She teased.

"Well to tell you the truth I'm not that bad at the old cooking stuff, it's shopping I hate." Andrew hinted, "I don't suppose you'd spare the time to show a mere helpless man where the nearest supermarket is? I mean think of the admin problems of getting a replacement when the new doctor is found starved to death!"

"How could I refuse such a plaintive cry for help?" Charmaine laughed. "When will you be ready?"

"I'm always ready to see you!" Andrew replied happily. "What time can you get away?"

"Well actually I worked through my lunch today.." Charmaine began looking at the clock on the office wall.

"Remind me to put rum punch on the top of the shopping list!" Andrew interrupted remembering the effects of the heady brew on an empty stomach. They both smiled at the memory of their first proper date.

"As I was saying..." continued Charmaine, aware her conversation was being overheard by her colleagues and trying to keep a more serious tone to her voice. "I should be able to get away from here by four. Shall I go ...straight there?"

"Where?" Teased Andrew, picturing her office and the two other girls who were probably hanging on her every word. Charmaine blushed and leaned further away from the desk. Her friends leaned over to shamelessly listen in.

"Your apartment." She whispered.

"Sorry? I didn't quite catch that." Andrew replied, having heard her perfectly well.

"Do you want to have to find the supermarket on your own?" Charmaine warned, as her friends collapsed with laughter.

"I'll meet you at my apartment." Andrew replied meekly. "You do know where it is don't you?"

"Of course I do! I showed you the apartment in the first place!" Charmaine said indignantly then groaned as she realised that she'd played right into his hands.

"I'll be waiting!" Said Andrew gleefully. "Oh and Charmaine..." he added innocently.

"Yes?"

"Do give my regards to the girls in the office. Bye for now"

"Bye Dr Kinloch." Charmaine said archly through gritted teeth.

It didn't take him long to move in. The apartment was a good size, but he had few personal effects with him to unpack. He wandered through the place revelling in his new home. It was on the second floor of a three level block. Facing the sea it afforded a beautiful view of Dover beach from the veranda leading off from the lounge. He slid open the glass doors and the warm breeze wafted in billowing out the net curtains. He went around the other rooms opening the slatted glass windows to allow the breeze to carry through. It had two bedrooms. One with a double bed and one with twin singles. A compact bathroom and a small, but well equipped kitchen. He switched on the fridge/ freezer so it would be ready when he returned with the groceries. Rinsing out the plastic ice trays he found in the freezer compartment he replaced them filled with fresh water. Opening a cupboard in the main bedroom he found a selection of freshly laundered linen. He was just making up the double bed when he heard a knock at the door.

"Charmaine, come in. I was just thinking about you." He exclaimed. He led her through into the lounge. "Can I offer you a ... glass of water?" He laughed, "I haven't even got any ice yet!" Charmaine smiled.

"Looks like I got here just in time. Come on there's a SuperCentre market just up the road. Let's get you organised."

The supermarket was an education to Andrew. There were the usual imported goods. Many brands he recognised from home but there were also a considerable variety of local goods, some of which he didn't even recognise. They spent considerable time shopping. Charmaine guided Andrew with his selections arguing when necessary.

"Bananas." Said Andrew definitely when they reached the fruit section.

"Fig or regular?" Asked Charmaine looking over the selection.

"Fig bananas?" Asked Andrew. Charmaine showed him some small fat bananas. "Well I don't care for them myself. I find them too starchy but some people love them."

"Regular then." Said Andrew; at least he knew where he was there. "Hey they're green!" He complained as she picked up a bunch and placed it in the trolley.

"They'll be yellow tomorrow." She said smoothly. "You've got a lot to learn about the tropics Andrew. Fruit ripens very quickly here." They continued around the busy shop until the trolley was fully loaded. Finally they added a bottle of rum punch and a jar of grated nutmeg.

"The ice should be ready by the time we get back." Said Andrew; "We can Christen my new home properly!" Charmaine laughed.

"Let's make sure we eat first this time!" She looked down at the groceries. There was a good selection of frozen ready meals. Andrew's idea of home cooking. It wouldn't take long to prepare a quick supper.

As they stood in line at the checkout Andrew smiled.

"What's funny?" Asked Charmaine, glancing up from her shopping list.

"Us!" Replied Andrew happily, "Look at us we're like an old married couple!"

"Thanks!" Charmaine retorted, "Who are you calling old?"

"I didn't mean it like that." He grinned. "It's just...well I feel so comfortable with you."

"Mystique gone already huh?" shrugged Charmaine. "Oh well so much for that."

The queue shifted forward and they moved closer to the checkout. Charmaine reached into the trolley and started to unpack the groceries. Andrew gently rested his hand on her arm. She stopped and for a moment they stood just looking at each other.

"There's still plenty I want to know about you. I feel I've known you forever and yet I really still don't know much about you." Said Andrew quietly. "How do you feel? What do you want?"

"Look I don't think this is really the time..." Charmaine began, aware suddenly of the crowds around them. The elderly lady behind looked on with undisguised curiosity.

"Why not? I've never felt the time was so right. Look I've been sensible all my life." He said earnestly, "There comes a time to seize the moment! I want you to know...."

"Andrew please, we're in the middle of a supermarket!" Charmaine looked around her.

"Who cares? Madam," he turned to the elderly woman behind them "Would you like to go ahead?"

"No don't worry bout me." She smiled and nodded her approval "I ain't in no hurry. No you jes carry on." She wasn't about to miss this one!

"Thank you Madam." He gave a small bow. Charmaine looked mortified. "Charmaine, I know it hasn't been long but I know how I feel. I love you and that's all there is to it. Love isn't determined by time. You can't govern when you're going to meet the right person. You just know when it's right. Tell me Charmaine what do you feel? Can you love me?"

He held his breath, the other shoppers held their breath, the checkout girl held her breath. The silence was electrifying. Charmaine stared at him, her eyes filled with tears.

"Yes Andrew" she whispered. She did say more but her words were lost in the spontaneous applause that resounded around the supermarket.

"That'll be ninety-four dollars and fifty cents please." the checkout girl said automatically as she stared open mouthed at the young couple. She had to repeat herself but she waited until Andrew and Charmaine finally broke free from their embrace. The young man who'd packed their groceries grinned at them as he followed them out to the car park. Loading the bags into the car he winked at Andrew.

"Have a great night sir!" He beamed, Andrew gave him a generous tip and hurried into the car.

"Er, good night." He mumbled, suddenly embarrassed.

It was getting dark as they drove back to the apartment. They were both deliriously happy, intoxicated with emotion.

"You know Andrew, we had dinner in the most romantic place in the world and where do you tell me you love me? In a supermarket check-out queue!" She laughed, "You really are one of the last great romantics aren't you?"

"Well anybody could be romantic at a place like the Carambola! Where's the challenge in that?" He protested. "No you have to admit - it's takes a truly great lover to transform an ordinary place into a..." he searched for the right words "...a passion palace!"

"I can honestly say I've never thought of the SuperCentre as a 'passion palace'" she giggled.

"Ah well now, perhaps that's because you've never been there with a truly great lover!" He boasted as they pulled into the car park.

"And are you?" She asked suddenly as she switched off the engine. Andrew leaned over and kissed her.

"Would you like to find out?" He whispered softly.

"I've never wanted anything more in my life." replied Charmaine slowly.

Andrew leapt out of the car and ran around to Charmaine's side. Charmaine stepped out of the car and Andrew literally swept her off her feet. Kicking the door shut he carried her into the apartment block and up the stairs to the apartment.

Once inside they left a trail of clothing through the apartment leading to the bedroom door. As the temperature rose in the bedroom the abandoned groceries melted outside in the car.

Chapter 21

The following morning Andrew walked into Sweetboy's room with a spring in his step. Despite his happy personal life though he felt strangely troubled. He glanced down at the results he'd received so far, he felt as if he were doing some sort of jigsaw puzzle - blindfolded. Some of the results fitted - some didn't - some merely added to the confusion, appearing to contradict each other. The initial blood test showed a dramatic deficiency of white cells which could be indicative of an AIDS related problem but the test for HIV had, as yet, revealed nothing - although the full result would take longer to develop. The haemolysis of red cells appeared to indicate malaria, yet the blood screening revealed no parasites thus totally ruling out not only that possibility but also most other forms of tropical disease.

Unfortunately the time required for all the test results to arrive added to the difficulty. There was also the presence of strange non-healing burn like lesions of the boy's face and hands - could it be some sort of allergy to a tropical plant? The sap from the Manchineel tree could cause burns, Andrew had learnt that already, but he wasn't sure how severe such burns could be.

Sweetboy was awake, he watched the young doctor enter the room, searching his face to some sort of verdict of his condition. The anti-sickness drugs he had been prescribed had brought the sickness under control and although relieved to be rid of one problem, others, were causing him more worries.

"Well Mr Richards, how do you feel today?" Andrew asked cheerfully, reading the charts, he looked up and smiled at his patient - a futile gesture as he was wearing a surgical mask.

"Not so good, Doc." Admitted Sweetboy, in truth he felt pretty terrible, gripped with an overwhelming fear and dread, he was afraid to confide in the doctor yet also afraid not to.

"Well I can't say I'm surprised, but don't worry you'll be fine." Andrew said reassuringly, with more confidence than he actually felt. "Once we've worked out what's wrong with you!" He added mentally.

Andrew drew up a chair and sat facing his patient, pen poised he prepared to take a few notes.

"Now, Mr Richards, I..."

"Call me Sweetboy" interrupted Sweetboy; being called "Mr Richards" made it all seem even more serious.

"Ok, Sweetboy, now I need you to be completely honest with me - you know that nothing you tell me need go beyond these walls, but I do need to know the truth if I'm going to be able to help you."

Sweetboy gulped, wondering how much the doctor knew. The truth was he didn't know what he'd touched - just that it was bad - and that he was in big trouble.

Andrew watched the boy's face. He looked guilty, that much he was pretty confident of, and nervous, well that all tied in with the AIDS theory, perhaps he felt ashamed of his disease. It wasn't uncommon - especially among the young.

"What you want to know, Doc?" Sweetboy hedged, was it that obvious?

"Well, is it possible that you could be HIV positive?" Andrew asked gently, reading the obvious fear in the boy's eyes.

"No!" Exploded Sweetboy, totally surprised by the doctor's assumption. "Well that is to say - I don't think so..." He paused and thought about it, he was a normal young man and had quite a few girlfriends - it was possible. "You think that's what I got?" Maybe it was nothing to do with the strange consignment he'd opened - though he had to admit - it was quite a coincidence.

"To be honest - I don't know, I'm just trying to gather as much information as I can. You've never been diagnosed HIV positive then? Do you know of any contact with an infected person?" He looked questioningly at the boy.

Sweetboy shook his head, "Not that I knows, no Sir." He replied truthfully.

The questioning continued, but Andrew drew a blank each time. Sweetboy knew of the caustic effect of the Manchineel tree, but had not had any contact with one. He didn't recall burning his fingers, although he looked evasive when questioned about the burn like sores. He had not, to the best of his knowledge, been in contact with any infectious diseases. He hadn't eaten anything strange. He did not take illegal substances of any kind. Nothing unusual had happened to him at all that he could recall.

Andrew was sure there was something the boy wasn't telling him. There were times when he'd looked as if on the verge of confiding in him, then he'd clam up again, steadfastly maintaining he knew of no apparent cause for his current condition. On and on the questioning continued until they were both pretty exhausted. Still Andrew could not assuage the feeling that he was definitely missing something. Finally he decided to take a break, the patient needed his rest and Andrew needed a coffee.

Pausing at the door, Andrew removed his mask, he turned and looked back at Sweetboy.

"You know, Mr Ri... Sweetboy, if there's anything else you can think of, something you think I ought to know, something you're not telling me perhaps..." He paused, trying to think of the right words to emphasis the danger the boy was putting himself in.

"It could be very, very dangerous not to tell me." There was no response so Andrew left it at that. Sweetboy miserably wondered if he'd made the right decision.

A few miles away Smiler Baines was also undergoing an intense line of questioning. He'd informed Randall Westfield of the boy's admittance to hospital, and kept him appraised of the steps he would be taking to ensure the boy's silence. Now he hesitated, wondering if he should mention the dead fish and the increased patrols. If Westfield retrieved the stuff quickly enough, he reasoned, the problem would be solved. All he had to do was get rid of the fisherman and make sure the enquiry by the marine biologists was delayed until the operation was over. There really was no necessity to inform Westfield the extent of his failure, Smiler decided. It would be better if the man thought Smiler had resolved the local situation, at least. That was the best option, he was certain he could handle the other aspects of the problem himself. The situation might be salvageable after all.

Randell Westfield intuitively felt Smiler was withholding something.

"Mr Baines, are you sure I am fully appraised of the current situation? I can assure you - it would be very dangerous to try and keep anything from me."

Smiler decided, whatever the cost, he would make sure he'd made the right decision. Sweetboy was history and as for the marine biologists - he shrugged, whatever was necessary.

Chapter 22

Smiler drove through the busy streets of Bridgetown towards the island's hospital. He parked his hired moke in the car park outside and walked over to a phone booth just outside the main entrance. Reading the number off the large sign over the entrance he quickly dialled the hospital.

"Queen Elizabeth hospital, may I help you?" A female voice answered the phone.

"I was just enquiring about a friend of mine... Sweetboy Richards, I understand he was admitted last night." In the background Smiler could hear other phones ringing and being answered. As he had assumed, it was a fairly busy switchboard, his call would never be remembered.

"One moment Sir, I'll check admission." There was a brief pause, "Yes Sir, I've located him. He's in isolation room 213. Are you a member of his family? I'm afraid it's family visiting only at present."

"No, just a friend, don't worry." Smiler only wanted the room number but couldn't afford to appear rude in case it caused the call to be remembered.

"I can give you the nurses' station if you'd like? They can pass on a message or perhaps tell you how he's doing." The operator was anxious to be helpful.

"No thank you, please don't trouble them - I'll be speaking to his family later. Thank you so much." He quickly severed the connection. In the switchboard the line rang again almost immediately and the operator took the next call, Smiler was quite safe in his assumption that his call would be swiftly forgotten.

There was a plan of the hospital outside the main building; his finger followed the contours as located the area he was seeking. A crowded Route Taxi pulled up outside and noisily disgorged a quite extraordinary group of people, clutching packets and parcels and somewhat battered bunches of flowers. Smiler surreptitiously joined onto the end of the group slipping into the hospital behind them.

Once inside the bustling building Smiler removed a folded manila envelope from under his jacket, unfolding it to its full size he walked briskly along the corridors. He had learnt from previous experience that, in any place of business, if he walked briskly carrying a large folder or envelope nobody ever took much notice. In some more sophisticated office blocks he occasionally wore a nondescript uniform but generally all he needed was a simple envelope.

He walked through the maze of corridors, avoiding eye contact, carefully watching the door numbers and signs, while maintaining an air of complete confidence in his surroundings.

A few doors away from room 213 a most convenient water cooler gave him an excuse to linger. Ostensibly quenching his thirst, he checked out the local area. The nurses' station was mid way down the corridor, set back in a recess, with a high fronted podium. A bank of lights and buttons faced the desk, presumably connected to the individual rooms. Wire trays, piled high with notes and charts heightened the podium still further, and effectively obstructed the view of anyone seated at the desk. One nurse was perched on the edge of the desk; her back to the corridor facing another who was seated looking up at her. They were engrossed in conversation, discussing a new doctor.

The door to room 213 was closed, Smiler judged he could get to it without being seen but he had no way of knowing if there was anyone else in there. If he walked in on an examination he was sure to be remembered. He inched closer to the nurse's station.

"...well from what I hear, he's already a taking up with that Charmaine Harrison. Hayley says that Eileen told her that Bob saw them down on Accra beach not one week after he done arrived!" The older nurse was saying, obviously relishing the tale. "Well I hope she keeps her mind on the job more than you do." She added pointedly then muttered under her breath. "Damn young doctors causing all this distraction."

"Anyway he seems like a good doctor..." the girl continued, "Look at the time he's spending with that young boy in 213 - couldn't be more dedicated if you ask me. That boy probably owes him his life..." she added dramatically, looking defiantly at her comrade.

"Well, that remains to be seen - he don't seem to be getting no better, does he? Your precious Doctor don't even know what the problem with he yet!" There was an unmistakable note of triumph in the older nurse's voice.

Smiler crouched down behind the water cooler pretending to tie his shoelaces and listened intently.

"Maybe not yet," The young girl interjected swiftly, not ready to relinquish the argument, "But I hear tell he says he's making real progress - he tells me the boy is finally opening up to him, they was talking half the night last night. That's a strange case and no mistake - I ain't never seen anything like it. Anyway, you mark my words, when that Doctor Kinloch comes on duty tonight I bet he goes straight in there again. He must be a good doctor - nobody else ain't got through to him. No Doctor Kinloch is the only one in on that boy's secret let me tell you!"

"Secret hah! Ain't no secret - that boy's got AIDS an maybe some new kinda bug too. Only reason that boy won't talk is 'cos he be ashamed. Secret! What nonsense - you sure got some fool notions, girl. Maybe that doctor been turning your head but not mine - I seen it all before."

The conversation carried on but Smiler had heard enough. The boy's doctor wasn't on duty yet, the coast should be clear. He frowned wondering how much Sweetboy had told that doctor - Kinloch - they'd called him. Damn - he should have got there sooner. He slipped quietly into room 213. Sweetboy was sleeping, a saline drip hung above his bed, feeding vital fluid into his parched body. Smiler shook his arm.

"Sweetboy - can you hear me?" He whispered urgently. He listened carefully for the sound of anyone approaching the door.

Sweetboy opened his eyes; a look of horror crossed his face, had the man come to punish him for opening the drums? Did he know what he'd done? Smiler noticed the look with a sense of satisfaction but he spoke to the boy in a soft, pleasant voice, wanting to gain his confidence. The call button was resting on the bed only a few inches from the boy's hand.

"Don't worry - I'm not mad at you - I guess you were curious huh?" He smiled.

"No, not me, no Sir. I wasn't curious - not me!" Sweetboy stammered.

"Look don't worry. I know what you must have done - that's why I'm here - I can help you." Smiler said smoothly. "In fact I'm the only one who can help you - especially if I'm the only one who knows what's wrong with you. I am the only one who knows, aren't I?" He watched Sweetboy carefully, trying to judge how accurate the boy's answer would be.

Sweetboy gulped, if he said "yes" the man would know for sure what he'd done - but he must know already, he reasoned, and maybe he'd know what the cure was for whatever ailed him. He took a deep breath.

"Yes Sir, I guess you are. I'm real sorry - I didn't mean no harm - I just... well...like you said...I guess I just got curious ...I'm real sorry. Can you help me?" He added hopefully, "I hurt real bad you know and that doctor - he don't know what it is, must be something real unusual like...."

"The doctor - what have you told him?" Smiler interrupted, this was the most crucial question.

"Nothing! Only he just keeps asking me - like he knows I done something wrong - sometimes I think it's written on my face or something but I ain't told him nothing - I swear!" He added earnestly.

"Do you know what was in those drums?" Smiler asked quickly.

"No, sir. I thought..." he hesitated, "well I didn't know what it could be and when it weren't...nothing I knows, well I just didn't know what it was. Was it something bad? My fingers are burnt up. I think where I touched it. Is that it? Is that what burnt me? What would do this?"

"You really don't know, do you boy?" His grin was pure evil. Sweetboy's heart started to race.

"No sir, and like I said I wouldn't tell no one. I swear. Can you help me mister? I swear I'd never tell. Just help me. Please mister no-one else knows and no-one else can help me." He broke down in tears of pain and terror. "Help me and I swear I'll do whatever you say. I haven't told that doctor nothing. I don't think he can help me. He don't know what I done but you do. You can help me. Please help me. I swear I ain't blabbed." He begged.

"Yeah like you swore you hadn't touched the drums." Thought Smiler angrily, this was a complication he could do without. There was no point pursuing it now though - he couldn't believe a word the boy said. He'd just have to check the doctor out later. There was a tray of instruments on a trolley near the bed, one of Smiler's trademark grins passed briefly across his face. "Just perfect!" Keeping his back to Sweetboy, he slipped a syringe into his pocket. Turning back to him, he spoke quietly. "Look I've got the cure here, but you gotta promise me - when you get better you don't tell a soul about this cure - right?" He leaned forward to emphasise his point and deftly pushed the call button out of the boy's reach. Reaching into his pocket he drew out the syringe, keeping one hand covering the body of the syringe he pulled out the plunger fully, totally filling the chamber with air. Sweetboy had no idea what he was doing.

"You going to give me an injection, Mister?" He asked, his voice betraying his fear.

Smiler hastily reassured him, he couldn't afford to alert the boy and have him call out. He spoke cheerfully to him, calming his fears. Sweetboy looked apprehensive but he wasn't about to stop the only person who could save him.

"Don't worry - I can put it into your drip. You won't feel a thing and I promise you, you'll be amazed. I guarantee you won't be in any pain within minutes. It's good stuff this." He carried on talking as he inserted the needle into the drip just before the point where it entered the boy's arm. Pushing the plunger in he injected an entire syringe of fresh air into the boy's blood stream. The massive air embolism travelled quickly to the young boy's heart. For precious seconds the strong healthy heart struggled to continue beating. Blood frothed up in the chamber before the simple pump failed under overwhelming odds. Mercifully Sweetboy felt no pain and death was instantaneous. Smiler had been quite correct in his reassurance; Sweetboy was no longer in pain.

The following morning Martha Richards did not switch her radio on to the national obituary column.

Chapter 23

Smiler left the hospital as discreetly as he had arrived pleased with his afternoon's work. He estimated it would take at least a couple of days to organise an autopsy on the boy. No one had known what was wrong with him, so they might not find his sudden death too suspicious. If he could just delay the marine biology investigation for long enough, it would wrap the whole thing up and he could be safely on his way.

He was determined to seek out the Institute of Marine Biology. Still concerned about the amount of information Sweetboy could have given the doctor, Smiler had to act swiftly. He drove out of Bridgetown towards the south coast and the small fishing town of Oistins. It was getting late, the traffic was heavy due to the early evening rush hour and the short journey took him far longer than he had anticipated.

It was getting dark as he drove along the coastal road. Sunset is a spectacular, but short-lived event in Barbados and the darkness fell swiftly. Smiler drove slowly along the south coast road, trying to read signs on buildings as he passed them. As he was passing a small, brightly lit bar a group of laughing tourists spilled out of the open door and onto the road, he swerved to miss them.

"Hey man - where you rushing off to - don't you know it's happy hour?" one of the group called cheerfully. They waved as they lurched off across the road towards yet another rum shop.

Smiler cursed silently as he drove on. He pulled into the car park of a small bar and checked his map by the neon lights radiating into the darkness. He drove on, an occasional street lamp shining like a diamond against the blue velvet night. Finally he found the building he was seeking.

Set back from the road, the forecourt was surrounded by tall trees. A single light shining from a window penetrated the blackness of the car park; he could barely make out the sign. "Barbados Institute of Marine Biology".

Leaving the moke at the side of the road, he slipped across the forecourt and tried the front door. It was unlocked. The building was in partial darkness. There were no immediate signs of life but then he noticed a light shining from under a door at the end of a small corridor.

"Hi there!" he called out cheerfully; having decided openness would be the best approach.

"That you Daddy?" a muffled voice called from behind the door; "You's early man! You's always early man - I told you another hour yet. I said I gotta finish up here yet a while. Come on in and have a coffee, I won't be long I..." The door opened and a young black man stopped speaking abruptly as he saw his guest was not the one he was expecting. "Sorry - thought you were someone else. Can I help you?" The man stood politely, but firmly blocking the entrance to the room. Over his shoulder Smiler could just about make out some scientific equipment, looked like a laboratory of some sort.

Smiler summed up the young man, local by the accent and appearance, dressed casually but smartly. Obviously not the office cleaner, he'd mentioned reports - could be just the person he was looking for. He'd decided previously that he'd use the story that he was from the Miami Herald worried that the fish problem could spread. Smiling, he reached out and shook the man's hand.

"Evening, glad to catch you. I'm from Miami...." he started his story.

"Oh right - friend of Brad's right? Come on in - sorry I thought you might be a reporter. Boss is real touchy about press leaks. I'm afraid you've missed Brad - got a hot date - you know Brad!" He grinned, then turned and led the way into the lab. "Come on through, I'll ring and see if he's left yet..."

"Oh don't bother I'll catch him later" Smiler interrupted, nonchalantly, relieved he hadn't yet mentioned his cover story, and grateful for the opportunity to get the man's confidence so quickly. "Me and Brad go way back. I only called in on the off chance, I didn't...say... great place you've got here." He paused, and looked around admiringly. In reality it meant nothing to him but the comment had the desired effect on his host.

"Yeah? Well it's not bad - could do with a bit more stuff, you know, but like I say it's not bad." His voice swelled with pride, "What did you say your name was? I didn't catch it."

"Bill, Bill Johnson," Smiler lied smoothly, extending his hand and smiling congenially.

"Nathan, Nathan Corbin - call me Corby - everyone does. So you interested in marine biology then? Are you in this line?" Corby asked.

"No, wish I was though, I've always been fascinated by it. What you working on now then? Don't let me hold you up though - it's just that...well...I guess I'm just a bit of a nut about this stuff. I expect you're too busy though." He looked wistfully at Corby.

"Hey no sweat - it's great to find someone else as keen as me - Brad reckons I'm obsessed - like he isn't! You know Brad - he can get just as wrapped up in a mystery as I can - he just makes out he's not bothered." Corby laughed, indicating the coffeepot he looked questioningly at Smiler.

"Thanks, I'd love one. What do you mean "mystery" I thought your work was mainly research?" He looked puzzled at Corby.

"Well perhaps "mystery" is a bit dramatic but like when someone gets a reaction and they don't know what they got it from.... we get calls from around the world you know." he said proudly. He poured two cups of coffee and handed one to Smiler, offering him the cream and sugar, he sat on a high stool and pulled another over for Smiler.

"Oh so it's mainly medical stuff then?" Smiler asked casually, adding cream to his coffee.

"Not always, there's also a lot of pollution work and that sort of stuff, and of course it's not just people that have medical problems - we're kind of fish doctors sometimes!" he laughed.

"Oh yeah, I've been reading about that problem over on the east coast.... hey...that's not you dealing with that is it? Now what did I read?" He paused thoughtfully, "Something about "our two finest minds or something" don't tell me that's you and Brad" He looked suitably impressed. Corby was delighted.

"There are no others! Actually there really are no others - least ways not free to deal with that at the moment. It's not because we're the best or anything." He added modestly.

"That's not the way I read it!" Smiler replied flatteringly, "So how's it going then? You two "great minds" solved the whole thing?" He added jokingly. "I suppose it's some kind of tropical fish disease or something huh?" He sipped his coffee and feigned mere idle curiosity.

"Well we haven't got all the information yet - but we will." Corby declared.

"Maybe the problem will go away of its own accord - sort of burn itself out - like an aquatic flu epidemic!" Smiler laughed, making light of the situation.

"No, it's nothing like that, too many different species affected." Corby became more serious, "No, personally I'm pretty sure it's a pollutant, but it's not one I've come across before..." His voice trailed off as he considered the options.

"So it's just you and Brad working on it then - I guess that must take up a lot of your time." Smiler asked quickly, dragging Corby away from his train of thought.

"Sure does at the moment. To be honest it's a pain 'cos I hate to leave my other work. We're compiling a paper on marine zoo toxicology...."

"Sounds a lot more interesting than dead fish. So you're pretty keen to get back to that then huh? Interrupted Smiler, determined to gather as much information as he needed. "Maybe you can just come up with some theory and the problem will be solved before you have to prove it. That way you could get back to the real stuff." He suggested.

"No we couldn't do that. Nice idea though!" laughed Corby. "No, there's no way I'm letting go that East Coast thing until it's resolved. We've got to find out what's doing it before the problem spreads. I don't care how long we've got to work at it really. You can't help getting intrigued by a new problem. I don't know what it is..." he paused thoughtfully, "but I'll tell you something, it's sure got me and Brad interested, we'll get to the bottom of it - I guarantee it."

"Wow you certainly sound keen! Is everyone here like this? Such dedication!" Smiler gently mocked, carefully sounding out the man. Corby seemed lost in reverie.

"What?" Startled, Corby suddenly laughed, "Sorry! You've started me off there. No don't worry about it - we're not all maniacs like me you know. Most people here just work a normal nine to five! I tend to get a bit engrossed - once I've started something I'm like a dog with a bone - I just won't let go - Brad's just the same! They all think we're crazy here!"

"Well a bit of enthusiasm never killed anyone." Smiler grinned, resting his cup on the surface; he casually put his hand in his pocket and felt for his knife.

"Hey," Corby suddenly jumped to his feet, "Let me show you what we're supposed to be doing here - you'll love it." He walked quickly through to a back room, "Come through here - I think you'll find this very interesting." He called over his shoulder.

"Right behind you." Smiler walked through, quietly closing the door behind him. He walked silently up to Corby, who was standing with his back to him, leaning over a large glass case. As he approached he again reached into his pocket for his knife. His fingers embracing its comforting weight like an old friend. Suddenly Corby spun around, his face animated by his enthusiasm for his work.

"What do you think?" He asked proudly, pointing at the cabinet, "Some of the deadliest poisons in the world - and their antidotes!" He gestured towards one of the exhibits. Smiler let go of the knife and leant forward, this was really becoming interesting now.

"Fish poison? You're kidding! But they only give you the belly ache right? I mean they couldn't kill you?" He peered into the case and lifted the lid.

"Careful! We normally keep this cabinet closed. " Corby quickly warned, "See those spines there? They're from one of the most dangerous fish we know - the stonefish. Under those spines are the venom glands - enough poison in there to kill a grown man in minutes."

"Really? Wow that's amazing! What is this tiny bottle thing then?" Smiler carefully picked up a tiny glass vial beside the spines.

"That's the anti-venin, developed in Australia, you know. We keep it right beside the spines - I mean you'd have to be pretty quick but even so.... hey careful..." he reached forward but was too late. Smiler dropped the glass vial, which smashed instantly on the tiled floor. As Corby reached across to save the vial Smiler moved swiftly, twisting his startled victim's wrist in an unbreakable arm lock he jammed Corby's hand down onto the deadly spines. The razor sharp needles embedding themselves into main radial artery of Corby's wrist sending a lethal injection into his blood stream.

Sinking to his knees, Corby stared incredulously at his own hand as he slid down the display case onto the cold, unforgiving floor tiles. The electric blue needles shimmered incongruously in the stark light of the lab. Perversely Corby thought how beautiful they looked before the venom reached its allotted destination, traumatising his heart, splitting his air starved lungs, his throat swelling as his own lymph nodes strangled him. Through his pain racked sobs he turned imploringly towards his killer. The cold face grinned down at him as Smiler casually raised his coffee cup in mock salute. Corby convulsed once more and drowned in his own vomit.

Corby's father arrived at the laboratory a short time later. Twenty minutes early and ten minutes too late.

Chapter 24

The ambulance arrived swiftly at the Institute but it was abundantly clear there was little they could do. The patient they had been summoned for was obviously beyond help, although they were able to help an elderly man by treating him for shock. Joseph Corbin was clearly heart-broken over the death of his youngest son and sat quietly in the reception area, dazed and confused. The police were summoned, as was the Director of the Institute. They arrived simultaneously. The police, used to dealing with accidents - even fatal ones - were brisk and efficient, Paul Scobie, by contrast was as bewildered as the victim's father.

"Well Shirley, what a terrible thing to happen. Such a very pleasant young man. Oh his poor father. Dear me. I just don't know how to face him. Poor soul. Just look at him. He's devastated." he muttered as he wandered around the foyer.

Winston Alleyne, Chief of Police, emerged from the incident room where he'd viewed the body. He stood for a moment looking at the two potential witnesses.

"Who've we got?" He quietly asked the uniformed officer standing by the door. He nodded his head to indicate Joseph Corbin.

"Victim's father. He found the body and rang the paramedics. He's been treated for shock and we're just waiting for the boy's brother to come and get him to take him home."

"Has anyone talked to him?"

"Not much Sir." Admitted the officer. "We got the basics. He was supposed to be meeting his son here. He arrived a bit early and found the boy on the floor. Sounds like he was already dead by then though. We couldn't get much else. He's in a pretty bad way; anyway he doesn't seem to know much about the place. He's very proud of his boy but he said he didn't really understand what he did here."

"Ok I'll catch up with him later." The inspector sighed, not much help there. "What about the other guy?"

"Paul Scobie, Sir." The officer consulted his notebook. "He runs the place. We brought him here as the key holder. I'm afraid he's.... well, that is to say, he hasn't been able to further our enquiries as yet."

"Who's he talking to, Sergeant?" They both looked over at Paul Scobie who continued wandering around muttering softly.

"I don't know sir. I thought it was the victim's father but he keeps mentioning "Shirley". I guess it must just be the shock. He certainly hasn't said anything which could help us, Sir." The officer replied quietly. "I've asked the paramedics to stand by but he's refused treatment. Says he's ok"

"Right well, I'll have a word. Seal that room." He indicated the laboratory. "Usual format. No one enters until forensics have finished. The photographer should be here any minute."

"Yes sir. I'll take care of it." He took up position in front of the door.

Paul Scobie ceased his wandering. He slumped down in a chair in the reception area opposite a still stunned Joseph Corbin.

"Dreadful, quite dreadful." He murmured, "Such a tragedy, dear oh dear, such a young man - and quite brilliant too..." He shook his head, then turning to Joseph he added. "May I offer my sincere condolences Sir; well I mean words fail me. What a terrible tragedy. I just can't understand it...." his voice trailed off and the two men sat staring into space. Captain Thomas viewed the scene with some dismay; he couldn't see either man capable of being much assistance. The director of the institute looked quite elderly really and certainly not strong enough to view the body and offer a possible theory as to what may have happened. Mr Corbin senior had identified the body but knew nothing of the work his son was involved in. Captain Thomas himself knew little of marine biology and questions needed to be asked. He approached Paul.

"Mr. Scobie? Sorry, Dr. Scobie I should say," he amended, consulting his notes. "I wonder if we might go somewhere more private? Your office perhaps?" He nodded towards a uniformed policeman to accompany them.

"Pardon? Oh yes, yes of course - umm... my office. Yes that would be best, my office I think, yes, yes, quite right. Of course." Paul rose somewhat unsteadily to his feet and stood looking around, as if unsure of the direction he should take. He led the way, hesitantly, towards his office. The familiar surroundings gave him some measure of comfort and he sank back into his comfortable leather button backed chair with a sigh.

"Dr Scobie," Inspector Thomas began, his junior colleague took out a notebook and prepared to take notes, "I wonder if you could tell me the nature of Mr Corbin's work here?" He decided to start with the basics, a few routine questions to get the man at ease.

"Ah yes well, um Nathan, er Mr Corbin, that is, er...was, well anyway he was involved in marine zoo toxicology." He looked across at the young policeman taking notes, "Um - would you like me to spell that for you?" He asked kindly.

"That won't be necessary, thank you." Inspector Thomas answered for the man, whose reply would have been quite different had he been given a chance to speak. "Perhaps you could elaborate a little on the meaning of ...er...the term."

"Yes of course Inspector, well it's the study of poisonous and venomous marine animals, do you see? Nathan is becoming quite an expert on the subject, very enthusiastic he is...was." His face clouded briefly, "Oh dear, such a tragic lose. Yes well, Nathan and the new chap er...Mr Tucker were to compile a complete paper on the subject, a catalogue of as many species and antidotes, as we are currently aware of. That's what all those glass cases are for you see Inspector, they're all being collated in there."

"Mr Tucker?" The Inspector asked, noting the name.

"Yes an American chap - seems very pleasant. Young fellow, very keen - oh I suppose someone ought to contact him, I believe they were pretty good pals you know. Oh dear, and he's not long arrived here, how dreadfully upsetting for him...." He frowned, picturing the young man.

"Do you have an address?" The inspector asked briskly interrupted the older man's rambling.

"Well I believe he is staying with Nathan at present. Oh dear - has anyone gone around to his apartment? It would be quite a shock for the poor young man you know...."

"I'm sure the matter is being dealt with." the inspector said dismissively, "Now you say Mr Corbin is compiling this er...paper. Does he usually work this late?"

"Well sometimes, like I said he is very keen but he's been doing a bit extra recently. He's been working on this business on the east coast...." Paul was off again, lost in thought as he remembered the young man's dedication to his work.

"So he's not actually been involved in the zootox.... er venom project at present then? He was found in the laboratory with all the glass cases. Have you any idea why he would be in there?"

"Well I'm afraid I asked him to take on this other project. I know he didn't want to shelve his other work, I suppose he was working on that in the evenings. Oh dear I feel so responsible - the poor boy must have been tired, that's how accidents happen you know...." He began to look quite distressed as he assumed responsibility for his employee's death.

At that moment the door burst open and Brad Tucker came running in. Paul Scobie's heart sank further as he saw the worried expression on the young man's face. How on earth could they break the terrible news to the lad?

"What's going on? The cops were waiting at Corby's apartment when I got back -they wouldn't tell me much - just that there's been an accident at the lab. Where's Corby? Is he okay?" It was obvious the accident was serious by the number of policemen on the premises. Inspector Thomas rose to his feet and formally shook the newcomer's hand. Paul Scobie looked close to breaking down.

"Oh you poor young man, what a dreadful shock for you - well for us all - who would ever have thought of such a thing." He sank back in his chair and shook his head sadly.

"Perhaps you'd better come with me Sir, Mr Tucker, isn't it?" He called over his shoulder as he led the young man from the room, "My sergeant here will arrange to take your statement Dr Scobie, and bring you some tea. If you'll excuse me...." He nodded towards his colleague who spoke rapidly into his radio with the request for refreshment then again reached for his notepad. Brad and the Inspector left the room.

Once out of earshot the Inspector turned to Brad.

"I'm afraid I have some very bad news for you sir." Brad stiffened, he'd known it was bad when he passed the ambulance outside.

"Corby." He whispered.

"I'm afraid there was an accident at the laboratory this evening Mr Corbin is dead." He stood for a moment in silence while Brad absorbed the fact.

"How?" Brad barely spoke the word.

"Well sir, to be honest. I would be grateful if you could shed any light on the matter. Do you feel able to help at present? Perhaps you'd like a few moments?" he paused, waiting for the man's reaction. Brad took a deep breath and shook his head.

"No, I'll be all right. How can I help?" He said quietly. He struggled to compose himself.

"Well Sir, I didn't want to distress Dr Scobie with the scene of the incident, he doesn't appear very strong, but we do need some expert help with the well...more technical details of the laboratory." He paused by the door of the room and looked questioningly at Brad. Brad gave a brief nod and braced himself to confront the sight. They entered the room; a sheet covered his friend's body but Brad still

shuddered when he saw the outline of the corpse. He took several deep breaths and turned away.

"What do you want to know?" His voice had a catch in it as he tried desperately to control his emotions.

"I understand Sir, It's not an easy task, you can see why we didn't want to bring the director in here." Inspector Thomas said sympathetically, then more briskly he continued.

"We haven't removed...anything...as yet because we wanted to try and ascertain the chain of events. Are you familiar with these glass cabinets?"

Brad concentrated on the cabinets, dragging his thoughts away from his friend.

"Yes, these are where we store the most dangerous samples - they're usually kept shut." He said, swallowing hard, and forcing his gaze onto the cabinet, trying to avoid seeing the white sheet on the floor just beside them.

"But not locked?" The policeman asked, puzzled by an apparent lack of security.

"Well we usually lock them up at night, or when they're not in use, but while we're working they're closed but not locked. It's thick enough glass and we all know the dangers..." He winced as he realised what he'd said. It would appear his friend hadn't been aware enough.

"These fish venom - are they strong enough to kill a man then?" The policeman was surprised. He had seen the wounds on Nathan's hand and wrists but was not sure of the cause of death as yet.

Brad steeled himself to check the cabinet, the stonefish sample had been disturbed and the antidote was missing. He looked around in surprise.

"The stonefish!" He cried alarmed, "The antidote is kept right beside it - where is it?" He looked around wildly and caught sight of the broken glass vial on the floor just beside the body. The inspector pulled him back as he bent down to retrieve it.

"Hold on Sir, I'd rather you didn't touch anything." He pulled the man's arm back away from the glass. "Did you say "stonefish?" - I take it that's a particularly lethal er...fish." He'd never heard of such a thing.

Brad slumped, realising what had killed his friend.

"Of course, stupid of me. Yes officer, the venom of the stonefish would kill. The victim would feel intense pain and lose consciousness within minutes, there would be swelling of the lymph nodes, respiratory distress, convulsions followed by death." He spoke mechanically, giving a text book answer. Tears filled his eyes as he imagined Corby's painful death.

"Mr Corbin would be aware of the effects of this ...fish?" It seemed incredible. The Inspector looked at the sample with renewed horror; it hardly looked like a lethal killer.

"Yes" whispered Brad.

"And presumably he also knew of the antidote then?" The Inspector looked down at the broken glass.

"He told me about it - said that's why it was kept right beside it - he said it would be the safest place to keep it...he said...." his voice broke and he sobbed.

The police Inspector patted the distraught man's shoulder. He looked thoughtfully down at the white sheet under which the young scientist's body lay.

"I guess he must have caught his hand and panicked, he probably dropped the antidote as he tried to save himself - poor guy!" He sighed as Brad's sobs filled the air.

Chapter 25

The inquest into the death of Nathan Corbin was a brief but ultimately dramatic affair. For Charmaine and Andrew the day began with them having breakfast together at a small bakery in Sunset Crest. They watched as a steady stream of people filed into the Civic Centre across the road.

"Terrible isn't it?" Sighed Charmaine, watching the sombre procession. "He was so young."

"Were you...er...close?" asked Andrew quietly, trying to quell the jealousy which rose so inappropriately within him.

"Oh yes. I suppose we were really." Replied Charmaine softly still staring out the window. Andrew's face fell and though he tried to hide it Charmaine caught a glimpse of his expression as she glanced back at him. She smiled.

"Not in a romantic sense, silly. He was just a friend. We met through work and just sort of hit it off I suppose." Her eyes filled. "I used to go over to the Institute with hospital stuff and we'd have a coffee together and just sit and talk."

Andrew patted her hand sympathetically. "It must be horrible to lose a good friend. I'm sorry. When did you see him last?"

"He called me a couple of weeks ago. Said he had a colleague coming over from the States and he wanted to arrange an evening out. I think he wanted me to bring along a friend to make up a foursome" She shook her head sadly remembering him pleading with her to fix him up with a date.

Andrew wanted to ask if the friend was for Corby or his guest but it didn't seem right under the circumstances. "Did you go?" he asked, trying to keep a casual tone.

"No," she looked up and smiled through her tears, "I found a ... 'friend' of my own and got a bit distracted."

Andrew felt a rush of tenderness overwhelm him and he leaned over and gently brushed her hand as it rested on the table.

"I think we're more than friends now, don't you? " he whispered softly. "I hope I continue to distract you for a very long time." Reluctantly he dragged his thoughts away from such pleasant prospects and back to the immediate future.

"This isn't the time for this I suppose." He stood up and held out his hand. "Are you ready? We ought to be getting over there." She stood up somewhat shakily and took a deep breath.

"Yes I suppose so. Ready as I'll ever be anyway."

Together they crossed the road and entered to Civic Centre. Lois Jones was just arriving to represent the Queen Elizabeth Hospital. She watched the couple walk into the courtroom hand in hand. Seeing her they hastily stepped apart and joined her. The usher called for silence mercifully sparing them any need for explanations and they quickly took their seats.

"Looks pretty serious." mused Lois. "Wonder how long it'll be before he's applying for a permanent post." She thought as she sat quietly waiting for the proceedings to begin.

Brad sat at the back of the small courtroom in the Civic Centre at Sunset Crest. Wearing a hastily bought, ill-fitting, dark suit he listened intently as the proceedings commenced. His tanned face was lined with sorrow and he occasionally shook his head in apparent disbelief as the formalities were observed. He winced as the clerk read out his friend's name and he heard the boy's mother sobbing pitifully.

The room was filled to capacity with friends, colleagues and family as well as an assortment of press reporters. Andrew sat attentively by Charmaine, very aware of his boss sitting on her other side. He didn't want Dr Jones thinking he was some sort of hospital Casanova. He glanced around the room, a couple of tourists sat at the back, presumably interested in the way a foreign court operated. He shook his head incredulously at their morbid curiosity. Despite the crowd there was almost complete silence as the evidence was presented, a silence broken only by the sobbing of the victim's mother and the faint rustling of paper as the reporters took notes.

It was a bright, airy room. The whitewashed walls were covered with official looking framed certificates. Several portraits of sombre looking government officials stared down on both the grieving and the merely curious. A faded portrait of a young Queen Elizabeth II smiling regally in formal pose with her equally youthful husband standing proudly at her side hung between two huge windows through which the bright sunlight streamed.

The windows each had three large slatted panes of glass that wound open by means of a small handle at the base. They were fully open and an ocean breeze, supplemented by huge ceiling fans, kept the room at a pleasant temperature. The Coroner, Mr Garfield Taylor, sat behind a huge mahogany bench, flanked by court officials. The Court stenographer sat in front of him and a mahogany witness box was to his right. A large table housed several tagged exhibits including the glass case that housed the fatal venom.

Chief Inspector Alleyne was describing the scene of the incident as he had found it on the night in question. The Coroner listened carefully before putting a few questions to the officer.

"Chief Inspector Alleyne, I understand you attended the incident personally."

"Yes sir. The operations room called me when they received the 112 call from the Institute. It was obviously a most serious incident so I drove straight there."

"I see. Were there any signs of a break-in?" he asked, jotting down a few notes as he spoke.

"None whatsoever." Replied the officer, firmly.

"Were there any signs of a struggle?" Continued the Coroner, nodding as he wrote.

"Aside from the broken glass vial containing the anti-venin nothing was disturbed at all." The officer checked his notes although the incident was fresh in his mind.

"This vial was kept beside the venom itself, I understand?" He peered across at the policeman; it was a very strange case, unprecedented in his experience. After years of experience in the Coroner's court he thought he'd heard it all but this was a new one on him.

"Yes, sir. His colleague confirmed this and there were several other er...exhibits...similarly displayed. The glass case in question is here as evidence." He indicated over towards the table. Everyone turned and looked over at the table. Mr Taylor nodded and made a few more notes. There was a moment's silence, then turning back to the Chief Inspector; he continued his line of questioning.

"Was there any evidence at all to suggest the presence of a third party when the incident occurred?" It appeared a straightforward enough case but Mr Taylor was renowned for being very thorough in his deliberations.

"No Sir, nothing to suggest that the victim was not entirely alone when the incident occurred." There was a brief murmur around the courtroom as those present pictured the unfortunate man dying all alone in such a terrible accident.

No one noticed a slight smile briefly cross the face of one of the "tourists" at the back of the courtroom. Smiler was very pleased he'd taken the time to wash and replace the coffee cups before leaving the scene. It was all going very well, he decided.

Mr Taylor continued with his questioning, upon learning how the victim's own father had discovered his son's body he acknowledged the man's suffering with a nod of respect towards the man. Joseph Corbin sat staunchly upright and stared forward, briefly the two men's eyes met and a look of respectful sympathy passed between them. Despite his solemn job, Mr Taylor was not an unfeeling man, and could greatly empathise with the victim's father. He was a father himself, and could well imagine the pain the man must be going through. Joseph Corbin gave a slight inclination of the head to acknowledge the man's sympathy before squaring his shoulders to continue with the ordeal of hearing the details of his son's untimely demise.

Captain Alleyne was thanked for his time and was replaced on the witness stand by Dr Malcolm Young, the police pathologist.

"Dr Young, I understand you are a British pathologist?" Asked the Coroner.

"Yes sir. I am Dr Malcolm Young, Royal College of Forensic Science. I am currently working here as part of an exchange scheme between the British and Barbadian police authorities." He explained. A large man with a florid complexion, he was sweating quite profusely and obviously finding it hard to adjust to the heat away from his cool air-conditioned work-place, despite the breeze which everyone else seemed to find refreshing.

"Thank you Dr Young. You may proceed."

"Thank you Sir." He nodded in respect to the Coroner. "I examined the deceased, Mr Nathan Corbin upon his arrival to the Queen Elizabeth Hospital morgue in Bridgetown. The victim died as a result of respiratory failure. This was caused by strong venom that I detected in the bloodstream. From the wounds on the deceased it was ascertained that the venom had been introduced through the wounds in his hands and in particular to the main artery in his wrist." In deference to the family he kept the details as clinical as possible.

"I have conferred with members of the Barbados Institute of Marine Biology to verify the biological details of this particular venom as I am unfamiliar with the field of marine zoo toxicology."

"But you are absolutely sure of the cause of death?" Mr Taylor asked.

"Absolutely Sir, all my conclusions were made before I conferred with the Institute. The Institute served to confirm my findings. There was no doubt in my mind that the death was caused by a venom, the lymph nodes were swollen and the heart and lungs showed conclusive evidence of respiratory failure. I could state quite categorically the exact cause of death but I couldn't identify the name of the venom which would cause such symptoms." Malcolm Young confirmed.

"And you are quite satisfied the venom was introduced by the wounds on the victim's hand?" The Coroner persisted.

"Yes Sir, the wounds were already showing signs of cyanosis indicating lack of oxygen in the blood, they were definitely where the venom was introduced." He stated firmly. "The spines had pierced the main radial artery which would have made death almost instantaneous." There was a general murmur of relief from the assembled public at this last piece of information. A small mercy - but a mercy nonetheless.

"From your observations, was there any indication as to how the victim could have sustained such an injury?" Mr Taylor asked. At the back of the courtroom Smiler tensed as he awaited the reply. Malcolm Young paused and wiped his brow while he contemplated his answer - Smiler held his breath.

"Well Sir, I've given the matter a great deal of thought - it was a most bizarre accident. The spines were embedded quite deeply, a couple of them had actually broken off inside the wound, which would indicate a certain amount of force - he didn't just brush against them. I examined the scene of the incident very carefully though and the only supposition I could come up with was that he must have dropped the anti-venin and in lunging to grab the falling vial, he jammed his hand on the spines. I can't see any other conclusion - but I'm afraid I can offer no concrete evidence to support my theory - apart from the broken glass."

Smiler quietly exhaled and relaxed. He was almost home free. He contemplated leaving but decided to stay for the duration, it was obviously a foregone conclusion now but even so his cautious nature forced him to stay for the final verdict. Brad Tucker vehemently shook his head.

The Director of the Barbados Institute of Marine Biology took the stand next; he confirmed everything those before him had said. To the best of his knowledge Nathan Corbin had been working alone that evening, he often put in a few extra hours so that was not in itself unusual. There had been no signs of a break-in at the laboratory when he arrived, indeed he couldn't even imagine why anyone should want to break in.

He described the stonefish and its venom, launching into a tedious monologue about dorsal spines, pelvic spines and venom glands until everyone present felt they knew more than enough about the deadly creature. He was however, also able to confirm the pathologist's description of the effects of the stonefish venom upon the respiratory system reiterating the former expert's conclusion.

Shaking his head sadly he admitted it was his own sad opinion that the pathologist was probably right in his supposition - it was a tragic accident.

"Thank you Dr Scobie. You may return to your seat." Mr Taylor nodded his thanks and looked down at the papers before him. He appeared to be summing up his notes and there was a few minutes silence while everyone present absorbed the information they had received.

Brad had been growing more agitated with every passing witness. Suddenly he rose to his feet, to the astonishment of those around him.

"Your honour." He called to the startled Coroner; "Can I say something? I worked with Corby, Mr Corbin and I just want to say..." he was practically shouting.

"Sir!" Mr Taylor interrupted the outburst. "This is not a court of law, you may address me as Sir or Mr Taylor, if you have something relevant to say which will add to our understanding of the case, you may approach the bench and take the stand." He glared across at the loud young man who had so rudely shattered the peace of the Coroners court. Brad scrambled along the row of spectators and hastily made his way up to the witness box. Reaching the stand he turned to the Coroner and began earnestly.

"I just don't buy it...." he began, fervently. "It just doesn't add up...." Across the room, Mr Taylor sighed.

"Could you please observe the formalities of the proceedings and state your name for the records Sir." He interrupted, frowning at the earnest young man stood before him.

"Bradley Tucker, Sir, currently working at the Institute...I" he looked exasperated as he was once again interrupted.

"For the record I assume you are referring to the Barbados Institute of Marine Biology?" Mr Taylor asked, hoping to return the proceedings to a more dignified level.

"Yes, yes of course...Sir," added Brad as an afterthought, before proceeding. "The thing is I just don't buy it!" he insisted.

"I beg your pardon?" Mr Taylor asked icily, "Do you have further information or not Sir?"

"Yes - well no - I mean - well not really I guess." His shoulders slumped as he realised he couldn't prove the unease he felt. "Look I worked with the guy - he was nobody's fool - he just wouldn't do anything so....so...dumb!" he finally concluded. Mr Taylor winced at the man's unfortunate choice of words and looked across at the bereaved parents. Brad followed his glance.

"I'm sorry Mr and Mrs Corbin - I don't mean to upset you but I just want to say your son was a brilliant man - a scientist - he knew exactly what he was dealing with - he knew the dangers - he was always so careful - he just wouldn't do it - he wouldn't.... I'll never believe that..." his voice trailed off as he struggled to put into words his gut feelings. He was obviously distraught and close to tears. There was an uncomfortable silence within the room as everyone strained to hear what the man had to say. Eventually the presiding Coroner took pity on the young man.

"Mr Tucker, I admire your loyalty to your friend - I'm sure we all do - and I appreciate you find his death hard to accept but you should understand the effect this sort of outburst has upon your late colleague's family. Accidents happen - it's a fact of life - even the most brilliant can make a mistake - believe me I've seen them happen so often." He sighed, then shaking his head he recommenced in a more formal tone. "It is the verdict of this court that the cause of death of Nathaniel Corbin is...accidental death."

"No!" retorted Brad in a fresh outburst, "No I refuse to accept that - no way!"

"Mr Tucker," replied the Coroner sternly, "Remember where you are. That is the verdict of this inquest and that will be an end to the matter!"

"Not while I'm around it won't" shouted Brad as he stormed out of the room, everyone stared after him in open astonishment, everyone except for one tourist at the back of the courtroom who looked at the back of the receding figure with grim determination.

Chapter 26

Andrew Kinloch sat in the hospital cafeteria lost in thought. The cafeteria was open to both staff and visitors; even the occasional patient came by to join their visitors for a break from the routine of the wards. It was a bustling place, always noisy and busy but today it could have been totally empty and quiet as far as Andrew was concerned. His coffee grew cold in front of him as he sat, folding and unfolding a sachet of sugar, oblivious to his surroundings. It wasn't as though the young man had been the first patient he had lost, he told himself, nor even, sadly, the youngest. Six months in the emergency room at Glasgow General had brought him his fair share of accident victims of every age. It was just that it had been so unexpected.

He blamed himself for not having the patient hooked up to a monitoring system. When the nurse had looked in on him he had appeared to have been dead for quite a few minutes. The crash team had been hastily summoned and every effort had been made to resuscitate the young man. It was all to no avail, eventually they had to admit defeat and declare him dead. Andrew had wanted to attend the post mortem himself but he was on duty this afternoon and it was scheduled for a time when he couldn't get away. He'd left a message for the pathologist asking him to send him the results as soon as possible.

"Damn" he thought angrily, "What did I miss?" He gave the sugar sachet an angry twist and the flimsy packet gave way. Pale golden grains of sugar spilled over the clean Formica table, in his haste to clear it up he knocked over his coffee which flooded across the table adding to the mess and to his growing sense of irritation.

"Having a bad day?" A cool voice inquired, handing over a stack of paper napkins. Charmaine stood over him, having witnessed the small accident as she passed.

"Well I've had better." he smiled ruefully, "Much better! " He gratefully accepted the paper towels and cleared away the debris from the table whilst Charmaine brought over fresh coffee.

"Do you want to drink this one or shall we just decorate the table with it?" Charmaine teased him gently, aware that something was troubling him deeply. "It's nice to see you." She smiled, discreetly touching his hand. "I'm sorry I haven't got long, I was just passing when I saw your er...problem. What's up? I hope I haven't upset you?"

"No, you wouldn't know how." He smiled at her before continuing softly, "I lost a patient this week. Do you remember that young guy I was telling you about? He just up and died on me." He shook his head, "Only a young man - I can't help feeling I should have been able to save him." Reaching over he picked up another sachet of sugar and again commenced folding and unfolding it. Charmaine deftly moved his coffee out of harm's way, earning a brief, grateful smile for her trouble.

"Come on - you're a doctor." She said gently, "You must have lost patients before? I'm sure you did your best." Surreptitiously she glanced at her watch, she didn't like to leave him like this, but she had little time to spare.

"Yeah I know - but he wasn't that sick!" Protested Andrew, still trying to work things out.

"Well he died didn't he? That's about as sick as they get!" she retorted, trying to humour him out of his melancholy mood. "Sorry I shouldn't say that but this is a hospital - people come here when they're sick - you can't expect them all to get better. You're a doctor - not a miracle worker! Look I've really got to go - I lost a day yesterday. I'm sorry but I really must get caught up - now are you going to be all right?" She looked anxiously at him.

"Yes of course, I'm fine. Listen when can I see you again? Maybe we can have another day out somewhere?" he added, brightening visibly at the prospect. "Though the last one would take some beating." Charmaine hesitated, her next day off was this coming Friday off when she was to attend Nathan Corbin's funeral but this hardly seemed an appropriate time to mention such an event. Andrew, noticing her hesitation, totally misread her response.

"Sorry maybe I'm rushing things? Have you made plans already" He blushed with embarrassment and quickly sipped his coffee to avoid eye contact.

Charmaine smiled, "Actually I have made other plans - though not very pleasant ones. I'm afraid I have to attend Corby's funeral on Friday that's why I hesitated. You know I'd love to spend a day out with you but..." she paused, a look of sadness crossed her face, "... you know what he meant to me. Although I'm dreading it, I must go and pay my respects. Actually since he was a sort of colleague too so I suppose they'll be quite a few going from here."

"Let me come with you. It'll be easier for me seeing as I didn't know him and I want to help you through this. I want to be there for you."

"If you're really sure you don't mind I would appreciate your support. I can't help worrying about that guy at the inquest yesterday. He looked like he could do with a friend. I guess he must be that American Corby rang me about..." she grinned as she remembered Corby begging her to fix them up for a double date shortly before his friend arrived, then her face clouded as she realised that was the last time they'd spoken. She drew a deep breath and continued, "...well anyway I feel I kind of owe it to Corby to make sure his pal is ok. You and he have a lot in common really - both new here and working for a while in 'foreign parts'. It must be a hell of a shock for the guy for this to have happened - maybe we can help him out between us."

"Yeah sure, maybe we can ...I don't know, take him out for lunch or something. Whatever - look you'd better go. I'll catch you later." Charmaine hurried off and nearly collided with a small, quite elderly black lady, dressed in sombre clothing who was entering the crowded cafeteria.

"Oh excuse me." She stammered, "I'm so sorry I wasn't looking where I was going - are you all right?"

The lady nodded, then in a voice that was barely a whisper she spoke. Charmaine had to lean forward and strain to catch the words.

"Do you work here?" Seeing Charmaine nod her affirmative, she continued. "They done told me I might find Dr Kinloch here. Do you know him?"

Charmaine caught her breath as she looked into the woman's face, she was obviously wracked with extreme pain, the sorrow was etched in her face and she was stooped over as if every step was an effort. Her urgency forgotten, she helped the older woman over to a seat.

"Are you all right Madam? Let me get you something - tea perhaps? Yes I know Dr Kinloch he's right...oh!" She glanced over towards the table she had just vacated and which she had left Andrew Kinloch sitting at - there was no one there. "That's odd," she added, looking all around the room, "Well he was right there a minute ago - oh there he is. You wait here - I'll bring him over. You will be all right here for a minute won't you?" The woman nodded briefly.

"Are you a patient of Dr Kinloch's? May I take your name?" She looked anxiously at the woman, who gently shook her head. "No Ma'am, not me, but my grandson is...was a patient of he. My name is Martha Richards. I jes needs to speak to the good doctor.

I got to know if it was the drugs - I got to know. He was a good boy but ...well I jes needs to know. " Her eyes filled with tears. Charmaine squeezed the woman's trembling hand in a gesture of sympathy and hurried over to where Andrew was standing.

Andrew was over by the far wall of the cafeteria speaking into a white courtesy phone. As she approached him she saw the colour drain from his face, he gripped the phone tightly and turned to face the wall obviously for more privacy. Charmaine stood close and waited for him to finish his call, glancing back at the waiting lady with great concern. Andrew raised his voice, his tone urgent and alarmed.

"...and you are absolutely positive there's no chance of it being an accident? ... Yes, yes I know, ...yes...I understand ...but it couldn't have been the drip? No of course, not that much. You're right." His shoulders slumped, "Have you notified the police yet? I see, yes thanks for letting me know first - I appreciate it.... Yes I'll be around all afternoon.... Yes I expect they will want to see me...well you can always have me paged. Yes...thanks." He replaced the receiver and leant against the wall. His eyes closed for a second.

"Andrew? Are you all right?" Charmaine asked concerned, what was going on around here? She looked over at the old lady again, waiting by the table. Andrew opened his eyes and smiled tiredly at her.

"Oh hi Charmaine, I thought you'd gone. They just paged me from the path lab..." he followed her glance back to the old lady, then looked back at her, puzzled, "Did you want me?"

"Andrew I'm sorry but I think you'd better go and see that old lady- she looks really upset, said her grandson was a patient of yours but I think he's died or something, she said he "was" a patient of yours, anyway she's real upset. I think she's worried about his medication or something - I couldn't really understand her. She said her name was Martha Richards - mean anything? Maybe I ought to go and get her some sweet tea - she don't look so good"

Andrew gave a ragged sigh and wiped his face with his hands. He looked across at the grieving Grandmother then back at a startled looking Charmaine.

"I think she's going to need that tea - at the very least! I'd better see her somewhere quieter - and I think you'd better go and fetch Dr Jones. I don't know the hospital procedure around here. I don't know if I should be the one who tells her that her Grandson has been murdered."

Chapter 27

The following morning Smiler lay in bed in his cool hotel room, listening to the soft drone of the air-conditioner and assessing the situation. He was expecting a call from Miami and he wanted to get his own pitch in first. The fisherman was gone, that was one problem solved - or was it? He frowned as he remembered the nurses' conversation. What exactly had they said? He prided himself on his excellent memory. Mentally he pictured the hospital corridor, the nurses' station, and the water cooler and then their whole conversation came back to him. "…he tells me the boy is finally opening up to him, they were talking half the night...".

If only he knew for sure what the boy had told him. Was it worth pursuing? Probably not, he decided but a faint unease crept into his mind as he considered ignoring that particular situation. Perhaps he'd better find a way of checking the good doctor out. Of course if the drums were moved quickly enough it might not make any difference what the doctor knew. Miami might not be too happy if they knew their diversion had been discovered but as long as no-one knew what had consequently happened to the drums, he couldn't see what difference it would make.

Then of course there was the tragic accident at the Barbados Institute of Marine Biology. Smiler grinned broadly as he stretched out and folded his hands under his head - that really had been a stroke of genius, he thought with an immense feeling of satisfaction. "Accidental death" that's what they'd put it down to. "Brilliant!" He declared to the empty room, he was almost sorry he couldn't tell anyone about it - it had to go down as one of his most inventive murders yet. The boss of the Institute looked like it would take him months to get the dead guy's work sorted out, which was another problem solved.

Once again a dark cloud intruded on his sunny disposition - the American guy - what had he said he name was? Tucker - yes that was it - Bradley Tucker. Of course, that made sense, the dead guy had assumed Smiler was a friend of Brad's - that must be the same guy, from Miami. How much of a threat was he? Smiler pictured the crowded courtroom and the young American's dramatic interruption. He was pretty confident the guy was just sounding off. He'd never be able to prove anything. No one had even made more than a passing reference to the dead man's work on the East Coast pollution problem. Everyone would be concentrating on his work on poisonous fish since that's what killed him, Smiler reasoned. Probably that Tucker guy would be so wrapped up in his friend's death he wouldn't even get back to his work for quite a while - long enough for the stuff to be moved and Smiler to be long gone.

Smiler gave a self-satisfied grin. He figured he'd handled things pretty well all things considered. Granted, he thought, there were perhaps a couple of loose ends, which he would not normally leave, but, it would probably arouse more suspicion to deal with them than to leave them as they were. The doctor would have no proof of what the fisherman told him. Smiler wasn't even sure if the boy had told him anything. The Marine guy could holler all he liked, once the drums were gone there was nothing he could do to prove anyone would want his friend out of the way - again even if he did work things out that far. No Smiler was pretty confident the whole thing was dealt with and he could safely leave. The sooner he was off this Island the better he decided.

Having decided to leave well enough alone, Smiler rose, showered and dressed. He set about planning what he assumed to be his last day in Barbados. He could catch the afternoon flight to New York and put the whole sorry episode behind him.

There was a knock at the door. "Room service." Called a female voice with a local accent. Smiler opened the door a fraction and peered around. A slightly built black woman stood in the corridor, dressed in an ill-fitting pink dress, the standard uniform of the hotel maid; she bore an assortment of cleaning materials. Smiler was on the point of leaving the room anyway to go to breakfast so he opened the door and stepped back into the room to collect his keys and jacket.

As he crossed the room the phone rang, quickly he checked his watch. It was too early for Miami to be calling him - the US were an hour behind local time. Puzzled he snatched up the phone. "Yes?" he enquired, giving nothing away. "Hold the line" a voice barked at him, a voice he recognised instantly as Westfield's from Miami. Why was he calling so early? He again checked his watch, one minute had passed, there wasn't even going to be the trivial talk until the line was secure, this must be important.

Suddenly he remembered the maid, he spun around but there was no sign of her. The door was shut and there was no trace of the tray of cleaning materials she had been carrying. She must have stepped back outside to wait for him to finish his call. Still holding the phone he tried to stretch over to the door and check she wasn't just outside the door and could hear him - the cord wouldn't reach.

"You still there?" Westfield asked brusquely, impatiently awaiting the line to be secure.

"Yeah sure." Smiler replied, abandoning his attempt to check the door and turning his face to the wall instead. He reasoned that no one would be able to hear him from outside the room anyway, and besides, the brief glimpse he'd caught of the maid had been reassuring enough. She hadn't appeared anything out of the ordinary. A bit old to be working as a maid but that wasn't his problem. "Peasants" he thought with disgust. It was just his usual sense of paranoia making him check every possibility.

Both parties on the phone heard a faint click and Smiler braced himself to hear what his employer had to say - he didn't wait long.

"What the hell is going on down there?" Westfield angrily demanded.

"What do you mean? Everything has been taken care of here. The fisherman is history and everything is just about wrapped up. I..." Smiler started, genuinely confused by the man's attitude. His earlier confidence started to dissipate rapidly.

"I mean the extra patrols! I send a team of divers down there and they get stopped by the local Coast Guard. It transpires that some Institute or something has warned the Coast Guard that the waters could be being polluted and they are to increase patrols to find out how!! For Christ's sake - who the hell is this Institute? What is their involvement?"

"Did they catch them then?" Smiler ignored the question, instead thinking rapidly how fast it would take him to get out if the game was up.

"No thank God - they warned them to be careful in case the pollution made them sick - Christ it's almost a bloody joke - that's what they were there for! What do you know about this Institute? I thought you'd got everything covered down there - just how bad is it?" Westfield was sweating, he'd received word early from the team of divers and now he was panicking. The South Americans would not tolerate waiting much longer.

"It's the Barbados Institute of Marine Biology. A small operation they've been called in to check the waters. Don't worry I've got it covered. I've already been down and checked them out. Two scientist types were dealing with the problem. I've dealt directly with one of them - he is no longer with us and I don't foresee any trouble from the other - I think the Institute has more important things to worry about than a bit of local pollution at present." Smiler spoke quickly, trying to reassure the other man.

"Is the other one definitely incapable of causing any further problem? Just how did you handle it?" Westfield asked, assuming, correctly, that the first scientist would be dead but wondering if his colleague would be injured or merely running scared.

"Very discreetly." Smiler still felt totally satisfied with Corbin's death, despite the latest news, "It was an accident at the lab - no-one has put any connection to anything at all. There was a note of pride in his voice.

"What about the other guy?" Westfield asked sharply, disinterested and unimpressed by the means Smiler had used to dispose of the problem.

"He's not a problem - like I said no-one linked the events at all. The guy's more concerned about his friend's death than work at the moment - trust me that's not a problem." He spoke confidently.

"There's no-one else dealing with it?" Westfield enquired, "How do you know that?"

"I checked that personally, it's only a tiny place, the title is bigger than the building!" Smiler's attempt at humour fell on deaf ears, getting no response he quickly continued. "Look if it comes to it I'll get rid of the other guy too but at the moment I don't think it's necessary - really. I know what I'm doing - another "accident" will only arouse suspicion - I do know what I'm doing!" He repeated, beginning to grow slightly angry with this man who plainly didn't trust his judgement.

"Well you haven't exactly proved it so far! You're not doing such a brilliant job for a man who's supposed to know what he's doing!" Westfield retorted, sarcastically. "Okay, okay, what about this fisherman - I take it he doesn't have a 'colleague' waiting in the wings?"

"No he's definitely out of the picture - he was a young guy with his own boat - worked alone. End of story." Smiler was at least confident of that, he decided not to mention the doctor.

"You're absolutely sure he didn't tell his friends what he was up to?" Westfield mentally ran through any more possible dangers to him.

"I'm sure - anyway he thought he was smuggling drugs right up until he died - not something he'd brag about really." Smiler replied dryly. "I'm telling you that part is dealt with." He stated firmly.

"I'm glad to hear you've got something right. What about the Coast Guard?" Demanded Westfield, "Any ideas how to overcome that little aspect of your failure?"

Smiler winced - he wasn't used to being spoken to like this - usually he demanded and received the respect he so craved. His voice grew dangerously quiet as he replied.

"Look I've covered as much here as I was told to - and more. Circumstances beyond my control caused the problem - how the hell was I supposed to know the dumb kid would open the drums? There's no point going over that again - at least I'm sorting it out. I..."

"Big of you!" Interrupted Westfield, angrily "You are being paid a fortune for this job, remember? You're in this thing too deep to walk away now so I suggest you see it through."

"I'm not going anywhere until this thing is over. I'm a professional - I don't leave a job until it's over. " stated Smiler, abandoning his plans of leaving almost immediately. "This is only a small place the Coast Guard can't be that vast - your people will just have to wait until the patrol has passed or something. Surely you can deal with that side - I'll watch this side of things and deal with anything else until the stuff is gone. The pressure's been taken off the Coast Guard now, they won't be that interested, these people are so laid back- unless there's constant pushing they soon relax. I'll bet they won't even bother patrolling now that the Institute has - shall we say - "lost interest" He learnt much about Island life. His cool reasoning came to the fore and he worked out a logical solution. "The main thing is to get that stuff away from here."

Westfield, felt slightly reassured by the man's confidence; maybe all wasn't lost after all.

"Ok I'll work on that. You just make sure you keep everything there covered - I don't want any more surprises." He severed the connection.

Smiler stood for a moment staring at the phone. He decided it was time to double check his two remaining possible problems. Remembering it was the young scientist's funeral that day he grabbed his keys and headed out the door. He intended to pay his own respects, from a discreet distance, and just make sure the American guy was not about to cause any trouble - then he'd deal with the doctor.

The maid in the pink uniform carried on cleaning the hotel room bathroom and breathed a sigh of relief when she heard the door slam behind the hotel guest.

Chapter 28

Al Garcia sat in the conference room in the penthouse suite of the Westfield Inc. Towers. He had been summoned early by Randall Westfield and appraised of the ongoing situation in the Caribbean. He was sitting at the huge, oval conference table with papers spread all around him when a group of Hispanic looking cleaners arrived. Al scowled at the men as they entered. Dressed in brown overalls, peaked caps pulled over their eyes, they were a scruffy looking crew. "Do you have to do that now?" He snapped at them. "Signor?" One of them asked, the others stood around dumbly. "Oh for Christ's sake - doesn't anyone speak English around here anymore." he muttered in disgust. Turning back to his papers, he decided to ignore the intrusion. He left the room shortly afterwards. He made the car park in record time but it was not something he was particularly proud of. Al Garcia left the room, reluctantly, via the window. Signor Javier Carenas had not taken the latest news from his supplier well.

Two floors below the conference room Ben Webb was just arriving at his office. He too had been told to get in early to deal with the growing crisis. He entered his office just in time to see Al Garcia hurtling past the window. Dropping his briefcase, he rushed over to the window behind his desk and stared, horrified down towards the car park below. It was not an attractive view. Al's body lay spread-eagled across the tarmac. Ben sank to his knees, fighting back the overwhelming feeling of nausea that swept over him. Sobbing with terror, he curled into a foetal position half under his desk. A sixth sense made him listen suddenly as a faint noise broke through his terror fogged brain. He broke out in a cold sweat and held his breath, it was the sound of the office door opening behind him.

Hardly daring to move, he squinted through the gap between his desk and the floor towards the door. He could just about see two men standing at the doorway looking into the room. They obviously hadn't seen him and they stood scanning around the room, presumably checking for the occupant. His briefcase! It was in the middle of the floor where he'd dropped it - they had to have seen it. He began to cry, tears rolled down his cheeks and he rocked silently back and forth waiting for his fate.

The room remained quiet. After what seemed like an eternity Ben cautiously opened his eyes and looked fearfully round, expecting to see a gun pointed at him at the very least. The room was empty - they hadn't seen him! How far away were they? The door was ajar, what if they were in the corridor just outside? He peered carefully over the edge of the desk and slowly pulled the phone towards him. Inch by inch the precious line of communication was tugged across the desk.

He winced as the receiver rattled as it crossed the edge of the ornate leather embossing. They mustn't hear it, he prayed, he had to reach the phone. He would call 911. Tell the police there'd been a break-in or something. Nothing mattered any more. He didn't care if he was locked away for his part in the dealings. At least he'd be safe. Finally the phone was at the edge of the desk; Ben reached up and slipped it down to his private sanctuary. He let out a tiny sigh of relief as he clutched it to his chest.

"Thank God!" he sighed under his breath. With trembling fingers he picked up the receiver. The phone line was dead. He stared at it in shock. It couldn't be! It had to work - it was his only hope. Sadly he replaced the phone and slumped back, leaning against the wall. It was over. He'd never get out alive.

He wiped the tears from his eyes and sat staring forward thinking about his wife. He loved his wife. She was a good woman. She deserved better than this. There had to be a way out. Suddenly he spotted it. The small panic button installed under his desk. He'd forgotten all about that. It was part of the elaborate alarm system Westfield had had installed recently. A bandit alarm had been installed in every main office. Was it working yet? He wasn't sure. What if it sounded and brought the assassins back? He gingerly touched the button with his finger then jerked his hand away as if burnt. He couldn't risk it.

Trembling, he staggered to his feet and over to the partially open door. He listened for a few minutes, trying to hear above the sound of his own beating heart if anyone was still around. There was silence. He had to get help. They could be anywhere, waiting for him behind any door. Again he thought of Hillary. A sudden image of their honeymoon in Antigua popped unexpectedly into his mind. He owed it to her to at least try.

He hesitated briefly then, taking a deep breath, he squared his shoulders and walked, almost defiantly, over to the desk and pressed the button. Silence. Frantically he pressed it again and again. Despair overwhelmed him. There was no help coming. He was alone. "Ok - you're on your own." He told himself sternly "Get a grip man you can do it." He resolved to get out by himself.

Barely suppressing the panic that threatened to overwhelm him he headed for the door. He crept out of the room, along the corridor, watching every door he passed. It seemed like hours until he reached the stairs and elevators. He hesitated then opted for the stairs. Keeping what little backbone he had pressed firmly to the wall so no one looking down the stair well would be able to see him, he inched carefully down the seemingly unending stairway to the ground floor. In the distance he could hear sirens approaching. It was the most beautiful sound he'd ever heard.

Officers' O'Reilly and Turner headed into the entrance of the Westfield Inc. Towers. Someone had pressed an emergency alarm.

The station had called the building but there appeared to be a temporary fault on the phone lines so they had to check it out.

"New system isn't it?" Turner said casually looking out the window as they approached. The building seemed quiet.

"Yeah, probably a fault. Maybe the cleaners set it off." O'Reilly replied unwrapping a fresh stick of gum. "No sign of any problem. Park out front and we'll give it the once over."

As Ben reached every new level he crawled on his hands and knees under the window of the door opening onto the corridor. He didn't even try to peek through to see if the coast was clear. He wouldn't risk being spotted. It seemed to take forever to reach the bottom. He was beginning to hyperventilate from breathing so rapidly. Finally he reached the ground floor. The sirens had stopped. He prayed they had not left. Surely they would see Al's body? He cringed as a mental image of the crumbled body flashed into his mind. Fighting back the nausea that again threatened him he peered through the small window in the door between the stairs and the reception.

A police car was pulling up outside the main entrance. He looked around as best he could, through the narrow window without taking the risk of opening the door. As far as he could tell the place looked deserted. He didn't like to think what had happened to the security man who was supposed to be there. Could he make it across the reception area? Surely they couldn't just shoot him down in front of two armed officers? He peeped quickly through the glass again. The officers were getting out the car. They didn't look particularly alert though. Their weapons were holstered and they looked rather bored. Perhaps they thought it was a false alarm? Who'd called them? Whatever they thought they were his salvation, he had to take a chance.

He took a deep breath, flung open the door and sprinted across the reception area. The uniformed police officer approaching the large glass doors was startled to see a small man with a tear-streaked face, dressed in an expensive, but filthy, suit burst through them.

To his amazement the man dashed past him, yanked open the rear door of the police car with such force he fell to the ground, hastily he scrambled towards the back of the vehicle and dived in. He lay cowering on the floor of the car - completely hysterical.

"Uh Sir? Do you have a problem?" asked the bemused officer, with a puzzled glance at his colleague who was approaching from the other side. Both officers shrugged and stared in at the gibbering wreck of a man.

"Quick, quick shut the door - let's get out of here! Quick they might still be in here - I think they're coming for me next. I know they are. I saw them - in my office. I saw them. The men who did it. I saw them but they didn't see me. Quick shut the door. They did it - I know they did and they'll get me next and you too if you don't hurry." He babbled on, desperately trying to pull the door closed. The officer held on fast to the open door and called in to him.

"Sir, calm down sir. What did you see? What men? What did they do? You're not making sense sir." The guy was obviously some kind of nut, Officer O'Reilly decided - he could see from his colleague's expression that he was not alone in reaching that conclusion. Pushing his hat back, he scratched his head and, casually chewing gum, he looked down at the weird guy. "Terrific" he thought, "What a great start to the day" He sighed.

With a sudden startling clarity Ben dramatically declared. "The men who did that!" pointing over towards the car park and Al Garcia's crushed body. Both men turned in the direction Ben was pointing. Officer O'Reilly lost his gum - and his breakfast. His colleague, Officer Turner, who was older and more experienced, drew his gun and quickly checked around the immediate area.

"Get in the car." he said urgently. "We'd better call this in fast." He didn't need to repeat his instruction.

Minutes later the area was a sea of flashing lights as reinforcements and an ambulance arrived. Photographs were taken before the body was draped in a sheet awaiting the arrival of the forensic team. The building was searched but found to be empty. There was no sign of the firm's night watchman. It was later discovered he been advised, by telephone, to take a short walk and deciding no job was worth his life he had done exactly as he was told. Ben was taken, much to his relief, down to Police Headquarters for questioning and by the time Randall Westfield III arrived at his prestigious office block, the investigation was well underway.

By the time they reached downtown Miami Police Headquarters Ben had made a monumental decision. Marching up to the sergeant behind the desk he announced.

"I want diplomatic immunity" He told the confused man.

"Excuse me? Are you a foreign national sir?" The sergeant asked looking dubiously at the dishevelled businessman who stood before him - he certainly looked and sounded American.

Ben's resolve crumbled. "That's wrong isn't it - oh God I'm just not cut out for this kind of thing - look I just want to tell everything and - well you know - like be protected and stuff." He looked about ready to drop on his feet, a pathetic creature with dirty clothes and a filthy face, his once manicured hands were grazed and bleeding where he'd scrambled across the ground trying to reach the sanctuary of the police car.

The desk phone rang and the sergeant automatically picked it up, his eyes never leaving Ben's face as he struggled to comprehend what on earth this maniac could be talking about. He spoke quietly into the phone for a couple of minutes then indicated for O'Reilly to take Ben along to an interview room.

Ben sat miserably in the room. He wondered if he had enough information to buy his own protection. He knew of a couple of shady dealings, but he had no evidence. He knew quite a bit about the plutonium smuggling, but again, not the really crucial details, Westfield was too clever to let any one person have enough information to actually harm him. Did he need actual written documentation to trade with the police? He simply didn't know. It was not something he'd ever dealt with. All he had to go on was stuff he'd seen or read in the news, how people gave evidence and got into witness protection - that's what he wanted - but did he have enough to offer?

He looked around the room as if for inspiration. There was a plain wooden table in the centre, with a couple of cheap plastic chairs on either side and a large white clock, with a particularly loud tick on the wall. It was not the most inviting room Ben had ever been in but at least he was away from Westfield Towers. Over and over he saw in his mind, Al's face as he hurtled past the window, again and again he pictured the crumpled body. The images wouldn't stop - he couldn't make them go away. The door opened and to his great surprise Warren Schreiber walked in. Ben leapt to his feet.

"Oh Warren, you're here too! Did they pick you up or did you come in like me? I'm going to give myself up - tell them everything - you should do the same - it's not worth it. It was horrible - you should have seen it! I'm lucky to be alive. Get out of there now - while you've got the chance." He grabbed at the man, desperately trying to convince him. He hadn't even noticed an older man who had walked in behind Schreiber.

"Mr Webb? I'm Detective Letts, I believe you're already acquainted with Detective Schreiber here." Said the man dryly. Ben stood staring at the two men - his mouth hanging open in shock.

The three men sat at the desk. Ben was gasping for air like a fish out of water. He kept opening and closing his mouth but no sound came out as he tried to digest the latest turn of events. The two officers sat waiting patiently for him to compose himself.

"But...you.... I" spluttered Ben eventually. "I don't understand. I thought...I thought.... I don't know what I thought." he mumbled then suddenly he straightened in his seat. "So you tipped them off about the ship! You were a ... a ... what do you call it? A plant?"

"Yeah, I guess you could call me that. I prefer "undercover agent"" Warren Schreiber replied with a wry smile. "But unfortunately that backfired. Word got back to Westfield..." He glanced across at his colleague, Detective Letts.

"Yeah well that was a mistake." Letts interjected quickly. "These things happen. I don't like it any more than you do. That's history now. The point is now..."

"The point is now..." continued Schreiber, "how do we wrap this thing up? I was getting pretty close but today...." he shrugged, "well let's just say we didn't anticipate this thing blowing wide open like this."

"Maybe I can help?" Ben asked eagerly, "I'll tell you anything I know." He nodded his head vigorously, anxious to be 'in with the good guys'!

"I think you know less than me but we'll go over everything." Schreiber reached for a notepad and prepared to interrogate his former colleague. Letts rose to his feet.

"I'll head on over to Westfield. He'll be at the Towers by now." At the door he paused and looked back at his colleague. "Maybe this will unglue him enough - he's got to break sometime."

The other two exchanged glances, knowing Westfield they did not share Letts optimism. The door closed behind him and Warren Schreiber turned back to Ben.

"We've been after him for some time, but he's pretty good at covering his tracks." He began. "He's gone too far this time though. It's become a Government investigation. This one's gone to the top." He said grimly.

Ben gasped. "Government?" He looked more shocked than ever, if such a thing were possible.

"Do you have any idea of the implications of an American aiding a foreign power? For Christ's sake he's handing them the means for assembling a nuclear weapon! You must realise what's involved here?" He said in exasperation. "That's why we had to go undercover. We've got to keep a lid on this!"

The enormity of the situation finally dawned on Ben. "What about me?" he whispered. "You know I didn't want to get involved. You know what Westfield's like. I couldn't get out.... he would never let me walk away." His eyes widened with horror as he pleaded with Warren for his understanding. Warren took pity on him.

"Yeah, I know what he's like." He sighed. "Look it's not up to me but... well off the record ok? I'll see what I can do. I expect they'll put you in a witness protection programme or something - it's Westfield we're after - and his contacts. We need to know exactly where the stuff is going."

"Al's the only one he really confides in....oh!" Ben stopped as he again relived Al's final moments.

"Exactly! Today has really screwed us. I was trying......"

"But something's gone wrong!" Ben interrupted excitedly. "Something else I mean, apart from the diversion. That's why we were in so early this morning. Westfield called me this morning, very early he told me to get straight in - he said...he said..." his voice trailed off then he added with a sigh. "He said Al would explain."

"Terrific! We better hope Letts comes up with something." There was a brief silence as they both contemplated how the detective would fare in his interrogation of Westfield.

In the conference room at Westfield Towers, Randall Westfield III was sweating uncomfortably despite the air conditioning. The detective seated in front of him looked perfectly cool and calm, totally at ease with his surroundings. A black and yellow tape cordoned off the window from which Al Garcia had fallen to his death. Randall, to his horror, kept finding his glance being pulled magnetically towards the grim sight. He shuddered as he imagined Al's body hitting the ground. He was astute enough to know they had brought him in here to unnerve him, and he was determined to keep his head - but it wasn't easy.

"Mr Westfield, you must be deeply shocked by this tragedy." The Detective began, smiling solicitously at the businessman he faced. "Have you spoken to other members of your senior staff? I would like to interview them all as soon as possible, naturally." he continued, smoothly.

"Oh er...yes of course, naturally. I er, well that is to say; I haven't really had time yet. I mean well of course Mr Garcia's tragic ...er... accident has come as such a shock." Randall babbled. The truth was that two members of his senior staff were missing - he had no idea where they were. He could only assume that whoever had murdered Al, presumably the South Americans had taken them as hostages. They probably intended using them as bargaining power, if they hadn't already killed them. He wondered if the police had searched the building. Wherever Schreiber and Webb were - he didn't give much for their chances although at present he was more concerned with saving his own neck.

Detective Letts watched the emotions crossing Westfield's face. He was too tough to crack that easily but maybe wondering where Schreiber and Webb were might just unnerve him enough. He decided not to mention their whereabouts just yet.

"You called Mr Garcia's death an accident. Do you really think it was?" He asked coolly.

"Well," Westfield used all his years of negotiating to bluff, "Well I suppose the only other real alternative is...suicide, I just find that so hard to accept." He sighed "The poor man, I knew nothing about his private life." He paused and looked sorrowful, "He must have been so unhappy."

Chapter 29

Brad Tucker paused as he was dressing in his sombre dark suit, and looked around the apartment. When he returned from the inquest a few days previously he'd embarked upon a frenzied cleaning campaign. He'd cleaned until he was exhausted, scouring away his anger and frustration, trying to do one last thing for his friend. When Corby's parents came around to collect his personal effects the place would be spotless. It was the only practical thing he could do for them. He didn't want Corby's mother to have to worry about preparing the place for the next occupant - although he couldn't bear to think of someone else taking over, he knew mothers worried about things like that.

The small apartment gleamed, every surface was shining. Every discarded shirt, every cast off sock was in the laundry basket. He'd collected a variety of coffee cups in various stages of abandonment, one or two showing signs of developing an interesting new life form. He and Corby would have had quite a laugh over it he thought, with increasing sadness. The cups had been scrubbed vigorously and replaced in the cupboards. All Corby's papers, including maps and charts of the East Coast as well as reports on fish venom he shoved hastily into a briefcase to return to the lab. Ironically the reason for Corby's death was buried under reports of the means by which he'd died.

The apartment showed little resemblance to the carefree 'bachelor pad' Brad had arrived at, so very recently. It was the only way Brad could bear to stay there, he realised his sudden domestic streak probably had more to do with wiping away memories than helping Mrs Corbin. His task over he slumped down and, opening a bottle of local rum and proceeded to get very, very drunk.

Although the apartment had stayed in the same condition since that evening, Brad, fortunately, was now very sober as he carried on dressing, wondering about his own future. There was no reason why he shouldn't stay on the Island and carry on their work. Perhaps that would be a fitting tribute to his friend, he remembered Corby's earnest face as he talked about producing a comprehensive paper on marine zoo toxicology. That had been on his first day at work, Brad recalled how eager Corby had been to avoid unnecessary suffering by people harmed by marine life, how knowing the proper treatment would save lives - it hadn't saved his.

It just didn't seem right, but, now he'd calmed down, Brad had to admit - he could see no other explanation for his friend's death. There was just a nagging, gut feeling that something somewhere was wrong, there was something they were all overlooking. Donning his black tie, he decided what he should do, namely, stay on the Island and continue Corby's work.

Of course, he suddenly remembered, he'd have to wrap up the East Coast thing first. He frowned, he'd forgotten all about it in light of recent events, well it shouldn't take long. "Concentrate on work" he told his reflection in the mirror, as he straightened his tie. It would be the only way he could envisage getting through the day ahead. Picking up his jacket he left the apartment.

A few miles away Andrew was also preparing for the funeral. He had few thoughts for the deceased, he wasn't callous but he'd never met the man. He was thinking more of Charmaine and also the young American she wanted him to meet - Brad Tucker and the man's outburst at the inquest. He seemed a volatile sort. Andrew hoped he wouldn't cause a scene at the funeral, with typical British reserve Andrew hated any sort of public display of emotion. He did sympathise with the guy though, must be terrible for him; Charmaine seemed to think he didn't know anyone else on the Island. Everyone was very friendly but even so, must be tough feeling so alone in your grief, Andrew thought as he tied his black tie.

Andrew's thoughts turned to the young fisherman who'd also died so recently. He pictured the boy's grandmother; she had been consumed with grief when he'd talked to her. She'd been most concerned about drugs, very anxious that her Grandson may have been taking something. It didn't make sense. Andrew had reassured her - there had been no trace of illegal substances in his blood. She was clearly very worried about something but had begged Andrew not to say anything of their conversation to the police. "I don't want he Mummy to think he was up to wicked things, don't go giving her bad memories of her boy - it be bad enough for her now." She'd pleaded mysteriously.

Andrew had no idea what she was talking about. He wondered why she should suspect her grandson of being involved with drugs, perhaps because he'd suddenly been taken so ill. Poor woman, probably seen something on TV. about young people and drugs, he thought, mind you, he reasoned, if he were involved in the drug scene that would account for him being killed.

It was all very strange he thought, as he mechanically slipped on his black jacket and then quickly removed it as he realised how hot it made him. He'd brought his dark suit with him from Scotland, not anticipating having to wear it much, and certainly not anticipating the heat of the Island. He decided to slip it on at the last minute and remove it as soon as decently possible at the funeral. The practicalities of his attendance wiping other thoughts from his mind.

A couple of hours later Andrew and Charmaine stood outside the church of The Holy Trinity in the parish of St. James and watched solemnly as the coffin was lowered into the grave. As Charmaine had predicted there was a vast crowd attending the service. The church had been packed to capacity, and several people had to stand outside throughout the proceedings. Dr Scobie read the eulogy and spoke of the tragic loss of a brilliant scientist cut down in his prime.

Other family members paid their own moving tributes to the young man. Many of the mourners wept openly as the flower bedecked coffin was brought in. Brad was one of the pall bearers and as he shouldered the weight of the coffin he found it hard to contain his own grief. "You must keep a grip" he told himself sternly, "You owe that much to Corby. Think about work, don't get emotional, get a hold of yourself man, the family need you to show respect." Suddenly an incredible thought entered his head - if Nathan Corbin's death hadn't been an accident - someone must have killed him - but why?

All through the service the same thought kept resounding in his head. Was it an accident or not? It had to be, no-one would ever want to harm Corby - he didn't have an enemy in the world. It was plain crazy to think anything else. Still the thought persisted in his mind, Corby knew the dangers of the stonefish so well, he'd been handling dangerous samples for years. The silent argument in his head served to keep Brad from breaking down completely throughout to long, sad service.

Afterwards Brad stood outside as the coffin was lowered into the parched ground, shading his eyes from the bright sunshine which seemed so inappropriate to this mournful scene. Charmaine and Andrew stood a few feet away, looking across at the young American, his every expression being keenly observed.

A short distance away Smiler Baines watched the scene unmoved. He felt no remorse as he observed the grieving going on around him. Mingling with the crowd, he was more intent on getting closer to the deceased man's colleague. As the members of the immediate family drew closer to the grave to ceremoniously drop earth on the coffin, Brad stepped back and bowed his head in respect. Charmaine nudged Andrew and they discreetly slipped over to where Brad was standing all alone in his grief.

"Excuse me." whispered Charmaine, "You don't know me but I was a friend of Corby's. How are you holding up?" She asked sympathetically.

Brad turned and looked at the young girl speaking to him, she was beautiful despite her red eyes and tear stained face. A young man, obviously recovering from a nasty case of sunburn stood awkwardly beside her, he thrust his hand forward towards Brad

"Er, Andrew Kinloch, pleased to m....well that is to say, under the circumstances, er...well, my name is Andrew Kinloch er...may I introduce Charmaine Harrison. " He blushed deeply making his already pink face an even deeper shade. Brad instantly liked the young man facing him. He shook hands firmly with them both.

"Brad Tucker. Even under the circumstances it's a pleasure to meet friends of Corby's." There was a moment's silence as all three turned and looked over to the open grave. Charmaine gave a small sob and Andrew, putting his arm protectively around her, led her gently away to the shade of a beautiful Flamboyant tree. They stood in silence, grateful at least for the cool shade proffered by the giant tree. Brad followed them and they watched the mourners file past the grave, Brad and Charmaine remembering Corby and Andrew wondering what to say. Smiler, watching from a few feet away frowned and sidled closer. Ostensibly sheltering from the hot sun he leaned against the other side of the huge tree and closed his eyes, wiping his brow with a handkerchief. From this vantage point he could hear every word the three young people said.

"How did you two know Corby?" Asked Brad, breaking the silence and turning to Charmaine and Andrew. Andrew looked a little uncomfortable.

"Well Andrew here never actually met him, he's new to the Island. He's come along as moral support." Charmaine interjected quickly smiling gratefully at Andrew. "I've known Corby for years - it's a pretty small community here you know. I work at the hospital and we have a lot of dealings with the Institute." Her thoughts again returned to Corby, and to the many good times they'd had over the years.

"I see," Brad smiled at Charmaine, turning to Andrew he asked casually, "So you're new here too? Vacation? I picked up on your accent - English?" He noted again the sunburn, the poor guy obviously wasn't from a hot climate.

"Scots. No I'm not on holiday - I'm working here. I'm a doctor, working at the same hospital as Charmaine here." From his shady seclusion Smiler stiffened. Could he be the new young doctor those nurses had been speaking about? There must be many hospitals around here. On reflection though he had to admit - it was only a very small island. How many new doctors would arrive at the same time? It didn't sound good to him, he strained to hear what the man was saying.

"Have you been on the Island long?" Andrew continued, he looked at the tall American. He was quite tanned and seemed very at ease with the heat, unlike Andrew himself who could feel a heat rash developing under his too heavy dark suit.

"No not long, but I'm from Miami so at least I'm used to the heat." He gave a small sympathetic grin at Andrew, who was clearly not used to it at all. "I'm thinking of staying on though, I want to carry on with Corby's work." He paused and thought about the paper on venom which Corby had been so keen to finish. Smiler thought about the East Coast problem.

"I'm sure it must be interesting work, you must tell me about it sometime." Andrew replied, politely, having little idea what a marine biologist's work would entail.

"Maybe you two should get together." Charmaine said enthusiastically, "You're both kind of new here. Especially over this holiday weekend. It's not a time to be alone. Perhaps we can all go to Kadooment together - I'm sure you'd both enjoy it."

Both men looked blankly at her. Neither had heard of Kadooment. Brad didn't even know it was a holiday weekend.

Andrew did, as he recalled being given Monday off as one of the older doctor's had mentioned it was a holiday a young man would enjoy more, but he didn't recall anywhere called Kadooment.

"Er, Charmaine, where's Kadooment? Andrew asked, "Anyway I'm working Saturday and Sunday remember?"

"Kadooment isn't a where - it's a what and it's on Monday - it's the biggest day of the year here." Charmaine laughed, at their bemused faces, and explained. "It's the grand finale of all the crop-over festivities. Like huge street party, there's a parade that goes on for hours then everyone goes down to Spring Garden Highway and parties for hours - the crowds are unbelievable. You just get swept along with them - lots of loud music and dancing, loads to eat and drink, anything can happen down there!"

Looking up she saw Dr Scobie approaching and quickly added, "Look now isn't the time or place, how about we meet at the entrance to Spring Garden Highway on Monday, say about 10 o'clock in the morning?" Both men nodded their agreement. "You're still at...at...the same apartment, aren't you?" she asked Brad, knowing Corby had planned for his friend to stay with him but not wanting to spoil the new found lightness of the conversation by mentioning his name. Brad nodded. "Fine well I'll ring you, oh good afternoon Dr Scobie. How are you?" The conversation changed to polite small talk and Smiler slipped away.

Later in his hotel room he thought again of Charmaine's description of the events due to take place on Monday, "swept along by the crowds" he recalled her saying, it would be an ideal opportunity to rid himself of the last two dangers - although he still wasn't entirely sure it would be necessary. The phone rang shrilly interrupting his reverie. After the customary timed delay Westfield said tersely.

"Look I haven't got long - things have taken a severe turn for the worse here. Whatever it costs make sure there is no-one - and I do mean no-one - left down there who could link anything back to me. I don't care if you have to sink the whole damn Island - there must be no witnesses left there."

Chapter 30

Monday dawned bright and clear and by the time Andrew and Charmaine arrived at the appointed rendezvous the temperature was already well in the eighties. Charmaine looked cool and attractive in a swimsuit and shorts set. A wide brimmed hat gave ample protection from the sun and she had sensibly worn comfortable shoes for the long day ahead. Andrew was also dressed in shorts; he wore a lightweight cotton shirt and again comfortable shoes having been well primed by Charmaine. He sported a straw hat but notwithstanding this precaution he also had the added protection of a wide band of sun cream down his nose, he was not about to risk sunburn again! Despite all his measures he still did not manage to look, or feel, as cool as his companion.

Brad approached the pair similarly dressed to Andrew although he looked far more at home in the climate. Having been warned by Charmaine to leave early he'd just beaten the deadline for the roads to be closed and made the rendezvous with little time to spare. The trio exchanged greetings but had little time for small talk as the first of many bands neared.

Loud throbbing calypso music filled the air and the colourful parade began. Lorries decorated with fluorescent colours passed by them, each carried a band of some description, rock bands vied with steel bands each playing loudly, trying to be heard above the others. Each float had two strong ropes coming out from the back corners held in place by large security men, they made a half-hearted attempt to keep the dancers belonging to each float in some semblance of order.

In elaborate costumes, dancers of every size, age and shape were dressed according to the theme of their float. Andrew watched in amazement as a crowd of around fifty bright yellow "sunflowers" male and female swept past him. A woman who must have weighed at least 250 pounds was dressed, like her compatriots, in a lurid green leotard, matching green tights and a bright yellow headdress. She waved enthusiastically at the trio. Brad and Charmaine grinned and waved back with equal vigour. Andrew gave a small smile and a discreet wave, totally overwhelmed by the incongruous sight.

The "sunflower" came over, much to Andrews's horror, slipping under the ropes containing her party she grabbed Andrew and did a quick dance with him, swirling him around with the strength of an Olympic hammer thrower. He wondered, with a medical detachment, if anyone had ever actually died of embarrassment! Eventually she let go and with a cheerful pat on his head she went on with the parade. Brad and Charmaine collapsed with laughter.

Eventually even Andrew loosened up as wave upon wave of colourful floats passed them. A Banks brewery float inched its way through the crowd. Girls in colourful costumes handed out cold beers, and held impromptu limbo competitions at the side of the road. The cherished prize for the inexpert dancers was a T-shirt extolling the virtues of the local brew. Andrew and Brad both won one, Brad for his dancing prowess and Andrew as a sympathy prize!

After watching the parade for a couple of hours they joined the back of one of the floats and commenced the slow journey along the highway, stopping frequently for refreshments. Local women had small stalls set up all along the route selling spicy fish cakes and hot rotis. The smell of hot-dogs pervaded the air vying for attention with the vapours rising from the beer tents and rum shops. The party atmosphere was tangible and everyone was in high spirits, singing and dancing and generally having a great time.

Smiler viewed the crowds with growing dismay. He thought he'd allowed plenty of time to reach the entrance to Spring Garden highway but had been stopped by a roadblock and turned back. Every route he took met with the same frustrating result and eventually he was forced to abandon the car and join the parade on foot. It was a nightmare. He stood no chance of finding his intended victims in this crush but before he could even consider abandoning his pursuit he was swept along by the crowd towards the harbour where the highway ended and the party began in earnest.

Several hours later he was exhausted, there was little hope of him returning to his hotel room. He couldn't get out of the crush of people and he had no idea where he'd left his car. He knew from his earlier excursions that the road ended at the harbour and that there were usually plenty of taxis nearby waiting for the cruise ships. Perhaps if he could just get through to the start of the parade that presumably must have reached its destination by now, he would be able to get a cab out. He started to push his way through the throng.

He was sprayed with icy cold beer from a passing brewery float. Although temporarily refreshing he realised that it would be a hot sticky mess within minutes. "Oh terrific!" He thought with disgust, surveying his ruined shirt. "Drowning in a sea of peasants and now covered in beer - great day!"

"Hey man - sorry about the shirt - here have another - compliments of the brewery - have a great holiday." A large black man dressed as a giant bumblebee thrust a T-shirt in his hands and buzzed off into the happy crowd.

"Doc! Hey Doc! Over here!" A deep voice was shouting during a brief lull in the music Smiler spun around hopefully, but then shrugged, disappointed, as he saw a local man bearing a

T-shirt proclaiming himself to be 'The Beach Doctor'. What the hell is a beach doctor? He thought angrily, the guy certainly didn't look like a medical man, in his scruffy shorts, battered straw hat and bare feet. He was on the point of turning back into the crush when he realised it was the "Beach Doctor" who was calling.

He followed the man's gaze and his spirits rose as he saw the object of the man's attention. It was the young British doctor, dancing along with the crowd. He couldn't see the American but he knew they should be together. He still wasn't entirely sure how to kill them both. He figured he could probably knife one of them and disappear into the crowd but that would still leave the other one. Maybe if he just disposed of one now. At least that would be one problem solved. He tried to get closer. The 'Beach doctor' was still calling to the British one.

"Hey man - how's that sunburn? Looking good man! You having a good time? Love the hat - flower power huh - better late than never!" The local man shouted. Andrew caught his words and grinned back.

Andrew managed to understand about half what the man was shouting, but recognising him from the beach, and buoyed up by copious amounts of rum punch and local beer, he responded in the same spirit. "You're looking pretty good yourself. How's the 'practice'?" he shouted back, but his words were lost as the crowd moved on and the men separated.

Smiler noted his quarry's straw hat; someone had stuck a sunflower into it, which bobbed above the crowd giving him a slightly easier target to aim for. A couple of times he got almost within reach but each time the crowds would shift slightly and Andrew moved out of range. To his great frustration he kept being pushed sideways towards the edge of the road.

Having struggled previously to get away from the throng now when he needed to be in the middle he found himself becalmed on the beach that bordered the Spring Garden highway. Cursing under his breath, Smiler threw himself back into the heaving mass and tried desperately to catch up with the young doctor.

Gradually he inched closer. After what seemed like an eternity of weaving through the swaying crowd the doctor's back was within a few inches. Smiler gave a huge grin of satisfaction, there was no way his victim could possibly fall to the ground in these crowds, and he'd be swept along for ages. Smiler calculated no one would ever know who'd stabbed the ill-fated doctor. The crowd was parting slightly as another lorry approached affording Smiler the opportunity to close in. The lorry continued at snail's pace as the crowd cheerfully waved it through. The band and dancers aboard cheered and blew whistles of appreciation in response.

Smiler glanced at the lorry, ironically it was funded by the Barbados Health Authority, decorated in silver and white, odd shaped balloons hung from it's sides and huge white discs covered every part of it. Briefly he considered the odds of pushing one victim under the huge wheels. It would be a neat trick if he could stab the other guy in the confusion that would arise from such an accident. He dismissed the thought contemptuously; the lorry was travelling too slowly.

The band aboard it struck up another loud calypso song. Smiler had no idea what everyone was singing but was grateful for the end refrain of each chorus when everyone within earshot threw their arms up with a loud shout. "Perfect!" He thought. As the lorry drew alongside he found himself almost pressed into the back of the British doctor. "Hold your hands up, Hey!" sang the happy crowd. Smiler grinned - it was almost poetic. He reached in his pocket and surreptitiously pulled out his flick knife. "Ok Doc," he thought nonchalantly, "I guess you're first!" With his infamous surgical skill he calculated the optimum point of entry for the blade on the young doctor's body. His fingers felt along the familiar carving of the bone-handled switchblade seeking the carved rose that would release the stiletto blade.

"Hey man! Do you know you're messing with your life? A cheery voice enquired, startled, Smiler looked up. A young woman dressed in a giant white disc was talking to him, before he had a chance to answer, she continued, "That's right man, have fun but be safe - courtesy of the Barbados Health Authority - have a good holiday!" She thrust a carrier bag over his extended hand, knocking his finger away from the trigger mechanism, and was swept away with the crowds. Smiler looked frantically around for the young doctor but he was nowhere to be seen.

The bobbing sunflower had vanished into the sea of Technicolor hats and headdresses. Totally bemused he looked inside the carrier bag - it contained a couple of condoms and a leaflet on safe sex! The irony of their concern for protecting life was not lost on Smiler. This has got to be the strangest place in the world he concluded.

"Pretty weird place huh?" A stranger beside him retorted, holding an identical bag and peering with equal amazement at the contents, "Hey Andrew, wait up" the man shouted. Smiler realised the stranger beside him was the American he was also supposed to be hunting. He tried frantically to disentangle his arm from the carrier bag but lost a vital couple of seconds in getting his arm free and securing the knife. The American was also swept forward and another opportunity was lost. He could just about make out the young American's words as he called to his rapidly disappearing friend. "Wait for me" he yelled.

"How???" drifted back the reply as the doctor struggled to stand still in the tidal wave of dancers. Andrew clung to Charmaine's hand; there was no way he was going to be separated from her.

"Well meet me..." Brad thought quickly, he didn't really know anywhere they could rendezvous. "Of course - the lab" Charmaine must know where the lab is. "I'll meet you at the lab tonight - Oistins - tonight ok?" he bellowed.

"Yeah sure, no problem!" A very happy Andrew called back over his shoulder, slipping into the local dialogue with surprising ease, as he was carried away by the dancing multitude.

Smiler knew when it was time to admit defeat, struggling back over to the side of the road he sought sanctuary in a tented rum shop on the edge of the beach. Well, he mused, as he sipped gratefully on his chilled rum and coke, at least he knew where the lab in Oistins was, and it was the scene of his most recent achievement after all. He could see no reason why his triumph could not be repeated.

Chapter 31

Charmaine pulled into the courtyard in front of the Barbados Institute of Marine Biology just before 8 o'clock. The beach bar next door was packed to capacity with the last few die- hard Kadooment party- goers. The roads were littered with bits of colourful crepe paper and tinsel like remnants of a children's party. The discarded glitter shone like stardust in the streetlights. The street cleaners would be up and about early clearing away the debris of yet another very successful Kadooment.

"Honestly when that lady in the sunflower costume grabbed you - it was so funny." Charmaine laughed, "You should have seen your face - it was hysterical!"

"Yeah well thanks for telling me she'd stuck a flower in my hat - I must have looked a right idiot." Andrew joined the laughter.

"Oh very out of place - with everyone else dressed so soberly! You really stood out - I expect you'll be struck off for 'conduct unbecoming'!" Charmaine tried to keep a serious tone but couldn't stop giggling. "Hey this is it - the Barbados Institute of Marine Biology - impressed?" She announced grandly.

"Very!" Andrew replied, peering through the darkness at the small single story stone building. "Er... where is it? I think I might have blinked and missed it!"

"This is it - yes I know it looks like a little beach front bungalow - but I tell you they do some good stuff here - Corby..." she stopped abruptly and tears sprang to her eyes. Andrew was immediately concerned. Charmaine turned off the engine and they sat in the darkness of the car park for a few minutes.

"Oh I'm sorry Charmaine, I was only kidding - I'm sure it's a great place. Please don't get upset." He felt helpless as he sat there in the dark, he could hear she was crying. He put his arm around her and pulled her close.

"I wish there was something I could say to make it better." he whispered.

"Don't be silly - it's not your fault. I'm just tired and I... well, I know it's the last thing he would have wanted but I can't help feeling guilty about having such a good time today. It just doesn't seem right." She looked across wistfully at the brightly-lit entranceway; Brad was already there and had turned on all the lights in the foyer to welcome them. The car park was very dark; being surrounded by tall trees and could be a foreboding place at night.

"I used to meet him here after work sometimes - oh, like I told you before, there was never anything in it - no big romance you understand. But sometimes we'd meet here after work and pop next door for a drink. I'm really going to miss him." She sighed, "I'm just so sorry you never got to meet him - you'd have really liked him - he was great fun." Her voice was a bare whisper.

"I'm sure he was" Andrew replied gently, "And I'm sorry too - look we don't have to go in you know, not if you don't want to. Would you like to go somewhere else?" He looked across at the building; there was only one other car in the car park so he assumed Brad was waiting for them alone in the building.

"If you like I'll pop in and tell Brad we can't make it - I'm sure he'll understand - it's been a long day." He continued, "I wonder why he asked us to meet him here? I..." he broke off Brad came into view, he was standing in the foyer of the building. He couldn't see them in the darkened car. As they watched he rubbed his face with his hands - he looked deeply unhappy.

"I don't think he wanted to go home." Charmaine said softly, looking across at the lonely figure. "Actually Andrew, if you don't mind..." she paused.

"Anything." Andrew interjected gallantly, seeing her hesitate.

"Well I'd kind of like to be alone for a while, but I don't want to leave that guy like that. It's easier for me I've got you. He must feel so alone. Would you mind? I mean, I don't know, have a guy talk or something.... drink beer and swap stories. You wouldn't have to stay long but I'd really appreciate it. I'm sure he'd drop you home." She realised he wouldn't have a car to get home.

"Of course, I quite understand - like they say here - no problem!" He laughed to show her he really didn't mind at all. "Actually I could probably walk it from here - it's only up the road. We're practically neighbours!"

"Oh yes of course - Dover beach is the next one along." Charmaine remembered suddenly, "I wouldn't walk along the beach at night though. It's only a few stops on a Route Taxi, they come along every five minutes...."

"You've got no faith in me! Like I said - I could walk it - it can only be a couple of miles. I quite fancy a moonlight stroll along the beach - of course it won't be quite the same alone, but there you go...if you're dumping me. " He tried to look heart-broken, which was rather a waste in the darkened car but she got the message.

"Listen Honey, seriously, take care if you do walk home, stick to the roads. Tell me you'll be careful. You haven't got your wallet on you, have you?" She sounded worried.

"No Mother." He gave a huge exaggerated sigh. "You told me not to take it to Kadooment remember? I've just got some spare cash in my pocket - enough for a few beers and my bus fare home. Anyway I thought this was paradise? You're not supposed to be mugged in paradise!"

"Not everyone here is an angel! You still have to be a bit sensible late at night. Now go on with you. Can you make my excuses to Brad?" She suddenly felt terribly tired and ready to go home, the last few days had been an emotional roller coaster.

"Yes of course, you get some rest. Don't worry about Brad - or me, well you could worry about me a bit - if you wanted to!" He leaned over and gave her a lingering kiss tenderly on the lips. "Thanks for a lovely day - remember I love you." He got out of the car, "I take it you'll see me safely into the building." He called jokingly as he walked towards the lighted entrance. Charmaine switched on her lights obligingly.

"Go on in you idiot. I love you too. I'll see you in the morning. Night!" She turned the car around and headed out of the car park. She took one last look in her rear view mirror and waved as she saw Andrew watching her leave.

Neither of them noticed a stranger standing among the tall trees that lined the car park. Smiler Baines waited until the car had pulled out onto the road before edging closer to the building. He slipped silently around the outside of the building until he reached the window. He already knew it opened onto a small recreation room.

Earlier he'd watched as Brad had gone into that room, put some beers into the small fridge and arranged three rather battered old armchairs. It was obvious he was expecting to entertain his guests there. The slatted windows gave a cool breeze off the ocean and afforded Smiler an excellent chance to eavesdrop. Hopefully he'd learn just how much the two men had worked out - then he could take whatever action was necessary.

Looking out over the deserted beach, he sat down on the soft white sand under the window. Safely hidden in the shadows he waited - he was in no hurry. Mechanically he checked the knife in his pocket, shame he couldn't pull the same stunt again with those fish spines, he thought, still something would turn up, it always did. He just had to be patient.

Chapter 32

As Andrew approached the building Brad sprang forward and opened the door, grateful for some company. His thoughts had been growing increasingly melancholy and he was in danger of becoming morose. He looked across Andrew's shoulder, surprised to see him alone.

"Charmaine not with you?" He queried, "Come on through - it's not much but the view is great!" He held open the door, and showed Andrew through to a small recreation area. He indicated a chair and Andrew sat down.

"No - she was absolutely exhausted. She sends her apologies. Hope you don't mind my company!" He laughed as he nodded his head in grateful acceptance of the beer Brad was offering.

"Well nothing personal buddy but she has got the edge over you!" Brad laughed, helping himself to a beer; he slumped down in a chair opposite Andrew and looked acutely disappointed.

"Well you weren't exactly my first choice for a hot date I can tell you!" Andrew pretended to be offended by his new friend's choice of company. The two men laughed together. They sat drinking their beer in companionable silence for a few minutes. Brad sat idly squeezed his beer can making a metallic clicking sound, muted sounds of merriment from the next door beach bar provided a vague background.

"Great day wasn't it?" Commented Andrew idly, watching a brightly-lit cruise ship meander slowly across the horizon.

"Yeah, especially for you! Picked any good sunflowers recently?" Brad asked innocently.

"God don't remind me! Charmaine's been giving me a hard time about that! This really is an incredible place, isn't it? I've never known such friendly people!" Andrew enthused.

"We noticed!" Brad commented dryly, then laughed as his companion blushed. "Another?" He pointed towards the fridge of beers.

"Why not!" Declared Andrew, he stretched over towards the fridge, it was just about within reach. "Hold on I'll get them - don't bother getting up." He pulled out a couple of beers and tossed one to Brad.

"I don't think I could!" Groaned Brad, "I can hardly move - do you know we must have entered about fifty limbo competitions today and walked miles!"

"Well two competitions - which you won! But it surely feels like fifty and we did walk miles!" Agreed Andrew, looking down at his tired feet.

Outside Smiler listened to the inconsequential chatter neither seemed to be on the point of making a startling revelation. He contemplated leaving them. They seemed set for the night.

"If I wasn't so beat I'd show you around the place - you'll have to come back another time." Brad murmured, putting his aching feet up onto the coffee table and slipping off his shoes.

"Yeah I'd like that. What is it you do here? Charmaine said you often help the hospital." Andrew asked, following his friend's suit and getting more comfortable.

"Well I've only been here a couple of weeks so I haven't exactly been called on to save lives yet..." Brad winced as he realised what he'd said. There was an awkward silence then he took a deep breath and continued, changing the subject "Actually our work is a bit more mundane at present, we're trying to sort out the East Coast problem. You might have heard of it?" He commented casually, struggling to restore the former easy mood.

"No, what's that?" Andrew asked, grateful to steer the conversation away from saving lives. Outside Smiler sat up straight and listened attentively.

"Where you been? It's made all the papers - well both the papers anyway" Brad laughed, "There's been a number of dead fish washed up on the East coast - you really should have read the papers. They were terrific! All these people wrote in and said what they thought was causing it - some of it was hilarious! One woman on the TV. reckoned it was God's vengeance for dirty lyrics in those calypso songs - another guy said he'd seen an alien space craft sending a ray down into the water!" Brad laughed at the memory.

"Ha those aliens!" Andrew laughed, "There should be a law against them!"

"Hang on - the guy had a witness!" Brad said seriously, Andrew looked suspiciously at him, what was he trying to pull?

"Oh yes" Brad continued, "He talked the whole thing over with Elvis who was standing right beside him at the time!"

The two men fell about in drunken laughter.

"They'll be catching fish in tiny sequinned suits next!" Roared Brad "Can't wait for the first fisherman to land a "kingfish" singing "All shook up".

Andrew exploded tears of laughter rolled down his cheeks as he collapsed with mirth. Suddenly he stopped - tiny alarm bells ringing in his head.

"Did you say the East Coast?" He asked seriously. Sweetboy had been fishing the East Coast - which was one of the few bits of information he'd managed to drag out of the boy.

"Yeah why? You an Elvis fan?" Brad chortled, then straightening up he noticed his friend had suddenly sobered up. "What's up?" He looked puzzled, half expecting his friend to burst forth with another joke.

"What is causing it?" Andrew asked quietly, thoughts chasing around his head.

"Well we don't know for sure yet, some kind of pollutant, but we don't know exactly where it's coming from yet. Why do you ask?" Alerted by Andrew's manner Brad was suddenly sober himself.

"I've just had a real strange case at the hospital..." Andrew said slowly, thinking deeply. "A young fisherman presents with strange non-healing burns, several seemingly unrelated symptoms, acting very strangely and obviously very sick." Andrew pictured Sweetboy arriving at the hospital; he had been very scared, could his problems be related? Perhaps he caught something from the fish? He put that very question to Brad.

"No, it's not a disease, there are too many different species affected - anyway I take it he's the only one you had like it?" Brad asked, Andrew nodded thoughtfully. "Well what happened to him - is he making progress?"

Andrew hesitated, the police had told him not to discuss the case until they could make their own enquiries but this might be of real help.

"He died." He said flatly.

"Of those few symptoms?" Brad asked incredulously. Andrew took a deep breath.

"No actually, but this mustn't go beyond these walls...he was murdered." He waited for Brad's reaction.

"What!! In the hospital? How?" Brad was quite amazed. Outside Smiler was squirming, he looked around, the tiny beach bar was still quite crowded. He'd never get away with just bursting in and killing them both, besides there were two of them - he decided to sit it out for a while longer.

"I know - it's incredible isn't it? It was neatly done though. Someone injected about 30cc of air into his drip. Showed up instantly in the post mortem. We still don't know what was wrong with him though - still doing tests." He shrugged, "It's one hell of a mystery."

"It's got to be connected - has to be, Corby was making some terrific progress on that, he.... Oh my God...." the colour drained from his face and he slumped back in the chair. "Corby!" He whispered.

"You don't think?" Andrew cried, alarmed. "Are you all right?" He asked, his medical knowledge coming to the fore as he watched his friend reeling with obvious shock.

"Yes, yes, I'm fine." Brad said impatiently, "But don't you see? If someone could get into a hospital and kill a patient they could easily just walk in here and..."

"But I thought it was an accident?" Andrew interrupted; worried Brad was perhaps reading too much into the basically circumstantial evidence.

"I never believed that - never!" Brad repeated vehemently. "Look at the facts here - you get a young man, working the East Coast, gets some sort of weird illness and then you have Corby working on what ever is killing fish in the same area and they both die suddenly! Surely you must see that's just too much of a coincidence."

"Perhaps we'd better go straight to the police!" Andrew declared, jumping to his feet.

"No! First we get our facts straight. We need something concrete to present them with. We can't just turn up with a story like this - they'd never buy it - they already think I'm some kind of nut after that stupid show I put on at the inquest." He thought for a moment then continued, "You find out as much as you can about that kid. See what else the autopsy comes up with. I'll check out things here, go over Corby's work. I've got to think this out - I wish I hadn't had all that beer." He added as an afterthought. Andrew looked at his watch.

"Look it's very late and we've both had quite a few. Let's sleep on it tonight - maybe it'll make more sense in the morning. I'll do some checking at the hospital tomorrow - I'll phone you if I come up with anything." As the excitement of the previous few minutes faded he found himself feeling very tired, although his thoughts were so disturbed he knew he'd find it hard to sleep.

"I'm going to walk home, maybe walk off a few of those beers. Perhaps it'll clear my head and I'll be able to make some reason of all this. Will you be all right?" Brad looked absolutely shattered.

"Yeah I'm fine - you're right, no sense going off raving at this time of night. Cop shop will probably be full of Kadooment drunks anyway." He gave a tired grin, "Or sunflowers being charged with assault! No you go ahead, I'm going to sit outside for a few minutes then head home myself. I've got some serious thinking to do."

They walked outside together and shook hands on the beach. Andrew set off towards Dover beach, lost in thought. Brad walked a few yards away from the noisy bar then sat down on a large rock and sat staring out to sea. Smiler Baines slipped out of the shadows, and quietly felt for the knife in his pocket.

Chapter 33

The waves broke gently on the shore as Andrew walked home. It was a soothing sound but Andrew didn't hear it. All he could hear was Brad's words. "... some kind of pollutant, but we don't know exactly where it's coming from yet..." Could Sweetboy have put some sort of chemical pollutant into the water? Why? Killing the fish would do him no good - his family lived off the sea. Perhaps he didn't know what it was - then why act so mysterious? He obviously knew it was something dodgy, Andrew decided or he would have come clean straight away. Andrew knew he was missing something. He tried to force his tired brain to work out the facts logically.

The image of the boy's Grandmother popped into his mind. "She knew he was up to something - she suspected him of dealing drugs - why? There were no track marks on his arms. He didn't act or sound drugged up and there was no trace of any narcotics in his blood. What made her suspect him? What else is linked to drugs? Money - it had to be. The boy must have suddenly got some unexplained money - it was the only explanation which made sense."

His legs were beginning to ache from treading through the soft sand. Suddenly he stopped, had the boy become rich overnight? It still didn't add up he thought, frowning, the boy's parents didn't seem to know about it. If he'd suddenly become wealthy surely they would have noticed it - he lived at home. Andrew trudged on, maybe he was barking up the wrong tree. Still the thought persisted, he could think of no other explanation for the Grandmother's fears.

"Okay" he said aloud, trying to clarify his thoughts, "The boy is paid a lot of money to put a pollutant into the sea, no - he wouldn't do that." He muttered. He hadn't seemed like an evil boy, he wouldn't take away his family's livelihood. "Right, " he started again more firmly, "The boy is paid to put something in the sea - which he doesn't know would cause problems then he gets sick and fish die and that's why he was killed."

He felt triumphant. It was becoming clearer. "Why?" He said suddenly, why put something in the sea? Of course, the truth dawned on him - to hide it! His thoughts raced ahead; okay so the boy was paid to hide something in the sea. He stopped again, dead in his tracks. Surely the people who had paid him to hide it must have known it would leak and cause all this trouble. Slowly he continued his walk. Sweetboy must have tampered with it.

He almost laughed as he worked out the remaining bits of the puzzle. The boy must have been paid to hide something, tampered with it, maybe he thought it was drugs like his Grandmother did, then all hell broke loose. "He opened Pandora's box!" Andrew said aloud. "Now," he muttered to himself, "What was in the box?" Mentally he ran through the symptoms, non-healing burns, he shrugged, presumably chemical burns, nausea, vomiting, RADIATION!

A voice screamed in his head. Radiation, radiation, radiation! How could he have been so blind! That would cause those symptoms and that would kill the fish - God only knew why anyone would want to hide radioactive material in the Caribbean Sea but it all fitted. Maybe it was radioactive waste en route somewhere else. As far as he was concerned he didn't care what it was - he just knew he had to find it, or, more accurately make sure someone - some expert - found it.

He was nearly home - what should he do? Should he go back to Brad? He hesitated for a moment then decided it was still probably best left to the morning. If he was right then it was very likely that Brad was right too - Corby had been murdered. He decided to ring Brad first thing in the morning and together they'd go to the police. He stopped to gather his bearings, there was a small group of palm trees just ahead, he was pretty sure that if he cut through them he'd reach the road and be nearly home. The moon slid behind a cloud and he suddenly realised just how dark it was.

Brad sat on the rock where staring with sightless eyes over the Caribbean sea, like Andrew he was oblivious to the sounds of the waves and deaf to the chirping of the tree frogs in the nearby Manchineel tree. All he could think of was Corby. He pictured his easy grin as Brad had walked through the customs hall and out into the bright sunshine. He saw again Corby's eager face as they'd driven home from the airport, remembering how keen he'd been to get into the boxes Brad had brought with him.

He was so dedicated to his work, tears slid down Brad's face as he became more and more convinced that it was his friend's devotion to marine life which had ultimately caused his death. He wondered about the faceless stranger who must have entered the lab that night. There had been no signs of a struggle, could it have been someone Corby knew? No, he dismissed that thought immediately - no one who knew him could ever harm him. He was the most open, honest and trusting person Brad had ever known. That was probably his downfall Brad concluded. Anyone who showed the slightest interest in Corby's work would have been welcomed with open arms.

Brad imagined Corby showing his killer around the lab, he may have even opened the cases himself to show the guy the samples. Brad cringed as he saw a mental image of Corby cheerfully showing his executioner around the lab. The pathologist had said that some of the spines had broken off in the wound, he could bet that the stranger had somehow forced his hand down on to them.

Tomorrow he'd find the proof. He'd check and double-check all Corby's work. The answer had to be laying somewhere off the

East Coast and Brad was grimly determined to find it. The moon flitted briefly behind a cloud and Brad felt a sudden shiver, despite the balmy evening. There was nothing more he could accomplish tonight he decided. Standing up he stretched and yawned, time to head home.

From his vantage point near the tree Smiler awaited his opportunity, he would act as soon as the man reached the trees, no sense going out into the open unnecessarily. Despite the occasional cloud the moonlight was bright enough most of the time to warn of his approach. As the moon temporarily vanished behind a cloud he saw his victim heading towards the trees. His moment had arrived. Silently he drew the knife from his pocket. His fingers finding the familiar carved rose.

"Do you know what the Bible says?" a soft voice asked him, Smiler spun around, he could barely make out the shape in front of him, it seemed to be a woman, a quite elderly woman. Some kind of religious nut - just what he needed.

"Beat it!" he whispered urgently, turning back to see where his prey was going. He was only a few feet away. The woman tugged at his arm.

"Mister you should read your Bible." She persisted, Smiler gave a small exasperated sigh, well he'd given her a chance, he drew back the knife. At that instant the moon shone through the clouds, reflecting briefly on the knife as it slipped expertly under the target's ribs, through the spleen and into the heart. The ruptured spleen pumped blood through the narrow wound rapidly saturating the victim's thin cotton clothing. Forty years of handling knives made for deadly accuracy. Martha Richards sank to her knees, her lips moving in silent prayer. There was a soft thud as Smiler Baines landed beside her.

"Exodus, chapter 21. 'Thou shalt give life for life, eye for eye, tooth for tooth..." Martha muttered, looking sorrowfully down at the man, she knew he was as good as dead. She'd been gutting fish for forty years; she was probably more of an expert with a knife than he was. Since the day she'd borrowed her daughter's maid's uniform and hidden in his bathroom she'd known what she would have to do. The only scrap of information she managed to glean was the fact that someone at The Barbados Institute of Marine Biology was causing this man trouble so she'd waited for two days outside the Institute. She had wanted to warn someone but didn't know who to warn.

She even hoped that just maybe her grandson's killer would repent, but as soon as she'd seen him waiting in the shadows, watching that poor man on the beach, she knew he was beyond redemption. He should be punished for his terrible sins, she knew that, and he should pay the ultimate price.

Technically Barbados did still have the death penalty but it was never used, and anyway there was no way an American tourist would be allowed to die, she thought scornfully. No there would be protests and arguments and them civil rights people would all get involved and the wicked sinner would end up being shipped back to the States and live the rest of his life in comfort. She couldn't allow that to happen, so she listened to her heart and read her Bible. Her instructions were clear. That didn't mean she felt no remorse for her actions - if only there had been some other way, she wept silently.

As Martha Richards knelt in prayer beside the body of her Grandson's killer, Brad Tucker walked past a few feet away - he never even saw them.

Smiler Baines lay on the sand feeling his life's blood ebb away. His life, as it was supposed to, flashed before him. He saw himself in street fights in New York. He relived episodes when dangerous men in dangerous cities had surrounded him. He'd survived bombs and shootings. It came to this. Stabbed to death by a little old lady. Out -witted by a religious fruitcake on some shit-hole island. For that reason alone he decided he deserved to die.

Chapter 34

Barbados - West Indies - August: Samuel Johnston walked home along the quiet deserted beach. The dawn was just breaking. The early rays quickly strengthening to dispel the morning coolness. Although he had grown up with the beautiful scenery he could still marvel at its beauty in the early light. He admired still, the way the waving fronds of the palms were silhouetted against the awakening sky. He was a contented man. He loved his job as a night security officer at the prestigious Treasure Beach Hotel. It was a good job. He particularly liked the uniform, felt it gave him an air of authority. The navy serge trousers and the crisp sky blue shirt gave him a dignified paramilitary appearance. Although in reality he had very little to do, he felt his presence gave quiet assurance to the tourists.

It had been a quiet night. The previous day had been the festival of the Kaddooment. An entire day of carnival and revelry. An annual event it was the highlight of the social calendar. Preparations for the following year would begin today. By the time Sam had gone on duty for the late shift most people had worn themselves out. The exertions of the long procession, the street dancing, blending smoothly with the copious amounts of rum that lubricated the entire proceedings made for an early nightcap. There had been one or two party stragglers but they'd stumbled off to bed shortly after he'd arrived, clutching their bright streamers and singing half remembered lines from the current calypso songs.

He had evicted a beach vendor from the bar and helped a wealthy but extremely drunk American back to his room, receiving a generous tip for his trouble. Walking along the beach, lost in reverie, contemplating how he would spend his bonus, he very nearly fell over the body of a man, lying face down on the soft white sand.

"Hey mister, you ok? Too much liquid sunshine eh my friend? Now you know why we call it rum punch. Come on then Mister rum head. Want a hand getting back to your hotel?" he grinned, someone had obviously enjoyed the Kaddooment. The man didn't move.

Sam frowned; hoping the man had not wandered away from his hotel. He was supposed to make sure the guests slept off any excesses in their rooms, not lying out on the beach. Leaning over he gently shook the man's shoulder. He was quite sure it was a visitor, he was wearing the typical garb of the tourist, shorts and T-shirt, the back bearing the logo of the local brewery. He carefully rolled him over on to his back and gasped in horror.

The man's shirt no longer urged people to drink the local beer - his shirt now told a different story. This man wasn't dead drunk. Just dead. A vast dark stain, spreading out from a small tear just under the heart, puckering the thin cotton, and leaving no doubt of its wearer's fate. The man's eyes were open and staring, flies buzzed around the congealed blood enjoying an unexpected yet welcome breakfast. There was so much blood for such a small wound. It saturated the white sand under the body. For a moment Samuel stood staring in total shock and disbelief at the gruesome sight. Glancing wildly around he spotted a beach vendor slowly approaching.

"Hey you!" he screamed.

"Oh man don't you go bugging me. What's your problem man?" Grumbled the salesman. "I ain't working yet - ain't a body round yet." He kept trudging through the soft sand, annoyed at being pestered by the hotel security so early.

"Get the police man!"

"What? What you talking bout?" He peered closer and suddenly caught a glimpse of the body. "What you done man? Sweet Jesus - what you done?" He gasped as he too saw the carnage.

"Just get help, Go, just go!" Sam wailed. The beach vendor turned and fled. The powdery sand flew up as he scrambled across the beach.

Sam fought to regain his composure - he was after all, a kind of policeman himself, he reasoned. He was a highly trained security officer, he told himself - he could handle any crisis. It was no use. His eyes were drawn back to the body. "All that blood" He gasped. A sickly stench filled the air as the virgin sand was turned an ugly liver brown. He clasped his hands over his mouth but he couldn't prevent the bile that rose in his throat spraying through his trembling fingers. He sat miserably in his ruined uniform and awaited the arrival of the police.

The new civic complex at Holetown on the West Coast of Barbados was a source of much community pride. It housed a post office, courtroom and police station. Candy-store paintwork of peppermint green with contrasting white shutters made it look more like a local attraction than an official government building.

Winston Alleyne, Chief of Police, Holetown division, groaned as he surveyed the building site that was supposed to be the new police station.

"I thought this was going to be finished last month?" he barked at the foreman as he picked his way across paint pots and ladders. It was his usual morning refrain as he arrived.

"Outside's finished, Boss." Proclaimed the builder proudly.

"What about the inside?"

"Jail cell's finished." Continued the builder cheerfully, "Ceptin the bars - they's coming soon though and we've painted a line to show where they be." He added helpfully.

"Oh terrific." He glared over towards the new prison area. A scruffy looking local man stood inside the recessed area. Their eyes locked and they both looked down at the painted white line at the prisoner's feet.

"Mango suspect Sir." The desk sergeant said brightly. The prisoner shrugged, reaching into his pocket he drew out a fruit and started to chew slowly.

"Sergeant." sighed Winston, "Don't let him eat all the evidence." He walked on into his office.

"Your office is finished." Called the builder after him, "More or less..."

He sat at his desk in his gleaming new office. It was at the front of the building, and from his window he could see the locals and tourists mingling in the small shopping mall at Sunset Crest opposite the Civic complex. Above the shops an air-conditioned gym did a good trade for the island's fitness fanatics, many building up enough energy to enjoy a late breakfast in the bakery below. Brightly painted mini mokes lined up along the car park, patiently awaiting the arrival of the next tourist, ready to do battle with the bumpy roads. Their ranks giving evidence of the popularity of the small Caribbean island.

He stared with unseeing eyes out of his window - this was trouble - big trouble. He hadn't actually seen the body himself yet. It had been discovered very early that morning, hastily photographed and taken directly to the morgue at The Queen Elizabeth Hospital in Bridgetown. There was no question of keeping it at the incident site due to the intense heat. There was also the question of minimising publicity. Although there had been no form of identification on the victim it had been quickly surmised that the deceased had been a tourist. Winston sighed deeply as he contemplated the immediate future - a dead tourist - worse; a murdered tourist would not exactly enhance the Island's reputation as a safe holiday destination. Tourists were, unfortunately, occasionally robbed, but rarely harmed physically. The locals knew better than to kill the golden goose, they may steal a few eggs or pull a few feathers but everyone knew where to draw the line.

He gave a wry smile as he remembered he was supposed to be interviewing the prisoner. A local man accused of stealing mangoes. He wondered briefly if the suspect was still waiting. "Mangoes! If only that was the biggest problem!" he thought dejectedly, the murder overshadowed everything. It was bound to make the foreign press; people would surely be deterred from visiting. There are lots of Caribbean islands; it would be only too easy to find another destination. His eyes rested fleetingly on the name plaque on his desk. Under his name was printed the Island's motto. "Tourism is our life - play your part" Like most Bajans he was acutely aware of the competition, everyone worked hard to make their island the most attractive.

The shrill ringing of the telephone interrupted his gloomy thoughts.

"Chief" he answered abruptly, "Oh hi Malcolm, are you down at the QEH?"

"Yup, already on the case - we foreigners don't waste time you know!" Malcolm stated cheerfully in his strong English accent. He was a British pathologist who had transferred from England as part of an exchange scheme within the police force. He continued in a more serious tone. "Actually I haven't officially started the full P.M. on your stabbing victim as yet, but I thought I'd fill you in on what I found in the prelim. I think I've found something rather interesting. It might help to get you started in the investigation"

"What have you got?" Winston reached for a notepad, his hopes rising that perhaps this thing could be wrapped up quickly.

"Well I know this sounds crazy, but I don't think this guy was unlucky." Malcolm said slowly, remembering his immediate thoughts as he examined the body upon arrival.

"Maybe in England you have a different notion of luck - out here in the tropics we tend to think being found stabbed to death is pretty unlucky. We're funny like that!" Winston commented dryly.

Malcolm laughed, "I guess I should have phrased that better! What I meant was, this was not just bad luck. It doesn't look like a mugging that went wrong or even an accidental stabbing in a fight. Certainly there are no immediate signs of a struggle. It's early days yet, but from my experience, and the evidence so far, I would say this was a professional job."

"What the hell are you suggesting? What "evidence so far?""

"Look this is all off the record right? It's just that...well... judging by the entry wound, whoever killed this man knew what he was doing. It was a neat job. It would have been an almost instantaneous death - no time to cry out and attract attention. Swift and deadly accurate."

He was standing with his back to the room, facing the wall phone his fingers traced the contours of the clinical white tiles as he spoke. He turned and looked over at the trolley behind him. The body was covered in a surgical green sheet that contrasted sharply with the ghostly white hand that had slipped out from under it.

"Someone who certainly knew how to handle a knife." He continued, "The blade entered under the rib cage. An old trick, removes any possibility of the blade being deflected by a rib. The weapon was intended to kill, not intimidate. Probably a stiletto or a boning knife, certainly a thin blade. Usually enters the heart via the spleen. That would account for the amount of blood lost. This wasn't your usual mugger, not with that degree of accuracy."

"You mean a professional, like a ... hitman? You're kidding! Are you sure?"

"No, I'm not sure - not yet. That's why I say it's off the record but I just thought I ought to warn you. I mean, if this man is someone important enough to be professionally killed - well the old solids are going to hit the ventilation system! Only a thought but you'd better be prepared and damn certain everything's being handled by the book right from the start. God knows who he is - was - but...I guess someone thought him a problem." Malcolm sighed, thoughtfully.

Outside Winston's office the prisoner finished his breakfast and strolled nonchalantly out the door. Winston caught a brief glimpse of him as he ambled past his window but his thoughts were preoccupied with the unknown murder victim.

"You don't recognise him at all do you? Does he look like a high ranking politician or someone?" He suggested.

"What does a high ranking politician look like? Anyway this guy just looks like Joe Public to me. I wouldn't say he was old enough to be a world leader - maybe someone important's son? I don't know - I leave that sort of thing to you lot!"

"Thanks Malcolm I appreciate you taking the time to warn me - when do you reckon you'll be finished?"

"I'll put it on priority, should be able to get back to you later on today - I'll keep you posted"

Winston hung up the phone and sat staring into space, his hand still resting on the phone as if to keep the line between him and the hospital open. His mind was whirling with the latest turn of events. A professional hitman? It couldn't be possible, no surely Malcolm was mistaken. After all, he wasn't Bajan. He didn't know the island and its people that well. Things like that just don't happen here - maybe in some rough inner city in England, London gangs or something but not here.

In the hospital morgue Malcolm unknowingly mimicked Winston's actions. He paused with his hand resting on the phone while he too pondered the identity of the mysterious victim. A faint noise behind him caused him to whirl around startled. To his surprise a stranger stood before him. The morgue was a restricted area and certainly not the sort of place anyone would casually walk into unannounced. For a moment the two men stood facing each other then the stranger smiled and reached into his pocket. Something in his manner made Malcolm step back. The man must have entered the room very quietly. Malcolm thought eyeing him suspiciously. He was dressed in a sharp dark suit, and sported a pair of all-concealing sunglasses. He had neatly crew cut hair and a generally clean-cut All-American appearance. The stranger smiled and flipped open a small leather wallet.

"Agent Dow, F.B.I. I wonder if I might take a look at your John Doe, Sir?" He asked with quiet authority.

"I beg your pardon?" Malcolm responded with full British reserve. The agent smiled.

"My apologies Sir, I was referring to your unidentified body. I am legally obliged to point out that I have no official jurisdiction on the Island but I believe I may be of some assistance." He walked over towards the trolley where Smiler's body lay and flipped back the sheet before Malcolm had time to consider his position.

He gave a brief, mirthless smile, clearly recognising the deceased.

"You know him?" asked Malcolm, totally astonished by the sudden appearance of the American F.B.I. agent.

"Let's just say he is known to us - we'll be in touch. I would appreciate this conversation being kept strictly confidential for the time being sir." Agent Dows spoke briefly and precisely then, as swiftly as he'd arrived, he was gone, walking rapidly along the corridor and speaking urgently into a tiny mobile phone as he went. Malcolm stood staring open-mouthed after him. He could just about make out the man's softly spoken words as he strode away - they made little sense to him.

"...it's him all right - looks like the South Americans beat us to it...yes I'll meet you there..." the words faded as he disappeared into the distance.

Winston Alleyne wondered briefly what the chances were of keeping the whole thing quiet - pretty slim, he decided. Maybe if the guy turned out to be from some small Scandinavian country. The country's main tourist trade came from Britain and America - the odds were stacked that this one was from either of those. The officer who had seen the body seemed to think so but these days, you never could tell. All they knew for now was that he was a white guy and looked like a tourist. 'Joe public' Malcolm had called him - so who was he? Was he someone important? Some VIP? Winston realised he should perhaps be feeling more sympathy for the victim than the island but he was too aware of the possible consequences of this one act of violence.

"Tourism" he declared to the empty room, "is our life's blood and something like this can bring on a very bad case of anaemia."

He spun around embarrassed as a small cough sounded behind him. His sergeant looked strangely excited by the stranger he was showing into his boss's office. The man remarkably like the one who'd just recently left the mortuary at the Queen Elizabeth Hospital, although neither policeman could have known that. Logically it was not possible for the man to have travelled so fast and indeed this was in fact not the same agent who had so surprised Malcolm Young. He was a colleague and could almost have been a twin. Same suit, same dark glasses, same clean-cut image. The sergeant stood looking in awe at the F.B.I. agent - he'd never seen one before.

Outside the police station Andrew, Charmaine and Brad screeched into the car park in Charmaine's car. Andrew was surprised to see Martha Richards at the door of the building. She didn't notice them though, as she stood proudly erect, her head held high. As they approached she appeared to take a deep breath and march resolutely into the police station. The unlikely group burst into the Inspector's office simultaneously, Martha quiet and dignified, Andrew and Brad in sharp contrast tense and plainly very animated. Charmaine bearing silent witness to the cacophony of emotions. Winston Alleyne stood in shocked silence as pandemonium broke out all around him.

"QUIET!!!" he roared. There was a stunned silence. "Thank you." he said quietly. "Now if someone could please do me the courtesy of explaining exactly what is occurring here. I..."

Martha spoke with quiet dignity, calmly talking her seat and awaiting her fate. "I've come to confess to a murder."

Everyone in the room turned in amazement to the little white-haired lady as they realised what she had said.

Chapter 35

Winston Alleyne eventually managed to restore order to his now crowded office. He arranged seating for everyone and, in an effort to return to a more civilised way of doing things, ordered coffee for his...guests. The sergeant reluctantly left. Andrew formally introduced Brad to Martha Richards. She shook his hand graciously but made no comment, both men wondered who on earth she could have killed. They knew nothing of the previous night's dramatic event.

"Surely she couldn't have? Not Corby?" He whispered to Andrew.

"Definitely not, she was rather busy with her own tragedy that evening." Andrew said grimly, remembering how the whole family had gathered at the hospital the night Sweetboy died. He recalled how they'd prayed by the dead boy's bedside for hours.

"Then who? What the hell is going on here? Do you think..."Inspector Alleyne called for silence, interrupting their whispered conversation. Brad looked sideways at the woman. She seemed so composed. He turned back to the Inspector as he started to speak.

"Now, let's try and sort this out." Winston began; he could feel a headache coming on and he pressed his throbbing temples as he wondered what on earth had metaphorically turned his life and his office upside down in the past few minutes.

"Perhaps if I may be allowed to speak." Agent Booth, F.B.I. rose to his feet. He paused and looked over to the door, his colleague Agent Dows had just arrived. Both men looked questioningly at the Inspector.

"Come on in!" He said wearily, "Why not - we're having a party." He slumped down at his desk and rested his head on his hands. The two F.B.I. men conferred quietly. After a moment Winston looked up and all eyes turned to Agent Booth.

"I should like to point out, first of all, that we have no legal jurisdiction on the Island but we would consider it a personal favour to the United States Government if you people gathered here would consider what we are about to reveal of the utmost secrecy." Everyone nodded.

"We have reason to believe," he continued, "that a covert operation has been taking place on this Island for the past few weeks." He paused and looked around the room, secretly relishing his moment of glory.

"Unfortunately we only received details of this operation very recently and were therefore too late to avert ...certain events. I am not at liberty to divulge the exact nature of our enquiry but I can confirm some aspects as they relate to incidents on the Island."

"Toxic waste!" Andrew interjected, triumphantly, he had been right. He and Brad looked at the agent waiting for confirmation of their suspicions. Martha stared straight ahead; it didn't matter anymore to her. Inspector Alleyne looked totally confused.

"Not quite, but you're close." The agent confirmed. He hesitated briefly then continued; they'd obviously worked most of it out anyway. "Our sources have discovered that a consignment of...a restricted substance...was temporarily diverted here to avoid detection at its ultimate destination. A local man was hired, to secrete this consignment just off shore of the island." There was an audible gasp from Martha; tears sprang to her eyes. Agent Booth uncharacteristically took pity of the quite elderly lady. "A very young, local man, who was used as a pawn in a much bigger game. He can have had no knowledge of the goods he was hired to hold. It would appear," he continued, "that the consignment met with some sort of accident and the seal was broken. We have no concrete evidence to explain this, we can only surmise that perhaps the young man was checking the contents to assure himself of their legality."

It was a charitable statement; everyone present guessed what the young man in question had been checking for but out of respect for Martha Richards no one spoke their thoughts.

Agent Booth continued his monologue. There was total silence in the room apart from his steady voice.

"The consignment then began to leak, causing the problems which I understand your Institute were investigating." He looked across at Brad, who nodded, too choked to speak as he again thought of his erstwhile friend. "This leakage caused obvious problems to the ... parties.... responsible for the... package, and therefore they attempted to contain these problems. The young fisherman was ...dealt with." Everyone's eyes turned to Martha who stared resolutely ahead. Agent Booth continued, "...as was the young man dealing with the contamination problem at the laboratory." All eyes turned this time towards Brad; Charmaine patted him on the shoulder in a gesture of sympathy. Agent Booth took a deep breath and came to the crunch.

"I have been asked - as a representative of the United States of America to request your co-operation to help us close this investigation. As I said earlier, I have no right to ask this of you but I'm sure you would all join me in wanting justice to prevail. As we speak our respective Governments are co-operating with each other to try and put an end to this sad episode. Our naval experts are currently, with permission of course, searching the East Coast for the damaged container. I'm very confident it will be properly dealt with very soon. It only remains to tie things up here." There was a moment's silence as everyone present wondered what he was going to ask of them.

"You may rest assured that the perpetrator of the heinous crimes which took place here in Barbados has already paid the ultimate price for his acts. His body was discovered this morning. My colleague has identified him as a hired assassin. " Brad and Andrew turned and stared at Martha in astonishment. Surely she hadn't.... she couldn't.... could she? Something in her expression told them she had. Brad wanted to leap up and congratulate her but decided that might not be appropriate under the circumstances. They all looked stunned that such a sweet old lady could be capable of such an act.

"How the hell did you find him?" He asked incredulously, it was a question they were all thinking, the guy was a professional - how did a little old lady track him down? Wordlessly Martha opened her handbag; she pulled out a battered picture post card showing Smiler's hotel. It was still folded over and contained the money Smiler had paid her Grandson. Neatly beside it she placed her fishing knife and also Smiler's flick knife. She wasn't going to leave that lying on the beach for anyone to happen upon. It could be dangerous, she thought, primly.

"When my boy was taken ill, I found this money - he was ashamed, I could see it in his eyes." Her words were softly spoken but everyone in the room listened intently, the matter had been puzzling the F.B.I. agents as well. "It was bad money and he was scared he Mummy would find it - so I hid it for him. When he died I went to the hotel on the picture. The room be marked. Soon as I see him I know. He was evil. I thought it was drugs he was doing - it was worse than drugs. I tried to make him repent. I told him to read the bible, but he wouldn't listen so I..." Agent Booth quickly interrupted her, he carried on his former explanation as if she hadn't even spoken.

"It is not our place to investigate his demise but we would suggest that he has been disposed of either by his former employers or, more likely by their customers, displeased by the delay in receiving their goods." Carefully avoiding Martha Richards he looked directly at Inspector Alleyne. "Off the record we could safely assume that whoever killed this particularly evil man not only did us a favour, but is most probably long gone from these shores." He gave them a moment to absorb the information before hitting them with his request. "It would greatly benefit our ongoing inquiries if this matter received as little publicity as possible. As I said before - we have no rights to request such a thing but, we believe nothing could be gained by a public investigation at local level."

Winston Alleyne looked at the man in total amazement - he was asking him to hush it up - to avoid publicity - not to cut the throat of the Island he loved. He'd have to get higher authority of course but, well, it could be the answer to his prayers.

"What about Corby?" Asked Brad quietly, he could see what they were driving at here, but his friend had been murdered.

"Mr Corbin's death has already gone on record as being accidental." Agent Booth replied, he'd been expecting this from his compatriot.

"But we all know it wasn't!" Insisted Brad.

"Yes we do - but does his mother have to know that? What useful purpose would it serve? His killer has been brought to justice. The only thing that re-opening the case would do is bring grief and pain to his family - why put them through it? We can find another way to serve the man's family. You have my word on it. For his family's sake if not for your Government's I'm asking you to think it over."

"What about Sweetboy's family?" Asked Andrew who had been quietly listening as the whole incredible tale was unravelled.

"His family don't want this to be known." Martha spoke with dignified conviction, "For my part I'm prepared to take my punishment, the Lord is my judge and I'm ready to take His punishment. I knowed what I did and I should be punished but don't go dragging the boy's name through the mud. I don't want he Mummy to know he was mixed up in trouble." To everyone's surprise Agent Booth knelt down before the trembling woman, he spoke gently.

"Mrs Richards, you say the Lord is your judge -let Him be the only one." He looked at Inspector Alleyne, who gave a barely perceptible nod; "If you insist on confessing to mere mortals about your crime then the whole thing will surely come out. Your grandson will always be remembered as a bad boy - you don't want that. Let it go - let me track down the men who organised all this, help me to bring them to justice." He deftly placed the knives and money back in her handbag. "Throw this away - give the money away if you want or even burn it. Don't punish yourself - only God knows how many lives you saved last night - the man was evil - he'd killed dozens, believe me. You're not a sinner - you're a saint!"

"I ain't no saint - I done wrong." She mumbled pleading with him to be allowed to accept her punishment.

"You took the only action you could and you saved a life - probably many lives. You know what that man was waiting for outside the Institute late last night - another chance to take an innocent life." He glanced across at Brad as he softly urged the woman to reconsider.

Brad gasped, it was nearly him! He hadn't realised where the event had happened. Chillingly he realised he would have been the next victim. He took the woman's hand.

"How can I thank you. You saved my life. Is my life not worth something to you? Surely I'm worth you forgiving yourself." He said gently. She looked at him and then across at the Inspector, he leant across and firmly closed her bag.

"Mrs Richards, thank you for bringing in the items you found. However they will not be necessary for our enquiries. That case is closed." There was a general sigh of relief around the room; everyone had taken her to their hearts.

They all sat back as the full impact of Agent Booth's words registered with them. They each had a part to play. Martha Richards wept silently as she came to terms with her own involvement in the whole sorry story. There was one question remaining in Winston's mind. Malcolm's words came back to him. "A professional job." He had to ask. It would finally prove to him that the whole incredible story was true. While the others were softly discussing the events he slipped over to Martha's side.

"I have to ask, not officially you understand, just for my own peace of mind. How did you? How did you know how to..." He faltered, how could he ask this frail woman how she'd committed such a crime?

Martha looked up at him, through her tears she spoke softly. "I been gutting fish for over forty years. Don't matter how big the fish is, you still go in the same way, through the soft bit." She bowed her head in sorrow; Winston bowed his head - in respect.

Across the ocean in downtown Miami Randall Westfield sat in an interview room at police headquarters and appeared surprisingly calm.

Detective Letts read the note he'd been handed and smiled. Randall Westfield smiled back, playing a dangerous game of cat and mouse.

"Mr Westfield, I have just received word that we have, in safe custody, an employee of yours in the Caribbean." He watched for a reaction, he figured the hospital morgue could justifiably be called "safe custody" - well he wasn't going anywhere that was certain.

Randall leant back and tried to look puzzled.

"Do I own any businesses in the Caribbean? How very remiss of me I don't seem to recall." He smirked; he was still to play his trump card.

Detective Letts abandoned the civility. "Look Westfield - we've got you. Give it up - there's no way you're getting out of this one!"

"Detective er...Letts wasn't it? I do believe you're right. If I may be allowed to call upon the Constitution of this great country of ours...." Randall began, pompously.

"Yeah, yeah I know, claim the fifth - it won't get you anywhere. We don't need a confession." Letts interrupted the monologue.

"On the contrary I don't wish to claim the fifth - just the opposite. I wish to claim freedom of speech. I want my day in court. I want to make a full and frank confession how I, an American citizen conspired to supply a militant group in a foreign country with nuclear arms. Perhaps I was acting out of patriotism. We'll let the people decide shall we? Of course it may prove a bit of a diplomatic embarrassment for our Government - I mean - some people may think I was somehow acting for- shall we say a higher authority? Some people might even think our own government wanted a change of power in that area. Who knows? I can't be held responsible for other people's thoughts - some of those Latin types are so quick to jump to the wrong conclusions. No you're quite right - I think I ought to make a full confession - publicly." He paused while the impact of his words registered with the officer who sat opposite him. "Then of course we could just forget the whole thing. You've got your plutonium I expect." He sat back and pressed his fingertips neatly together smugly, "We could decide the whole thing never happened." He waited for a reply. Grim faced, Detective Letts rose to his feet and walked silently out of the room.

He returned an hour later, his good humour surprisingly restored.

"Well Mr Westfield, I've got some good news for you. You're being released - pending further investigations. You're free to go."

Westfield rose to his feet. "Thank you officer, I'm glad we understand each other I...free to go? I can't just leave - I want protection!" He grabbed at the man who firmly disengaged his grip.

"Sorry Mr Westfield, protection from what? We've forgotten the whole thing - just like you said." He smiled warmly, "Have a nice day." He walked briskly away.

"Al!" Thought Randall desperately, "I must get hold of Al, I..." He remembered he wouldn't be getting hold of Al ever again.

Randall walked down the steps of the police station to where Charlie, his faithful "personal assistant" was waiting. The man was red faced from exertion, having run several yards to meet his employer.

"Sorry Boss, they wouldn't let me park any closer. I tried but the cops moved me on.... it's plain crazy, not like there ain't no space...." he babbled on with his earnest explanation. Randall turned and at looked up at the police building, Detective Letts stood looking out of the window at him. He gave the policeman a brief salute - acknowledging, with a wry smile, his own defeat.

The official police report was that it had been a drive-by shooting by person or persons unknown. The unofficial police report, mysteriously leaked, said it was a pay-off from a South American drug smuggling cartel. Most people had little difficulty choosing the version they believed - except strangely, Charlie who swore he'd caught a glimpse of the driver of the speeding car from which his boss received his fatal wound. He said the man certainly didn't look South American, he thought he looked like a clean -cut All-American boy. The driver appeared to be very smartly dressed, Charlie got the impression he was wearing a sharp dark suit but he couldn't see his face, apparently the assassin was wearing all-concealing sunglasses. Charlie was adamant it wasn't a foreigner - but then what did he know?

The assets of Westfield Inc. were seized as being obtained via illicit means. A move totally uncontested by the board of directors, none of whom were prosecuted for their part in any illegal activities.

The Nathan Corbin Institute for Marine Biology received a substantial grant enabling it to become one of the world's foremost authorities in marine zoo toxicology. An anonymous American businessman donated a beautiful stained glass window depicting St Andrew casting out his nets to Martha Richard' s church. It was in memory of her beloved grandson who had died after contracting a rare but fatal illness. As she sat in church one Sunday, praying for the soul of her dear departed grandson Martha looked up at "his" window - it gave her no small measure of comfort. Outside the church the sunlight sparkled, it shone brightly reflecting the beautiful shades of the window and the glittering Caribbean Sea. Charmaine and Andrew were walking arm in arm along a deserted beach nearby.

"What are you thinking my love?" Charmaine asked dreamily.

"Oh I was just thinking this really is paradise. Truly a lovely quiet Island." He stopped and looked into her eyes. "It's almost perfect."

"Almost?" teased Charmaine.

"Well it is a shame supermarkets aren't open on Sundays here. There's something really romantic I want to ask you."

Biography

Christine Brooks lived in Barbados as a child and learned to love the island and its people. She still has family and friends there and has maintained her bond with the country. She now divides her time between her home in a small Berkshire village and her home in Spain where she writes short stories for a Costa Blanca magazine. She is married to Paul and they have two grown children, Kate and Tim.

Printed in the United Kingdom by
Lightning Source UK Ltd., Milton Keynes
136707UK00002B/100-135/P